ANOTHER BODY IN THE GRAVEYARD

Taylor turned to Abby and said, "You better wait here."

Abby linked her arm through Mac's and the three of them started toward the graveyard, Taylor leading, Mac swinging his light left and right, not sure what he expected to find. The path soon narrowed and they had to continue single file.

Taylor stopped suddenly and Mac swept his light forward until both beams centered on the fur-coated form lying next to Jacob Schneider's tombstone.

Abby gasped and started toward the figure on the ground but Mac held her arm.

"Don't muck up the ground." He moved forward cautiously, avoiding any spot that looked as though someone had recently passed. He knelt and felt for a pulse at her throat. The skin was cool to the touch. He moved the coat collar, which partially concealed her head. "It looks like she fell against the edge of this tombstone."

"Is she . . . ?"

"Yes, she is."

GRAVE MURDER

AL GUTHRIE

ZEBRA BOOKS
KENSINGTON PUBLISHING CORP.

ZEBRA BOOKS

are published by

Kensington Publishing Corp.
475 Park Avenue South
New York, NY 10016

First printing: July, 1990

Printed in the United States of America

Chapter 1

Mac McKenzie leaned on the roof of his Plymouth station wagon and gazed at the seventy-year-old Queen Anne house. A deep porch ran the width of the front, shaded two bay windows that flanked the door, and continued around the right side of the first floor. A corner turret, fish-scale siding newly painted, bulged from the left side of the second floor. He had to agree with his wife, Abby—it was a handsome building.

He looked at the roof of the turret where a weathervane, locked in rust, pointed forever southeast and wondered, for the hundreth time, if buying the house had been a mistake. What lurked behind its plaster walls? Dry rot? Pipes leaking at rusted joints? He turned his back on the house and surveyed the short, graveled cul-de-sac known as Twilly Place. The Chicago Loop was only forty-five minutes away, yet little had changed since the days when Sarahville had been a farmer's crossroad community. Well, maybe the potholes were deeper.

For business, they say, location is everything. Was this *really* the place for an art supply and craft shop? Hard to imagine customers trudging through the mud for a skein of yarn or tube of ochre. But what did he know? Abby was the expert.

Mac slid a carton to the edge of the tailgate and lifted it as the front door to the house opened. Abby McKenzie stepped onto the threshhold, barring the way.

"You're not going to track mud in here!" she said. "Take that stuff around back." She retreated and closed the door without waiting for an answer.

Mac grinned briefly. Abby was getting a bit frayed, and he was ready to quit for the day himself. He started to set the box down on the porch when Abby reappeared and took it from him. "Sorry, Mac." She leaned forward and kissed him briefly. "Trying to bring order out of this mess is getting to me." She put the box down inside the door and gestured vaguely, taking in the outdoors and the house. "Do you think it was a mistake?"

"Of course not. Once they pave the street and put up some more shops—"

"And if we don't go broke first."

Mac studied her face. Her fine brown hair was drawn back to reveal delicate ears and a tiny mole on the left side of her throat. Her mouth, so often curved in a smile, drooped. He kissed the tip of her nose. "You put the coffee on and let me worry about this stuff."

Her answering smile was a little left of center. "Mac, I hate to mention it, but that old bookcase—"

"Goes on sale, along with the rest of the leftovers."

"Okay. We'll talk about it later."

He wrestled an oak bench to the ground and dragged it onto the porch. Removing his boots just inside the door, where warm air smelled of coffee and cinnamon, he hung his windbreaker over the newel and walked a trail of newspaper laid over varnished oak floors. The trail ended at a swinging door. He pushed it open and entered the kitchen as Abby removed a batch of cinnamon rolls from the oven. He sat at the kitchen table and propped his stockinged feet on a chair.

Abby poured coffee and sat down, resting her chin in her hand. "Maybe you're right about the bookcase. The place is starting to look like a Salvation Army store."

"Cheer up. The bedroom and kitchen are livable, so what else do you need?"

"I know that's all *you* need."

6

Grinning, he said, "In a pinch, I could do without the kitchen."

"In a pinch, you'd manage *in* the kitchen." She nibbled at a roll. "You could get your office straightened up without much trouble. Just a question of arranging—"

"Let's not go into that again. I've quit the business. I'm a full-time junior partner in the store."

"Then you'll have to learn to knit."

Mac laughed. "There's a limit, woman. Maybe we can put in a line of model trains. I'd be great with model trains." He saw Abby's lids half close. She had barely touched her coffee. "You've been working too hard," he said. "Go soak in the tub. I'll spring for dinner out."

The Running Fox Tavern was on the northeast corner of Old Main Street and Harper Road. Until a year ago it was just Main, and outside of the area designated as Olde Sarahville, it was still Main. Except for the March thaw that had left snow in sheltered corners and mud everywhere else, it would have been a pleasant walk from Twilly Place. As it was, they drove, parked in the lot behind the Tavern, and still had to navigate a fair amount of mud on the way to the back door.

They picked a table in the far corner, away from the draft that swirled in each time the door opened. A smiling, fox-faced man approached the table. "Good evening," he said. "I am Rudy Wilking, the owner. You are the McKenzies, are you not?"

"Yes. How did you know?" Abby spoke over the sound of voices from the barroom.

Wilking was a bit less than six feet tall, thin and erect, wearing a white shirt and maroon tie under a brown cardigan. "You were pointed out to me at the bank last week." His speech was precise, as though he had worked hard to eradicate an accent or dialect. "I have wanted to talk to you about the Merchants Association. I am the membership chairman." Mid-sixties, he had sparse black hair untouched by gray.

Dye, Mac thought.

"Monday is a slow night." He sat and motioned to the waitress. "Ready to order? I recommend the beef tips with noodles."

Mac and Abby took his recommendation. Mac ordered bourbon and water and a Manhattan for Abby. By the time the drinks arrived, enough small talk had passed to establish a friendly first-name relationship.

Abby, always less reticent than Mac, responded to Rudy's questions. "I'm from California. Mac was a widower. We met, we married, and I immediately dragged him into what may be a disaster."

Rudy smiled. "Surely not."

"She means business disaster. At least—I think she does," Mac said.

"And the moving seems to take forever. When you have to dispose of three households—"

"Three?"

"My things—Mac's. And I inherited my sister's place, so that makes three sets of furniture. It would have been simpler to just sell it all and start over."

"As I suggested," Mac said.

Rudy's pale blue, almost gray, eyes narrowed. "Your sister. Yes, of course. Tragic affair."

There was a moment of silence, then Mac asked, "You've been here a long time, haven't you?"

"Since 1945. The tavern has been here since 1857."

"It's in remarkable shape," Abby said.

"The foundation, beams, and bar are old. As for the rest, it has been worked over so many times, it is hard to say what is original and what is not."

"So what do you think?" Mac asked. "Will this Olde Sarahville scheme work?"

"If you have patience, and the resources to wait. We need a certain critical mass of shops before we can attract more than local trade."

"Being established, I suppose it doesn't matter as much

8

to you as it does to us newcomers," Abby said.

"It could expand summer trade. I plan a beer garden out back." He chuckled. "Josie Horvath, my cook, refers to the idea as beer and brots for the weary shopper, ice cream for the shopper's brats." Rudy leaned forward on folded arms. "But—I am sure you thought about it— Twilly is narrow, a cul-de-sac. With five or six, or more, shops to be built, how are you going to move traffic? Where to park?"

Abby toyed with her glass and frowned at the table-cloth. "I guess I *should* have thought." She smiled at Mac. "But I fell in love with the Twilly house."

"Understandable," Rudy said. "It is a fine old house, and well suited for your purpose. Have you retail experience?"

"Abby's the entreprenuer," Mac said. "Uncle fed me three times a day, most of my life. This free enterprise stuff makes me nervous."

"I had a store in California," Abby said. "About fifteen years."

"Then you know what to expect." Turning to Mac, Rudy said, "I take it from your remark you were something in the military?"

"Army Air Corps—until it became Air Force. Retired."

Rudy leaned back. "Air Corps. That places you in World War II. I would have thought you too young."

"Just made the last year. So, you bought this place right about the time I enlisted. Must have been tough to open a new business then."

"Yes, indeed. The shortages—it was no time to start a saloon. Well, at least your pension will put groceries on the table until the shop is established."

"Oh, Mac has been in business for himself for quite a while," Abby said. "He's a—"

"Consultant," Mac interrupted.

"Perhaps you can pick up some clients through the Association," Rudy said.

"I've dropped that. Plan to spend full time on the

9

store." Mac drained his glass. "It must be interesting to live in an old building like this. You do live here, don't you?"

"Interesting? Well, sometimes the plumbing is interesting. Excuse me a moment. Your food should have been served by now."

As Rudy Wilking left, Abby asked, "Why didn't you let me tell Rudy what you do?"

"Did." He shook his head in mock sadness. "And I know you. You were about to call me something colorful, like private eye."

"I was not." She paused, grinning. "Even though you are a gumshoe."

Mac scowled. "Corporate clients. Nice clean work, no tailing errant husbands, and no heavy lifting."

Abby answered with a gentle snort and conversation lapsed.

Mac could see Abby had become preoccupied. No doubt adding the parking problem to her other misgivings. Her California business had been on the verge of bankruptcy before she sold it, and that had shaken her self-confidence. If this one failed too . . .

Rudy returned, saying, "Your dinner is on the way. I won't worry you now with a sales talk, but the Olde Branch meets the third Tuesday of the month, which is tomorrow. Why not drop in?"

"Olde Branch?"

"The Olde Sarahville Branch of the Merchants Association, known as the Olde Branch and the Merchants."

"Are they worried about the parking?" Abby asked.

Mac said, "Maybe we could park customers on the vacant land behind us and let them wade the creek."

He was surprised when Rudy seemed to take him seriously. "That property is not available. Here comes your food. You folks enjoy your meal, and before you leave, stop in my office. I have a brochure on the Olde Branch that will interest you. And don't worry. The parking will work itself out."

Mac attacked his plate immediately. Abby pushed her glass in circles with her forefinger. "Mac, you know it'll be quite a while before we can open the store. And quite a bit longer before we hit break-even."

He shoved a forkful of noodles in his mouth.

"If one of those corporate clients you talked about should call—well, we could use the money."

They finished dinner, agreeing it was excellent. On the way out through the hall to the parking lot, they passed Rudy Wilking's office. The door was ajar. Mac knocked and pushed it open.

A man in his mid-forties standing before an old-fashioned safe turned sharply. He had a long, bony face, deep eye sockets, and sandy hair. His shirt cuffs were folded back two turns and his tie was pulled loose. "Can I help you?" he said.

"Rudy Wilking said we could get a brochure on the local Merchants Association," Mac answered.

"Sure thing." He rummaged in the middle drawer of a three-drawer file cabinet. "Here it is. Starting a business here?"

Abby nodded. "I'm starting an arts and crafts place, across the way on Twilly place."

"Then you must be the McKenzies." He extended his hand. "I'm Horace Arly. Good luck to you." He smiled at Mac. "Arts and crafts should do well, but I don't know if Sarahville has a lot of call for a private detective."

Mac winced, thanked him for the brochure, and turned to go.

As they left, Abby grinned. "Your reputation is getting around, Sherlock. Might as well hang out a shingle."

Chapter 2

March being March, morning brought a solid overcast and a resolve by the McKenzies that this was the day to straighten the mess in the attic. Mac had one foot on the hall stairs when Abby stopped him. She pointed to the glass above the door and said, "That fanlight has been speaking to me ever since we moved in."

Mac nodded. "I can hear it now. 'What can I do about this pane?' it says. 'Take two aspirin,' I answer. Then—"

"No puns before lunch. What it's telling me is, it should be stained glass."

Mac sat on the stairs. "And where are you going to find a stained glass window to fit?"

"You'll think of something."

"Restore the original appearance of the house, you said. There's no reason to think it ever had anything but plain glass."

"I'm not a fanatic; if it wasn't stained glass, it should have been."

"You'll have to prove the original house had stained glass."

"That's a deal. Now, according to the club news in the paper, there's a Sarahville Historical Society, and they meet tonight. Why don't we go? We can ask if they have information on the house."

"Tonight is the Olde Branch meeting."

"I belonged to a group like that once. The only woman.

Whenever I attended, they'd try to hold their stomachs in, and they called me honey."

"You have the same effect on me."

"Then they'd all light cigars."

"Business before stained glass, I say."

"Let's compromise. You go to the Olde Boys meeting and—"

"And you go to the Olde Broads?"

"Why old broads, particularly?"

"History of a Chicago bedroom suburb? Sounds like a substitute for knitting."

"I make my living from knitters. Could be good for business." Abby dragged Mac to his feet. "Let's get at those boxes."

The attic, where the movers had stored the remnants of two households as yet imperfectly merged, was gloomy. Abby sat on a box of old magazines. "You know, that creek in back of us looks a mess. Nothing but trash and weeds."

"Should be the Village's responsibility, I think." Mac went to the window at the south end of the attic. Through the grimy glass he could see the shallow gully, cut by Running Fox Creek, that marked their southern lot line. Melting snow had raised its level to the weed-choked banks and there was a skim of ice on the water. Beyond the creek the land was covered with sumac, cottonwood saplings, and assorted weeds. Farther south a low hill topped with three pin oaks rose nearly level with the attic window. There was something else on the hill he couldn't quite make out. He raised the window for a better look.

"Mac, are you trying to freeze me out?"

"Take a look at this."

Abby, hugging herself against the chill breeze, came to the window. "What?"

"On the hill, there. Is that a tombstone?"

"I don't see . . . Wait. You're right, I think. It's nearly hidden by weeds. A family plot? From the farm that used to be there."

13

Mac closed the window. "Not many family cemeteries in this part of the country."

"Your idea of a parking lot back there—"

"That was a joke, dear."

"I know, but Rudy seemed to take it seriously, which made me think it might have come up before. Like, maybe the village bridging the creek and extending Twilly."

"Sounds expensive," Mac said. "I can't see the village—"

"More important, you can't dig up a graveyard anytime you feel like it."

"Not without a legal hassle."

"I guess that's what Rudy Wilking meant when he said the property wasn't available. Why didn't he just say it was a cemetery?"

"Maybe he didn't want to bury your hopes."

Abby threw a magazine at him.

The Sarahville Historical Society meeting had been scheduled for seven-thirty. Abby checked her watch against the clock on the wall. A quarter to eight. The room, located in the basement of the library, was large enough for community groups of thirty or forty. The normal quiet of a library, filled with faint rustlings and murmurs, faded to an occasional creak from a heating vent and the imagined sound of a pulse beat in her ear.

Abby, lacking outside stimuli, found time passed at a glacial pace. She shifted her position frequently, examined the acoustic ceiling tile, imagined distant voices, brooded about Mac's stubborn insistence on abandoning his work.

All very well now: Setting up the store and the house kept him busy. He had some skill as a carpenter, could handle plumbing and electrical repairs if they weren't too extensive. But he would never be happy selling sable brushes and crochet hooks.

Eight o'clock. The meeting must have been canceled. Abby started to leave and was almost run over by an attractive blonde wearing jeans and a bulky sweater and carrying a white pasteboard box.

"Sorry," the woman said. "I'm Karen Canelli. Are you looking for the Historical Society?"

Abby introduced herself. "I'd about given up hope."

"It's the fog, I guess." Karen Canelli put the box on a card table in the corner. "We're usually on time. Well, not this late anyway. Excuse me." She hurried from the room. There was the sound of running water and then she returned with a coffeepot beaded with moisture. "Are you going to join?"

Before Abby could answer, a man in his late thirties, dark haired, with a small mustache, and wearing a three-piece suit tailored to his slim form, came in. Karen introduced him as Jerome Bedford.

Jerome smiled and took Abby's hand. "We are in *dire* need of new blood. This organization is becoming positively moribund. Do join."

Again Abby was saved a decision. This time the interruption came from a large man in his late fifties or early sixties, draped in an ancient green sweater. His hair consisted of a neatly trimmed gray fringe around a bald pate. "That's the ticket, Jerome," he said. "Tell her the group's dying and then expect her to join. You have a talent for PR work."

"Well, it's true, you know," Jerome said. "Sometimes I think I'm the only one with any *real* interest in historical research."

"Right, Jerome. You're the driving force that keeps—"

Karen hastily interrupted. "Abby, this is Al Rhine. Al is one of our oldest members—"

Al laughed. "She's right, whichever way you take that."

Abby smiled. "Rhine? I spoke to a Helen Rhine this afternoon—"

Karen, measuring coffee into the pot, said, "Helen is—"

"Where *is* our worthy chairperson?" Jerome asked.

"Right here, Jerome." These words came from a woman just entering. "I stopped at the desk upstairs." She removed her coat and hung it on a hook next to the door. She wore a tan blouse with a large bow at the throat and a brown skirt slit at the side.

"Helen, come meet Abby." Al Rhine gestured toward the latest arrival with his thumb. "My wife runs this show, and me too, I might add."

"You haven't run in years, Al," Helen Rhine said. "Abigail McKenzie? So glad you could come." Addressing the group, she said, "Abby has a problem, and we're going to try and help her."

"A problem?" Jerome asked. "What—?"

"We'll get to that, Jerome," Helen said. The four members sat around the folding conference table. Abby followed their lead and found herself between Karen and Jerome.

Helen took a notepad from the bookbag she carried and began to doodle. "I don't think anyone else is coming."

"Typical!" Jerome Bedford said. "Our fair-weather members let a little fog—"

"Yes. Well." Helen Rhine stretched, lifting an ample bosom into greater prominence. "Agnes Ketchall is leaving early tomorrow to visit relatives in Iowa. And—"

"I haven't missed a single meeting since the first," Jerome said.

Helen shoved a strand of nearly blond hair back behind her ear with an impatient gesture. "And the Arlys—"

"Well, just one—but Mother was being difficult that day."

Helen began to look a bit strained. "Please, Jerome, we'd like to get on with this. The Arlys both have the flu, and my personal sympathy. Al just got over it, and no doubt the Arlys got it from him." She glanced toward her husband. "He was impossible to live with for over a week."

Jerome leaned toward Abby and whispered, "Al Rhine is impossible, flu or no flu."

Surprised at hearing that sort of remark from someone

16

she'd just met, Abby glanced toward him. He smiled, as though his words were meant to be taken as a joke.

"Alice Hillman isn't here, so we'll dispense with reading the minutes. Would you mind filling in tonight, Karen?" Helen asked.

Karen nodded and Jerome said, "I'd like the minutes to show that whereas last month the meeting room was a veritable refrigerator, this month it is much too hot. It is always one or the other; the library seeming helpless to correct the situation."

Ignoring Jerome, Helen said, "And without Horace Arly, no treasurer's report." She looked up from the notepad, where she had drawn a series of nested boxes in perspective. "Now, we all want to know what the Plan Commission is up to, but Al had his bout with the flu right at the time of their last meeting, and couldn't attend. Has anyone heard anything?"

Karen looked up from her note taking. "I heard they want to convert the old schoolhouse into a storage shed for the Park District."

"That talk has come up before." Al Rhine allowed his bulky form to slide farther down in his chair. "I don't think it will happen."

"Well, at least they've given up the idea of tearing it down," Karen said.

Leaning toward Abby, Jerome whispered, "That shade of blue suits you." Abby mumbled thanks, and Jerome went on. "Helen should take lessons. Never seems to find anything but muddy browns in her closet." Then, raising his voice, he said, "We need better coordination with the Olde Branch. James Farrell should be here."

"Can't have it both ways, Jerome," Al said. "He's at the Olde Branch now."

"Poor man is doing his best to stay active in both groups," Helen said.

Al nodded. "Horace Arly too. He's always complaining because he'd like to attend both."

Now Helen nodded. "And I think Rudy Wilking would

join us, if it weren't for the conflict. We really should find some way to change our meeting night."

"I agree," Karen Canelli said. "I'd like to join the Olde Branch myself."

Jerome's eyebrows rose to his hairline. "You know how difficult it is to get a regular night at the library. *They*, on the other hand, could change easily. After all, they meet in a saloon, of all places."

"Tell you what, Jerome," Al said. "Instead of changing the meeting night, why don't we switch meeting places? I'll swap our coffeepot for a glass of draft any day."

"I suggest we draft a letter pointing out—"

"Well, we can't settle that problem tonight," Helen said. "Let's get on to something more productive."

Abby, following these exchanges as best she could, was beginning to feel sorry for Jerome Bedford, despite his annoying mannerisms. She didn't know which was worse—Al Rhine's putdowns or Helen Rhine's determination to ignore him.

Well, they knew him better than she did. Maybe the treatment was deserved. But he seemed so pathetically eager to—to what? Make his mark? Gain their attention? Abby had thought seriously of joining the Society. She was no longer sure that was a good idea. Not if general bitchiness was the regular order of business.

"In view of our poor attendance," Helen said, "I suggest we conduct the rest of the meeting over coffee, and proceed to Abby's problem."

Jerome rose and said to Abby, "I'll see to your coffee. What would you like in it?"

"Black will do fine. Thank you."

Addressing the group now clustered around the coffeepot, Helen said, "Abby McKenzie would like—"

"McKenzie? Of course." Jerome handed Abby a slice of cake wrapped in a paper napkin. "I should have realized when we were introduced. You're the one who bought the Twilly house."

"Yes. As a matter of fact, that's—"

18

"Did you know they wanted to rename Twilly Place? Sarah's Alley. Really! If you want an historic area, the least you can do is be historic."

"That's interesting," Abby said. "I—"

"Did you know the house dates back to 1907?" Jerome continued. "I've never been inside—I wonder—do you suppose we might have a peek?"

Helen frowned. "Really, Jerome, she's just moved in. I'm sure she doesn't want all of us trooping through the place before they've had a chance to get settled."

Jerome straightened his vest. "Well, I didn't mean this *instant*, Helen."

"As a matter of fact, the house is what brought me here," Abby said. "We'd like to restore it, within reason, to the way it looked originally. I was hoping the Society might have some information?"

"I'm keeper-of-odds-and-ends," Karen said, "or society archivist, if you prefer. We do have a collection of pictures."

"Would it be possible for me to see them?" Abby asked.

"Why don't you come for lunch and you can rummage around."

"There *is* a photograph taken about 1920," Jerome said, "I ran across it while I was researching the Schneider farm." He wiped a crumb from his lip, neatly folded his paper napkin, and dropped it in the waste basket. "Why don't I come along? I'm sure I can lay my hands on that picture directly."

"That's not necessary," Karen said. "I'll dig it out tonight and have it ready. Tomorrow all right, Abby?"

The snub could not be clearer, but Jerome seemed not to notice. "Speaking of the Schneider farm, I would like to request a special meeting next week. I have a *grave* matter to discuss."

"Grave? What do you mean, 'grave,' Jerome?" Al asked.

"I'll say no more. But *do* try to arrange the meeting, Helen."

Helen shrugged. "If the library is available. And the other members are agreeable."

Jerome seemed prepared to remain close-mouthed and mysterious against an onslaught of questions, but Helen Rhine began talking about the Society's Sarahville history booklet.

Abby looked at Jerome and wondered how it must feel to be persistently ignored. If it bothered him, he showed no sign.

"I'm off, everyone," Jerome said. "A rendezvous in the fog-shrouded night, and I'll have the key to a mystery!"

Al looked bored and Helen said, "Good night, Jerome."

Karen who, with the exception of cutting off his attempt to join her at lunch, had not joined the Rhines in Jerome-baiting, said, "Bundle up, Jerome. You don't want to catch the flu like Horace."

Jerome laughed. "I shall avoid the mythical flu bug." He shrugged on his coat, looked at his watch, and grimaced. "For want of a battery." A glance at the wall clock, a jaunty wave, and he was gone.

Abby looked at her own watch and wondered how Mac's meeting was coming along.

"Now what the hell do you suppose that was all about?" Al Rhine asked the ceiling.

"You'll have to come to that special meeting, Abby," Karen said. "I'm sure Jerome was talking about your neighbors to the south."

"Neighbors?"

"The residents of the Schneider graveyard."

20

Chapter 3

Mac sat through the Olde Branch meeting learning little, except that the members were more concerned with cold cuts and coffee, courtesy of Rudy Wilking, than with business. A circulating waitress added to the social atmosphere and, in the case of one member, to a loss of coherence.

As a newcomer he had been introduced to the group—about a dozen members—but for the most part the names had evaporated from his memory almost as soon as he'd heard them. Except for Rudy, of course, and for James Farrell, a short, wiry, redhead in his forties.

Farrell (Jim as he preferred to be called) explained he was a neighbor of the McKenzies, proprietor of the Twilly Feed and Farm Implement Antique Shop at the corner of Twilly and Olde Main. He took a seat next to Mac and kept up a running commentary on the proceedings.

"Half of these guys look at this as a night out. The other half just want an audience while they complain about the village garbage pickup or license fees. Not much gets done here."

"Why do *you* come?"

"Beer and sandwiches, and you never know what you might hear. Pays to know how the other businesses are getting along."

"Do you think this little corner of nostalgia will make it?"

21

Jim Farrell shrugged. "Jury's still out. They made a great success of this kind of thing up in Long Grove, but they didn't have our village board to contend with."

Mac sighed. It would be a crushing disappointment for Abby if her business failed. All the more reason the store should be his only interest.

Jim Farrell nudged him. "If you want to doze off, now's a good time. The chairman is about to tell us why we have to elect one of us mayor. Namely himself, though he won't say so. This usually takes about fifteen minutes."

Mac took Farrell's advice and let his mind wander. Abby kept telling him he wasn't cut out to be a shopkeeper, and tonight he was inclined to believe her. But it had been interesting so far. He smiled, almost chuckled aloud. The honeymoon in Arizona might have something to do with that, he admitted. Then visiting his daughter and his newborn grandson. Moving. Planning Abby's store. And Abby.

True, things would be different once the store was open. Waiting on customers, keeping books, ordering stock. Well, he'd manage. And he'd be there when she needed him, not off on some client's business.

Mac hoped Abby was having a better time than he was.

At adjournment most of the Olde Branch members drifted off home or to the bar downstairs. Mac lingered to talk to Rudy. James Farrell stayed to have a sandwich.

A tall, well-built man, mid-thirties, beer in hand, joined them and introduced himself as Jack Taylor. He had come in late and, like Mac, was new to the group. When asked, he said he had an idea for an old-fashioned ice cream parlor, and Olde Sarahville looked like a promising site. "Except it don't look like you can handle a whole lot more business with the little bit of parking available," he said.

"The way the Plan Commission has arranged matters," Rudy said, "each business will have room to park three, four cars tops, in front. Like horses at a hitching rail. Totally inadequate. So, what will the customers do? Park in my lot, of course. It is larger, and also close to where the new shops will be."

"Can't they enlarge Olde Sarahville to include a parking lot?" Jack Taylor asked.

Jim Farrell said, "If there was just one developer, the Zoning Board could do its usual extortion. Make him cough up some public use land."

"There is no room," Rudy added. "For example, the land to the north is a flood plain, owned by the Park District."

Farrell laughed. "Hear what they paid for that swamp? Belonged to one of the park commissioners, you know."

Rudy ignored the diversion. "West of Harper Road, except for the corner, is residential."

"Farther east on Main, then," Mac suggested. "Beyond where the creek runs under the street."

"Too far from the center of things. Who would walk that far to get to your place, Mac? Or yours, Jim?"

"McKenzie might solve his own problem," Farrell said. "The vacant lot next to him—"

"Is an eyesore." Mac accepted his first beer of the evening from the waitress. "An old foundation poking up through the weeds. I've been meaning to find out who owns it."

Rudy looked stricken. "I am so sorry. The lot is mine. I intend to build on the old foundation eventually. I will arrange to have it cleaned up immediately."

Conversation lapsed for a bit until Farrell said, "Maybe the village should buy your parking lot, Rudy."

"Not big enough," Jack Taylor said. "Waste of taxpayer money."

"Yes, but the property east of me belongs to the village, and we have adjoining driveways." Rudy shook his head gloomily. "Somebody is bound to think of combining the two properties into one large parking lot." He sighed. "And I wish to put a beer garden on part of my lot."

"The old one-room schoolhouse is there," Farrell said. "People wouldn't stand for it."

"Your amateur historians would not like it, I know. But

23

the Plan Commission wanted to tear it down before."

"Well, it's your property," Taylor said. "You don't have to sell to the Village."

"I'd be reluctant, that's true." Rudy frowned. "But if everyone pushed for it, I suppose I'd have to consider."

"Anyway, there's probably a better solution," Taylor said.

"Like what?" Farrell asked.

"Something will turn up."

"I'm glad you are confident," Rudy said. "Does that mean you have made your decision?"

"Decision?"

"About the ice cream parlor. You have run such a business before?"

Taylor swallowed the last of his beer. "Up until last year I was making a career of the Navy. One hitch short of retirement, and I decided enough was enough."

"The military life is difficult," Rudy said.

Taylor grinned. "So far, you haven't said anything to make me believe running a business will be easier. I saved up my reenlistment bonuses and I can see it all melting away with the ice cream."

Conversation turned to the Cubs' dismal performance in spring training, and what that might, or might not, say about the coming season. Then Rudy, suggesting the others might wish to visit the bar downstairs, excused himself.

The three, noting everyone else had left, agreed it was time to be going. Mac retrieved his windbreaker, and Taylor a Navy pea coat. Farrell said good night and headed for the men's room while Mac and Taylor walked to the parking lot.

"That Wilking is as reluctant as a shark after cut bait," Taylor said, pulling a watch cap over his black hair.

"About selling his parking lot? Not a bad scam from his viewpoint. Some cash in the pocket, a lower tax bill, the same old parking lot in the same old place, and maintained by the taxpayers to boot."

"Yeah. But he needs somebody else to push it so he won't look too eager."

"No parking problems tonight," Mac said. "Only a couple of cars in the lot. Which is yours?"

"Way back there," Taylor said, pointing toward the back of the lot. He laughed. "I got confused coming here and turned in the wrong drive. I think I'm parked on the grounds of that schoolhouse Wilking talked about. Where's yours?"

"I walked over."

"Can I give you a lift?"

Mac looked back at the tavern where the light over the door had acquired a fog-induced halo. "No thanks. It's not far." He could see the dark bulk of a car at the rear of the lot, but the hedge that he knew marked the border between tavern and school ground had vanished in white mist. "Take care. The fog's getting thicker."

Chapter 4

Abby had stopped for gas after the Society meeting and drove home at ten miles per hour, straining to see the center line of the road. By the time she arrived, Mac was already upstairs preparing for bed. "How were the Olde Boys?" she asked.

"About as foggy as the weather. How about the Olde Broads?"

"The only Olde Broad was named Jerome."

"No women at all?"

"Two women, two men." Abby slipped off her dress and went into the bathroom. "But it was a smaller than usual turnout. Did you meet someone named Farrell?"

"Yeah. He owns the antique place at the corner. The Feed and Farm Implement Store."

"I thought the name was familiar. Did he have any luck getting a change in the meeting night? He belongs to the Society too, you know."

"So he said. The Olde Boys see the Society as meddlers." Mac turned on the TV and settled on the bed.

"I think that's shortsighted, don't you?"

"Who's Jerome?"

"A mainstay of the Society. Probably forty, improbably neat, unmarried and unlikely. Tends to swoop and flutter."

"Flutter? You mean he's—"

Abby chuckled. "Oh, I don't think so. As a matter of fact, I think he was trying to hit on me."

"Can't quarrel with his taste."

"I'm probably wrong about that. He seemed . . . He's pathetically eager to be accepted. Appreciated. And he gets no chance from that bunch."

"How about your project?"

"I'm having lunch with the local archivist. There's a collection of old photographs."

"Archivist? Who's he?"

Abby came out of the bathroom and slipped into bed. "What are you watching?"

"Rio Bravo."

"Haven't you seen that before?"

"Only twice. Who's the archivist?"

"Karen Cannelli. And your meeting?"

"Complaints. The village doesn't give the project enough support, the zoning people discourage developers, the Plan Commission doesn't know what the hell it's doing."

"That's all?"

"Rudy had a lot to say about parking. You want something to eat?"

Abby yawned. "I had cake and coffee."

Mac explained Wilking's apparent reluctance and probable intent.

"What about his beer garden?"

"I think that's just a way of jacking up the price." Mac got out of bed. "I'm going to the kitchen. Want anything?"

"Mac, have you thought any more about taking a client?"

"No."

"Why not? You know that meeting tonight bored you silly."

"There's too much to do around here. You need shelves put up, the stairs need repairing, the—well you know."

This topic was going nowhere, Abby knew. But she couldn't let it rest. Her voice sharpened. "With the money you'd make from one good case we could hire a carpenter and get it done right."

"What's wrong with my—"

"You've tried fixing the screen door twice and it still rattles dishes when it slams."

Mac headed for the stairs. "I asked if you wanted anything from the kitchen." There was an edge to his voice now.

Abby turned her back to him and adjusted her pillow. "Just turn down the volume. Gunfire keeps me awake."

Mac's resentment of Abby's nagging evaporated as he watched John Wayne, several years his senior, pursued by Angie Dickinson. Unfortunately, Abby was sound asleep.

The next day started early for Mac with a shower that delivered a tepid, rust-brown stream, followed by a silent breakfast of dry cereal. His conciliatory inquiry as to how Abby had slept was answered with a shrug.

The condition of the shower now struck him as an opportunity for a practical demonstration of one of his arguments for staying with the store. He got his toolbox from the garage and descended into the cellar.

By twelve-thirty, satisfied a new water heater was the only solution, he put away his tools. For some reason this softened Abby and she offered to get his lunch. The sound of the screendoor slamming interrupted her on the way to the refrigerator.

She opened the door to the porch, admitting Captain Stanley Pawlowski, Sarahville's chief of detectives. He was also Mac's closest friend, the two having grown up together on Chicago's Division Street. "Come in, Stan," Abby said. "You're just in time to join Mac for lunch."

"Thanks. I can use it."

"I have to go out," Abby said, "so try to keep him from falling asleep after he eats. He has to pick out a new water heater."

"Napping after meals? I warned him to be careful. Getting married at his age can be a strain."

28

"Don't let your promotion go to your head, Captain," Mac said. "Think of me as a taxpayer. Show a little respect."

Stan removed his coat and hat, uncovering black hair, gray at the temples. He dropped the coat and hat on one vacant chair, himself on another, and accepted a beer from Mac.

"Congratulations, Stan," Abby said. "We were glad to hear Sarahville finally recognized your worth."

"The hell they did." He took a long pull at his beer and grimaced as though it had left a bad taste. "John Allmeir wants to be captain and his buddy the mayor wants to oblige. The only captain we got is the chief's assistant, and no way to bump him out of his job; he's got seniority up the kazoo and friends on the Village Board. So, His Honor waves his wand and the captain becomes deputy chief, no change in salary. We ain't heard the last of that."

"What does that have to do with your—"

"I'm telling you. Allmeir is chief of the blue suits, which is now declared a captaincy. So, since Lieutenant Pawlowski is chief of detectives, they have to make him a captain for symmetry. And don't think His Honor didn't try to figure a way around that."

"Well, that's big-city politics," Mac said.

"Small-town crap," Stan said. He waved his hand as if pushing the matter aside. "Were you folks home last night?"

"I was at a Historical Society meeting," Abby said. "Why?"

"Historical Society? You're really getting into this old-timers stuff, aren't you?" He shook his head sadly. "Nip it in the bud, Mac. Two years ago Julie found a chair at a garage sale. One leg a quarter inch short and six coats of paint. Made me strip the damn thing down to bare wood."

Mac got a bag of pretzels from the pantry and placed it in front of Stan. "Turned out to be an antique?"

"Turned out to be junk. But she bought it for two dollars and sold it at our garage sale for three-and-a-half. To her, it's a profit; to me, it's damn small pay for two days' work. Now she goes to every garage sale and country auction she can find."

"I'll have to ask her to be on the lookout for a stained glass fanlight," Abby said.

"Anyway, the reason I asked where you were," Stan said, "did either of you hear any shooting last night?"

"Shooting?" Abby asked. "Why? What happened?"

"Just answer the question, ma'am."

Abby removed the bag as Stan reached for it. "Jack Webb you ain't."

"What are we talking about?" Mac asked. "Disturbing the peace, or what?"

"Homicide."

"My God! Around here?" Abby asked.

Mac frowned. "What time last night?"

"We don't have a good fix on that yet. Just for argument, let's say after dark and before six this morning."

Mac shook his head. "Must have been close by or you wouldn't ask."

"At the old schoolhouse," Stan said.

Mac looked at Abby. "Okay to feed him now?"

Abby shuddered. "That close?"

"Here," Mac said, passing the bag, "but no sandwich till we get the rest of the story."

"Not much story yet. A village crew showed up this morning to do some work on the grounds. They found a car parked on the grass and—"

"Not Taylor?!"

Stan looked at Mac in surprise. "Taylor? No. Who's Taylor?"

"Never mind. Go ahead."

"Well, they called in to have it towed. You have to ticket before you tow, so a patrol came by. They noticed the padlock on the schoolhouse pried loose. Found the body inside."

Abby glanced at the clock. "I came by there less than three hours ago. Come to think of it, there *was* a police car."

"That must have been right about when the body was discovered, or you'd have seen more than one," Mac said. "So why are you lounging around here, Stan? You haven't been on the case very long."

"I've seen all I want. The evidence tech is still working and I've got a couple of men checking on who heard, or saw, what. I'm here so I can put my feet up a minute. It'll be a long day."

Abby got up and began to pull the makings of sandwiches from the refrigerator. "You can't live on beer and pretzels. Have you called Julie? No? Do it now, before you get so wrapped up in this you forget where you live."

"Since you know it wasn't Taylor, you must have an ID," Mac said.

"Guy by the name of Jerome Bedford."

Abby dropped the mustard.

Chapter 5

While Mac carried mustard-stained glass to the trash can, Abby wiped the tile floor with a paper towel. "I can't believe it," she said. "Jerome?"

Stan made himself a mustardless ham on rye and listened to what little Abby knew of Jerome's movements the night before. "If Bedford left the meeting at nine-fifteen," Stan said, "and if he went directly to the schoolhouse, he couldn't have been shot before, say, nine-thirty. What time did the meeting break up?"

"We all left when the library made its closing announcement. About ten-thirty."

"Nobody left early? Besides Bedford?"

"No. You don't think—?"

"Too early to think anything."

"Really, Stan," Abby said. "If he wanted to talk to one of the members he could have done it right there."

Mac joined Stan at the table. "Maybe not. It sounds like he was gearing up for a big announcement at the next meeting. He didn't want anyone to know what he was up to."

"He'd have kept quiet about his appointment." Abby, rinsing her hands at the sink, raised her voice above the sound of running water and knocking pipes. "Then he could talk to the person after the meeting. No one would think a thing about it. Anyway, his remarks would sound foolish, if the person was present. If there's one thing I'm sure of on short acquaintance, it's that Jerome would not want to sound foolish."

"Which remarks you mean?" Stan asked.

"Something about a fog-shrouded rendezvous. I think he left early as a kind of dramatic exit. He hinted about this grave business and everyone ignored the poor man. I think his feelings were hurt."

Stan checked his watch. "At least nobody can say I wasted my time coming here. Any last words, before I leave?"

"Call Julie," Abby said.

"How about me, Officer?" Mac asked. "Don't I get a turn in the barrel?"

Stan paused with one arm in the sleeve of his coat. "What do you know about it?"

"I was at a meeting too. At the Running Fox. I left about a quarter to eleven, along with a guy named Taylor. He mentioned turning in the wrong driveway and parking on the grass east of the tavern. You can see why I jumped the gun."

"How many cars did you see over there?"

"None. Lots of fog, and I'm not sure I even glanced that way. But Taylor must have seen Bedford's car, if it was there."

"Where can I find Taylor?"

Mac shook his head. "Maybe Rudy Wilking can tell you. Talk to Jim Farrell too; he left after me, so he might have seen something. Could it have been a parking lot mugger?"

"Bedford was wearing an expensive watch, and his wallet was in his pocket."

"If a robbery got out of hand—"

"Maybe. But what was Bedford doing in the schoolhouse? And who broke in? Him, or the killer?"

Uncertain whether Karen Cannelli had heard of

Jerome's death, or how she would take it when she did, Abby phoned to give her a chance to cancel their lunch. Karen had heard the news from Jean Arly; she assured Abby that company would be welcome.

The building was the center one of three, each three stories, that made up the Winslow apartment complex. All were set well back from Winslow Avenue. Having been buzzed in, Abby stepped out of the elevator on the top floor to find Karen waiting in the open doorway of her apartment.

Wearing jeans and a bulky blue sweater, her blond hair cut short, she waved to Abby. "I'm glad you could make it," Karen said. "I've got cabin fever and need the company."

Another blond head, at knee level, peered around the door jamb. Abby smiled at the boy as he looked up at her with open curiosity. "And who is this?"

"I'm Jason. I've got two guns. Want to see?"

"Better let him show you. We won't get any peace until he has."

Jason ran off. He was back, fumbling with the buckle of a two-holster belt by the time Abby reached the small living room. "I got a cowboy hat too," he said. "But Mommy lost it."

"No, Jason. You left it in the playground."

He looked sidelong at Abby. "I left it in the playground, and Mommy lost it."

"Well, maybe it'll turn up again," Abby said.

Karen sighed and shook her head. "Okay, Jason. Go play now." Jason ran from the room, guns blazing.

"He's a doll. How old is he?"

"Four. More devil than doll." Karen started to lead the way to a kitchen that doubled as a dining area, then hesitated. "Want to see the pictures now? Or eat first?"

"Why don't we eat, since it's ready." Seeing Karen in daylight, Abby moved her estimate of age from the early to the late twenties. Her fair coloring contrasted with the Italian 'Cannelli.' An attractive woman. Perhaps a bit

34

tense; there were three ashtrays in the room, each with a half-smoked, dead cigarette.

Taking her place at the table, Abby said, "This is a lovely apartment."

"I'll be glad to move. Jason doesn't get out enough. You know how it is. Energy confined tends to explode." She put a tuna salad on the table along with rolls and butter. "I hear from the people downstairs."

"You're leaving Sarahville?"

"I'll be your neighbor this time next year. East side of Twilly, one down from the corner."

"Really? Last time I looked, that was mostly mud."

"You haven't heard?" Karen paid no attention to her tuna. "They break ground this year. A row of stores, you know, common walls, but different fronts and roof lines. The architect's drawing looks like an old-time business street." She lit a cigarette. "But the best part is, each one has a flat upstairs."

"That's great!" Abby said, glad things were moving at last. "We knew there'd be something there someday. But right now we're exposed and lonely. And it'll be so nice to have you for a neighbor. You're renting one of the flats?"

"The unit—store and flat—is a package deal. If you don't want the flat, you can sublease, but the combination is the main appeal for me."

Abby sat back in surprise. "You're going into business, then. Come to think of it, you *did* say you wanted to join the Olde Branch."

Karen's face lit with enthusiasm as she nodded. "Ice cream parlor. Tiffany lamps, marble-top tables, the whole Gay Nineties shtick. What do you think?"

"I'll guarantee one steady customer. I'm an ice cream addict." Abby paused with a morsel of tomato halfway to her mouth. "Have you ever run a business?"

"Managed an ice cream store in Palatine for about three years. One of a chain. Not the same as owning, maybe, but—"

"Then you're not going into this blind."

"Just scared to death." Karen's attempt at a smile was not entirely successful.

Abby nodded in sympathy. "I know the feeling. I was a nervous wreck when I opened my first shop. Even now, opening a new store, I wonder if it's not a mistake."

"Vito, that was my husband, believed in insurance. I invested it for Jason's education. Now—well, I feel like I'm gambling with his future." Karen shrugged and waved the subject aside. "I don't usually bore people with my troubles." She started on the tuna salad. "I heard you were just recently married?"

"Yes."

"Late blooming—oh, I didn't mean—I mean, forty's not *old*."

Abby, pleased with the underestimate, laughed. "How did you come to join the Historical Society?"

"When I was twelve, an aunt showed me our family tree, and I got hooked on genealogy. My side, the Knudsens, are pretty well covered but I wanted to do something on the Cannellis. Helen Rhine works on the library reference desk and I met her while doing research."

"She got you interested in local history?"

"I attended a few meetings, got friendly with her and Jean Arly. And it *is* fascinating once you get into it."

"How did Jean Arly come to hear about Jerome? I didn't hear until just before I called you."

Karen poured coffee for them. "Isn't that awful? Poor Jerome. I still have trouble believing it." She sipped her coffee. "Horse—" She laughed in embarrassment. "Sorry. That slipped out. Al Rhine always calls him Horse, and if you knew H.A.—"

Abby shook her head. "I think you lost me. Which one is Horse and who's H.A.?"

"Sorry. Horace Arly, Jean Arly's husband. He prefers H.A., but like I said, Al Rhine calls him Horse. Mostly because of his name, but he *does* have one of those long, bony faces."

"Oh, yes. We met him at the Running Fox Tavern. He

works there, doesn't he?"

"He's an accountant. Rudy's one of his clients." Karen looked a bit rueful. "I called him Horse once, to my embarrassment. He takes it from Al, but you can see he resents it. Don't you find most men cherish their nicknames, like little kids?"

"Men are peculiar that way," Abby said. "Never really grow up."

Karen grinned. "Yeah. Isn't it great?" They both laughed. "Would you believe, when I joined the group I thought I might meet a man with compatible interests? But they're all married." She sobered abruptly. "Except Jerome, of course."

"And Jerome wasn't exactly—"

"Exactly. I'm sorry you took the brunt of it last night. Agnes Ketchall usually sits next to Jerome and she seemed to enjoy those bitchy asides. She's out of town." Karen stubbed out her cigarette. "This will be a real shock to her." She reached for another cigarette, apparently changed her mind, and stuffed it back in the pack.

"You were saying, about Horace Arly?"

"Oh, yes. Well, I told you the Running Fox Tavern is one of his clients and he happened to call there right after the police had been in asking questions." Karen lit the cigarette she had briefly denied herself. "I get depressed every time I think of it. Let's change the subject."

Abby nodded. "Back to men, then. Surely the Society isn't the last word on eligible males."

Sighing, Karen said, "Raising a kid doesn't leave much time to meet people. More coffee?" Abby shook her head, and Karen said, "Mom took care of Jason while I worked. Then Dad retired and they moved to Florida. Babysitters were okay, but chickenpox, and then flu, finally did me in. I'm hoping the store will support us and let me keep an eye on him at the same time."

Karen led the way to the living room, where Jason had stretched a blanket between the couch and the coffee table to form a tent. "All right, Jason. Now where are we going

37

to sit?"

Jason tried hard to wrinkle his smooth brow in a frown. "I've had it with this place." He yanked the blanket loose "If you want me, I'll be in my room."

Abby tried to suppress a grin. Karen sighed. "He's spent too much time in the company of a frustrated adult. He's got some peculiar expressions for a four-year-old."

"Better that, than some he'll pick up from his peers." Abby sat on the couch. "Tell me about the graveyard. Any idea what Jerome Bedford's mysterious hints referred to?" Then, remembering Karen's plea to stop talking about Jerome, she said "Oh, sorry. I forgot."

"That's all right. He's going to be uppermost in everybody's thoughts for a while." Karen picked up her cigarettes and turned the pack in her hands twice. "I've got to quit smoking. It's a bad example for Jason." She laid the pack back on the end table.

Uncertain whether to pursue her question or let it drop, Abby remained silent.

"Jerome could be a royal pain in the butt. Still, I felt sorry for him. He wanted to be accepted and didn't have a clue as to how to go about it."

"I only met him the one time. He seemed sort of . . ." Abby searched for words that would not sound unkind.

"He was a real perfectionist. If you read our Sarahville history, you'll see the chapter on the Schneider farm is the most complete. By far. Jerome's work. Makes the rest of us look bad."

"Where is the Schneider farm? Or is the graveyard all that's left?"

"No, the house and barn are still there. Can't imagine— unless . . . See, the first thing settlers did was dig a hole, put a roof over it, and move in. The second thing was build a church. All burials around here were in the churchyard. Maybe he found out why the Schneiders were an exception."

"Has anyone asked the Schneiders?"

"Too late now. None left. Matter of fact, Jerome *did*

interview the old man once. It didn't go too well. A clash of personalities."

Abby arrived home to see Mac climbing a ladder to the porch roof. "What are you doing? Besides getting ready to break your neck?"

"There's a touch of rot on the porch floor. Must be a leak somewhere. How was lunch?"

"Rot? Don't tell me we have to replace the porch!"

"Don't get excited. It's just one board." Mac shifted his weight and the ladder moved. "Hold the ladder. The ground's a little rough here."

Steadying the ladder, she said, "I found out six new stores are going up this spring."

"On Twilly? That's good news."

"But you'll never guess who's building them. Elmer Johnson."

"Well. Then I guess *he's* not worried about traffic."

She watched Mac climb down. "Funny he didn't say anything about it when he sold us this place."

Following Abby inside, he said, "A little goop on a trowel will fix the leak."

"I just wonder what else he didn't tell us." She handed him a sepia-toned, slightly faded photo. Easily recognizable, it had a sapling where the oak now shaded the west side of their house. A line of hollyhocks bloomed along the porch. "Read it and weep. That's definitely a stained glass fanlight."

"I know he's not exactly your favorite person, but . . ." Mac held the photo up to the fading light from the west window. "All I see is a glimmer in the middle of the porch shadow."

"Your eyes are going bad, old man. That is a stained glass fanlight, so let's have no argument."

"She let you have this?"

"Be careful with it. I borrowed it to have a copy made. What do you think about an enlargement? To hang in the store."

"Nice touch." He handed back the photo. "I'll have a talk with Elmer."

"And a caption explaining the history." Taking up the Society's pamphlet, she leafed through it. "Here it is. Oh, did you know that Farrell's place used to be Twilly's Feed and Farm Implement? It says here the Twillys lived in the back of the store until 1907, when they built this house." Reading a bit further, she said, "My God! They had twelve children! No wonder the house is so big."

Mac, again taking up the picture, said, "Damned if I can make out stained glass." He laid it on the table. "What's in the bag?"

"That's a cowboy hat for Jason."

"Who?"

"Karen Cannelli's four-year old. He's a doll."

"I guess you got on pretty well with this Cannelli."

"She's uptight about her first business venture. I remember how it was with me. I had sweaty palms every month until the accounts balanced and I knew bankruptcy had been postponed. Part of the problem is, Jason keeps her tied to the apartment. She needs some social life. An eligible man wouldn't hurt, either."

"I'm going to have a beer. Want one?"

Abby nodded and went back to the book. "Jerome Bedford really did a job on the Schneiders. A complete family tree, starting with Jacob Schneider, born in Germany." She turned back to the section on the Twilly family.

He set a can of Stroh's beside her and looked over her shoulder. "Anything on the graveyard?"

She riffled the pages. "Here it is. All family members that remained on the farm were buried there, starting with Anna, wife of Jacob, who begat . . . et cetera." She read in silence for a moment. "The last burial is Heinrich Schneider, born 1893, died 1974. Let's see—that made him eighty-one. And the end of the line for the Schneiders."

Mac yawned. "I'm going into Chicago tommorrow, to a salvage yard. They might have some gingerbread trim like the piece that's missing from the gable. Want to come along?"

"I can't. Karen's coming to see how we're laying out the store. Oh, I almost forgot. What about the water heater?"

"All taken care of."

"Good. When will it be installed?"

"When I said it was taken care of, I meant I got a new heater."

"They've already put it in? That's great! I can shower before you take me out to dinner."

"Not exactly. I *got* a heater and wrestled it into the house and down the cellar stairs."

Abby glared at him. "You didn't! Yes, you did. I can see by the way you sit. You've got a sore back and it'll be the heating pad tonight. Whatever possessed you—"

"You know what a plumber charges? You're the one saying we need the money."

"One good case—"

"Anyway, it's all taken care of. Stan's coming by to give me a hand tonight."

"You shouldn't have done that. With this murder case, Julie and the kids see little enough of—"

"Don't worry. I asked the whole family for supper."

"Mac! We don't have a thing in the house. The place is a mess. Did you think of that?"

"Sure. We can defrost that chili I made—"

"Oh no you don't. I'll call Julie and tell her you're taking us all out."

Stan wiped his hand across his brow, leaving a trail of rust and plumber's putty. "Someday I'm going to put in a screen porch like this one. Just sit on it all summer listening to the mosquitoes trying to get in."

"A little early in the season for porch-sitting," Mac said. "We better not stay too long."

"Porch-standing is okay. I need to cool off. What you going to do with that big boiler in the basement?"

41

"Leave it. I'd have to cut it up with a torch. Wonder how they got the old coal furnace out when they converted to gas."

Stan walked over to the screen. "Nice clear night." He lit a cigarette. "I talked to Farrell, like you suggested. He came out as you were walking away, and he saw a silhouette he figures was this guy Taylor stop next to a car near the back of the lot. But you say Taylor parked outside the lot."

"Yeah. He missed the turn in the fog and wound up on the schoolhouse property. Is he sure it was Taylor?"

"Says it was the silhouette of a Navy pea coat with the collar up. That's what Taylor wore, right?"

"Right. What do you hear from the other people in the tavern?"

"Only two others. They left about midnight, in no condition to see much, and walked home. Wilking relieved the bartender, who left by the front door; he walks home too. At closing Wilking takes the receipts to the bank, leaving by the kitchen door, which opens on the service drive. That's on the north side where you can't see much of the back."

Mac joined Stan at the screen. "No other possible witnesses?"

"A patrol car makes a habit of coming by at closing time and following Wilking to the night deposit. On the way back to their beat they passed the tavern and noticed the lot was empty, but there was a car on the school grounds."

"They didn't check it out?"

"It's not unusual. People mix up the driveways. The day shift tickets them if they're still there."

The night was becoming decidedly chilly, but they lingered on the porch, watching a cloud move across the moon. Stan broke the silence.

"So, how's it going?"

"Going?"

"Married life."

"Fine."

"Abby was frosted about this heater deal."

"If I was still taking clients, and had done this in my spare time, she'd be glad enough to save the money. It's giving up the license that bugs her. Figures I'm just doing it for her sake."

"Aren't you?"

"I figure this place will take care of me in my old age."

"Which starts next week, right?" Stan lit another cigarette. "I give it six months. For one thing, Abby's the only one smart enough to make change. For another, you'll be bored."

"A chance to be home evenings and weekends. A little quiet boredom couldn't hurt." To change the subject, Mac pointed to a bobbing light on top of the hill. "What's that?"

"Kids," Stan said. "Probably like to creep around the tombstones and scare themselves."

Chapter 6

By the last day of March the shock of Jerome Bedford's murder had receded and both Abby and Karen Cannelli were deep into store planning. The two of them leaned over the drawing board while Mac watched Jason launch a paper airplane from halfway up the Twilly house stairs. The flight ended on the floor plan of an ice cream parlor.

Without raising her head, Karen pushed the plane off the board and said, "Jason, don't play on the stairs."

Mac said, "Why don't Jason and I go look at the creek."

"Good idea," Abby agreed. "Just make sure both of you bundle up. A little sunshine in March does not a spring make." She watched them leave hand-in-hand.

Karen pushed at a strand of hair with her pencil. "I'm afraid it's not such a good idea, bringing Jason here when we're trying to work."

Abby disagreed. "We love having him around."

"But we've been here four days this week and Mac got stuck babysitting every time. I'm sure he'd rather be helping you with the store plans."

"He loves playing uncle. To tell the truth, the store bores him. He helps with the handyman work, and moving things around, but . . ." Abby straightened up and rubbed the small of her back. "I wish I could convince him not to give up his own business."

44

"What business is that?"

Abby hesitated. She and Karen had been visiting each other regularly and had become fast friends despite the difference in their ages. Abby wasn't sure why. Perhaps Karen reminded her of her first attempt at launching a business at a similar age. She wandered over to the window and watched Mac point out an abandoned bird's nest, then lift Jason to his shoulders for a better view.

"If you asked him," Abby said, "he'd say he was a consultant. The truth is, he's a private detective."

"Really? How exciting! No wonder all this store talk bores him. Why is he giving it up?"

"It's a long story."

Karen, joining Abby at the window, pointed to the pair outside. "Look. Jason wants Mac to put him up in the tree where that squirrel's chattering." Turning to Abby, she said, "You never had children, did you?"

Abby watched Mac and Jason, hand in hand again, disappear around the back of the house. "No. Mac has a daughter. And a grandson."

"Was he a lot like Mac? Your first husband?"

Abby laughed. "God, no. Bill Norris was a professional con artist. Always one step ahead of the posse."

"Oh, I'm sorry. I didn't mean to pry."

Abby shrugged. "It doesn't matter anymore. The story got to be common knowledge in some circles. Any number of people could tell you everything that happened, and a lot that didn't."

"The reason I asked is, I've always heard that people repeat — you know. And I know, when I meet someone, I tend to compare them to Vito. They usually come up short."

Abby considered the implied question. It had never occured to her to compare Mac and Bill Norris. The idea struck her as ludicrous. Still . . . "Now that you mention it, when Mac's working on a case, he can be just as devious as Bill. And there's that sense of excitement when he's . . ." Abby shook her head. "No.

45

They're completely different. For one thing, Mac has in-
tegrity."

Karen nodded. "Sure. But that sense of excitement.
Will you miss it? If Mac quits being a private eye?"

"Nonsense." Abby turned back to the drawing board.
"Now let's see where you're going to put your office."

Unpredictable March gave way to uncertain April, and
nature celebrated with a little joke—a lonely tulip leaf
rose from the mud and was promptly eaten by a rabbit.
The McKenzies watched the drama from their parlor
window.

A tall man wearing a Navy pea coat and watch cap,
carrying a roll of paper tucked under his arm, watched
from the street. As the rabbit departed, the man turned
and looked back along Twilly Place. Then to his right
and left, as if surveying the area.

"What do you suppose he's up to?" Abby asked.

"That's what's-his-name—Taylor. Jack Taylor. He was
at the Olde Branch meeting last month."

"Did you ask him over?"

"Before seven in the morning?" The last week of
March had been cloudy and windy with two occasions
on which it rained ice water. This had led to a lingering
cold. Mac was not feeling hospitable.

"You put something on," Abby said, following him to
the door.

Mac shrugged into a windbreaker and stepped onto
the porch.

Jack Taylor, smiling, started up the walk. "I was
afraid it might be too early."

"Come on in. There's some coffee left."

"Thanks, but I just had breakfast." He stepped inside
and nodded toward a drafting table standing in front of
the window. "Planning your store layout?"

"This is my wife, Abby. She does the planning. I plan
on getting out of as much of the work as I can. What

46

brings you here so early?"

Taylor took off his watch cap and stuffed it into his pocket, revealing black hair with a few strands of gray at the temples. "Remember all that talk about traffic problems? You know, Wilking's idea about a parking lot?"

"Sure. What about it?"

"I'd like to show you something." Taylor unrolled a hand-drawn map of Olde Sarahville, and placed it over the floor plan. "Here you can see—just like Wilking said—the four corners of Harper and Main are commercial, but west of that it's residential. Both sides of east Main are commercial, but the creek parallels the street on the north, and the flood plain is north of that. Then the creek swings south and crosses Main through a culvert. Farther east is too far out." Turning to Mac, he said, "Right?"

Taylor was concentrating on his pitch, as if he'd taken a crash course in door-to-door sales. Mac wondered if an interruption would force him to start over from the beginning.

"So far," Abby said, "so good."

Taylor drew a pencil from his pocket, and used it as a pointer. "The creek forms a retention pond here, south of Main, where it turns back west and then runs along behind your place, and south again along Harper. So Olde Sarahville is boxed in by this loop in Running Fox Creek, and the main development, except for a few empty lots on Main, has to be on Twilly." He turned to Mac again.

"Don't look at me. Talk to the boss." Mac, once he had absorbed what the map could tell him, studied Taylor, wondering what made a career sailor an expert in retail development. And wondering what he was leading up to.

"The Village plans another short street, parallel to and east of Twilly." Taylor pointed to a dashed line on his drawing. "That makes two streets with poor traffic flow

47

and no parking."

"But that's not definite," Abby said. "First the general concept has to prove itself on Twilly."

"Suppose," Taylor said, "they did this." He traced a line with his pencil from the end of Twilly to the end of the unnamed street. "Suppose they connected the two streets, making the whole thing into Twilly Circle, with a couple of jogs for the creek meander." He looked from Mac to Abby.

"Now that you point it out," Mac said, "I'm surprised they didn't plan it that way."

"The planning people botched this from the beginning."

Who was he quoting, Mac wondered.

"If the shops on this circle want to stay in business, a lot of traffic has to move along a narrow street," Taylor continued.

"Something tells me you're about to get to the point," Abby said.

"Right." With the air of someone pulling a rabbit from a hat, he said, "Turn Twilly into a pedestrian mall. No cars!"

Abby's smile spoke of great patience. "No cars, no customers."

"Unless the Village buys Wilking's lot," Mac said. "Is that what you're leading up to?"

Taylor shook his head. "Suppose we put a parking lot on the other side of the creek." Taylor sketched in an area directly behind the McKenzies' property, then added an access drive to Schneider Road. "Add a foot bridge connecting it to Twilly." He looked at Abby. "What do you think?"

Abby leaned on the drafting table and studied the pencil lines. "You glossed over a few problems. For example, we've been told that property is not available."

"Who told you that?"

"Rudy Wilking."

"Assume it's not true. What else?"

48

"The Village doesn't have the money."

"Assume the land's donated."

"That's a hell of an assumption," Mac said. "But even so, there's the graveyard. I don't know if you noticed, but it's right in the middle of your parking lot."

"It can be moved."

Abby's eyebrows rose. "Aren't there problems doing that?"

With a grin, he said, "There's no one buried there except us Schneiders."

"Us? What do you mean—oh!"

"Right. I'm the last of the line."

"I see." Mac waited for Abby to say something, but she remained lost in study of the map. "Okay," he said. "You can donate the land. You can move the graveyard. But what's in it for you?"

Taylor pointed to a strip of land running from Schneider Road, north along the east side of his proposed parking lot, all the way to the creek. "The Schneiders sold off bits and pieces of the farm until all that's left is the original farmhouse and barn on this piece, and the adjoining piece with the graveyard. The farmhouse strip has some value, but the rest isn't worth the taxes I pay on it."

Abby nodded. "So in return for the parking lot, you want the Village to put in the access road. Just gravel probably. And a foot bridge, also cheap. I should think they'd jump at it."

"The deal would have to include zoning approval for commercial use of my property. Pick up the cost of moving the graves, too."

"Why tell us?" Mac asked. "Why not at the Olde Branch last month? Wilking gave you a perfect opening."

"I can guess," Abby said. "We'd have to agree to an easement from the footbridge to the Circle for a walkway."

"Right. And I'd need"—his pencil swept along the

49

street he had sketched in— "an easement for the street here. You know Wilking owns the one next to you. I'd like to have my ducks in a row before I spring this on the Plan Commission. Wilking won't like it, but if everybody already agreed, he won't have much choice."

Mac and Abby straightened up from bending over the drafting table. Mac said, "How come everybody around here thinks the Schneider line died with Henry Schneider?"

Taylor relaxed visibly, as if his well-coached presentation was over and he could return to his natural manner. "Fritz Schneider married my grandma, a California girl. He died in World War One and Grandma took her son, John, and went home to her folks. By the time John Junior, that's me, was born, the name had been changed to Taylor. Dad died in the second war."

"Still," Abby said, "the Historical Society has a whole chapter on Schneiders, and no mention of living relatives."

"According to Grandma, the Schneiders were PO'd about her taking Dad to California. Figured the kid should be raised on the farm, like all the Schneiders. Anyway, I don't remember any Christmas cards going back and forth. I guess there was a complete break."

"But you were in the will?" Abby asked.

Taylor shrugged. "Old Man Schneider lost track of the West Coast branch. But he wanted to keep the old place in the family. Left everything to the oldest male in direct descent, if any. That's me. Oldest and only."

"Sounds medieval," Abby said.

"Well, what do you think?" Taylor asked, waving his hand over the map.

Mac opened his mouth, but Abby spoke first. "We'll have to think it over. Tell you what, why don't you come by for dinner. Say seven?"

When Taylor reluctantly accepted the delay, and the invitation, and left, Abby said, "You should take it easy today, Mac. You look terrible."

"I'm all right."

"I could rub your chest with chicken fat and tie garlic around your neck."

"Sounds tempting, but duty calls," Mac said. "I can't see anything wrong with the easement. Seems to me it's in our interest. Why delay?"

"Obviously, you haven't considered all the pertinent facts."

"Such as?"

"He's single, eligible, and gorgeous."

"You mean—this is good-bye?"

"I mean—Karen Cannelli is coming to dinner."

By evening Mac's cold had loosened its grip and he looked forward to the roast beef Abby was preparing. Karen arrived early and offered to help. She wore a blue dress with a cowl neckline instead of the jeans and sweater he had come to expect. Mother and son having been inseparable in their almost daily visits, Mac asked, "Where's Jason?"

"I left him with a babysitter, on Abby's advice. The last thing he said to me was, 'Tell Uncle Mac not to forget my wings,' whatever that means."

"Yeah, I promised him Air Force wings. I've got an extra pair somewhere in the attic. I'll dig them out before you leave."

"Abby, about your suggestion," Karen said, "putting a little office near the delivery door? How about if I put it upstairs? And take a tax deduction on part of the living quarters?"

Abby shook her head, but Mac spoke before she could answer. "You two aren't going to talk shop again, are you?"

"No, we have something else to discuss, so why don't you go look for those wings?"

Recognizing an invitation to leave when he heard one, he climbed the stairs, and took care not to return until the doorbell rang and he heard Jack Taylor's voice.

After introducing Karen, Abby said, "Hope you don't mind eating in the kitchen. A home in a store has its problems. Living quarters are mostly on the second floor, but moving the kitchen was too expensive, and carrying food upstairs too much trouble."

Without taking his eyes off Karen, Jack Taylor said he preferred kitchens.

Karen, after a quick appraising look at Taylor, studied the ceiling. "I love these old kitchens," she said. "You can't get that kind of plaster work at any price nowadays."

"Looks great," Mac said. "Until you have to climb a ladder to knock down the cobwebs that form on that relief pattern."

"Karen will have an ice cream parlor right down the street," Abby said.

Mac took the rolled-up map from Taylor and put it on top of the refrigerator. "Come to think of it, Jack, didn't you mention ice cream at the Olde Branch meeting?"

"Might as well come clean," Jack said. "I needed a reason for asking questions without giving away my scheme. Ice cream just popped into my head."

"What scheme are you talking about?" Karen asked.

"You haven't told her?"

Abby said, "Why don't you explain it, Jack, while Mac helps me set the table? Take Karen to the parlor, where you can spread out your map."

When they had left the kitchen, Mac said, "Did you spray the room with musk?"

"Enough sarcasm. Besides, the way he looked at Karen, I don't think they'll need any help from me."

"Good. I like a woman who can mind her own business." He climbed up on a folding ladder to reach the cabinet shelf nearest the twelve-foot ceiling. "Why didn't you put this stuff lower down?"

"You're the one that unpacked the good dishes," Abby

said. "I think Karen's interested, don't you?"

"How the hell should I know?"

"There's a gravy boat up there somewhere. And don't give me that above-it-all 'we men mind our own business' routine." She opened the oven door and the aroma of the roast filled the room.

"Maybe if she gets a husband, the kid won't be over here, running up and down the stairs, every day."

"Yes, Uncle Mac. But she's been a big help to me setting up the store. Anyway, I think she and Jack—"

At that moment Karen's raised voice floated down the hall. "That's totally irresponsible." The voice came closer. "If you don't care about . . ." Passing through the swinging door to the kitchen, she changed the subject in midsentence. "Can I help with anything, Abby?" she asked.

Abby raised one brow but Karen merely shook her head.

Jack Taylor, following slowly, looked at Mac, and shrugged. Who can figure women? was the obvious message.

"I was afraid it might get too warm in here, with the oven going," Abby said. "But it seems fairly comfortable, don't you think?"

"Fine," Jack said. Karen nodded.

"It's the high ceilings, I think."

After a strained silence, Mac asked if anyone wanted a drink and received no takers. Abby said they might as well eat. Jack and Karen took their places at the table and watched Mac carve the roast.

Abby forced a smile. "Looks like spring may be a bit early this year," she said, passing the potatoes. "I can't wait for the ground to dry enough so I can work on the garden. Do you like to garden, Karen?"

Karen pushed her peas with a fork. "He's going to tear down the Schneider farmhouse."

Abby looked at Mac, who immediately became interested in his plate.

"*And* dig up the graves of his ancestors."

This remark seemed to sting Jack. "What do you expect me to do? Give the whole works to the bank?"

"There *are* other alternatives," Karen said.

"Such as?"

"I'm sure you could think of something."

Taylor speared another slice of beef. "That's a real constructive suggestion!"

Abby twice attempted a neutral subject, without drawing a response. Finally she said, "Maybe between the two of you, you could think of a way—"

"It's really none of my business," Karen said. "Although I'm sure the Historical Society will be interested. And perhaps the Plan Commission will take our views into consideration before they approve this—this . . ."

"Irresponsible behavior?" Taylor volunteered.

Karen ignored him, and began asking Abby questions about her plans to restore the Twilly house. Taylor passed the rest of the meal in silence.

When Karen refused brandy and said the babysitter had to be home early, Mac saw her to the door with a definite sense of relief.

Jack, looking glum, admitted he wasn't too fond of brandy, and accepted beer.

"Your fan club doesn't seem to be growing," Mac said.

Jack sighed. "She's one of those—what do you call 'em?" He searched for a word. "Preservationists. No common sense."

"If you want to be part of Olde Sarahville, I think having the very first farmhouse would be an asset," Abby said.

"That place was built before the Civil War, and it looks like the old man hadn't done any repairs since the Spanish-American. It'd cost a fortune to fix."

"She didn't agree?" Mac asked.

"Hell, she didn't even listen. I think the part about the graves is what really got her water hot." He sipped a

54

little beer. "I don't know any of those people buried there. As far as I'm concerned, they're strangers. And it's not like I'm going to dump 'em in a landfill. I got arrangements to put 'em in the churchyard, all together, just the way they are now."

"Maybe when she thinks it over . . . Why don't you give her a call tomorrow?" Abby asked. "I can give you her number."

"Why bother?"

Mac was inclined to agree, and decided it was time to change the subject. "Did the police ever contact you about the Bedford killing?"

"I wasn't much help," Taylor said. "They wanted to know if there was another car on the school grounds and I said no. There *was* a car at the back of Wilking's lot, with a man in it."

"He was just sitting there?"

"Yeah. The cops were pretty interested in that, but like I said, I wasn't much help. Just didn't pay much attention to him, or his car."

"I wonder if that was Jerome, or the person he went to meet," Abby said.

"If it was Bedford, why would he move his car from there to the schoolhouse?" Mac asked. "It was probably just a tavern customer waiting for his head to clear before driving home."

Taylor nodded. "Probably. The guy asked me for the time as I passed."

"Jerome's watch *had* stopped," Abby said. "He needed a battery. I remember him saying something about it as he left the meeting that night."

"The cops showed me a picture of this Bedford guy, but like I say, I wasn't much help."

When Jack had finished his beer and left, Mac said, "So much for matchmaking."

"You realize he was so upset by Karen that he forgot all about the easement? In fact, he left his map behind. This is just a temporary setback."

55

"That's what Hitler said about Stalingrad. In any case, your scheme to get your girlfriend a propertied husband sprung more than one leak."

"You caught that bit about giving it all to the bank?"

"He's in trouble. Another thing: How did an ex-swabby get so smart about real estate and shops and what-not?"

"Just because he wasn't in the Air Force—"

"The guy was a chief machinist's mate. Let him be smart about anchor chains, or whatever a—"

"You private dicks are all alike. Don't trust anybody." Abby sat on Mac's lap and touched her forehead to his. "But since I'm responsible for getting them together—"

"Together?"

"—maybe you should check him out a little."

Chapter 7

Ten days of April weather had produced only two days that could be thought of as springlike, and on the second of these Abby took an early morning walk to the Kurtz bakery on Main. As she left the store carrying a bag of assorted sweet rolls and a loaf of bread, she came face to face with a radiantly smiling Karen.

"Karen! I haven't been able to get hold of you for a week now. What have you been up to?"

"Sorry, Abby. I've been meaning to call, but we've been awfully busy."

"We?"

Karen's smile became a wide grin. "Jack and I."

Abby's eyebrows rose. "Well. You and Jack Taylor. Let's see. The day after you ripped him at my house, you said he called. You thought you should talk to him just once, to persuade him to your view. The next day you came by and told me he was absolutely impossible. That night I called and got a babysitter on the line. There's where the story ends. So what happened?"

"Well, he came by to apologize for what he'd said—"

"What did he say?"

"I forget. It was silly for me to get so upset anyway. I mean the poor man is under a lot of pressure. He's doing the best he can."

"Okay. He apologized. Then . . . ?"

"Naturally I asked him in. And the wonderful thing is, he took to Jason right away. Well, we talked. He said he was willing to do what he could about saving the farmhouse."

"What about the graves?"

Karen's bubbling spirits seemed to simmer down momentarily. "I still think it's a shame to move them. But I can see his point. If he doesn't, he'll lose it all."

"That's been puzzling me," Abby said. "Why would the bank want the graveyard? They couldn't do anything with that piece of property without Jack's okay."

"Oh, that piece isn't mortgaged. The bank wouldn't. But he'd lose the valuable part, where the house and barn are. The bank would sell that and somebody would tear everything down and put up something ugly and modern."

Abby touched Karen's arm. "I know I introduced you two. And I admit, I sort of hoped you'd find each other interesting. But are you sure you're not moving too fast?"

Karen smiled and patted Abby's hand. "Thanks for worrying about me. All I know is, I haven't been happy in a long time. And I'm happy now."

Abby dropped the bakery bag on the kitchen table, where Mac sat reading the newspaper, and said, "Isn't it time for the master detective to be on his way?"

He leaned back in his chair and looked up from the sports page. "Who? On the way where?"

"You promised to check on Jack Taylor over a week ago."

"It's Saturday."

"Sam Spade didn't work a forty-hour week."

"Thought I'd give you a hand. Any bales to lift? Barges to tote?"

"I'll call when there's heavy lifting. While you've been wasting time, Jack Taylor has been making time. Are you waiting for the wedding?"

Mac folded the newspaper and put it on the table. "They patched things up?"

"Karen has been wandering around in a fog and her babysitter is earning overtime."

"In a fog? Come to think of it, I haven't seen her for a while."

"You wouldn't see a brick wall if you ran into it. How did you *ever* make it as a detective?"

Mac stretched, but didn't get up. "I could drop in on Stan, I suppose. What will you be doing today?"

"I'm ready for a break myself. Think I'll take the day off and do some sketching." She came around behind him and leaned on his shoulder. "Think of me as a client. Go find out about Jack Taylor."

"Can you afford my fee?"

Abby tugged gently at the hair on the back of his neck. "Maybe we can use the barter system. Do I have anything you want?"

The old Sarahville Bank building had gone through several incarnations following the bank's failure in 1930, and currently held the overflow from the Municipal Center, including Stan Pawlowski's office. It was the same crowded, poorly ventilated cubbyhole he had occupied before his promotion to captain.

Mac drew back the chair jammed against the front of the desk and sat down. "So what perks go with the job?" he asked.

"I get to appear before the Village Board," Stan said, "in person, to plead for money, to fix the goddamn window in my office, it should open."

"Put an ashtray through it. Then they'd *have* to get it fixed."

"Would they? Can't afford the chance until the weather gets warmer. So, what brings you here? It's Saturday and I'd like to get home while the kids still remember me."

"I just wondered what you found out about John Taylor."

Stan pulled out the lower right drawer of his desk, settled back in his chair, and propped up his feet. "Why?"

Mac sighed. "Abby played matchmaker with him and Karen Cannelli."

"What is it with women? Julie's the same. Can't mind her own business."

"They figure an unattached man is a loose cannon on the deck of life. Some woman has to tie him down. Anyway, looked to me like they couldn't stand each other. But I must have been wrong. Abby says they get along okay now. So the question is, is he on the level?"

"About women? I couldn't say. We did a quick check. Sixteen years in the Navy with a clean record. Came here when Metlaff notified him he was heir to the Schneider place."

"Metlaff? He handled the estate?"

"Yeah. Since he's *your* lawyer, you can ask *him* about Taylor."

"How's the Bedford case coming along?"

"Lousy. Nobody knows anything. Everybody agrees—Bedford was a pain in the ass. But nobody really hated the guy, as far as we can tell. He was purchasing agent for a chain store. We followed up on that for a while, looking for a kickback scheme or something. Mr. Clean."

"Abby mentioned he—how did she put it?—swooped and fluttered. Was he a homosexual?"

"Straight, I'm pretty sure. Probably overmothered. You know what I mean?"

"Yeah. Like the kid lived over the tavern, on Division Street. Remember? Instead of hitching up his pants legs when he sat, he'd pull them out to the side, like a skirt. What was his name?" Mac asked.

"I remember. Name ended in a *-ski,* like the rest of us Americans. Bernie ran around with his sister."

"That's the one," Mac agreed. "No man around to

60

copy. The old bat wouldn't let him out to learn bad habits in the natural way, like the rest of us."

"Jerome Bedford wasn't quite in *his* class," Stan said. "Anyway, we can't find a problem, male or female. At least in the last few years."

"It's been—what?—three weeks?"

"Twenty-four days."

"You always told me you make 'em in the first forty-eight hours or maybe never. Is this one never?"

Stan swore and kicked his desk drawer shut. "We talked to everybody this guy knew, but one. We tossed his apartment, checked his bank accounts and deposit box, searched the ground for a half-mile radius, and dragged the creek. You got any suggestions?"

"Everybody but one? Who's the one?"

"Agnes Ketchall. She's out of town—nobody's been able to reach her. Due back this week."

"What about the gun?"

"Probably at the bottom of a lake by now. We found a cartridge case. Nine-millimeter Parabellum. From the position of the body in relation to the cartridge, shooter and shootee were about four feet apart. Just speculating, I'd say shooter walked in first, Bedford followed. Then Bedford turned back, either to close the door or to run, and the shot took him in the back of the head."

"So Bedford went in willingly. Not at gunpoint."

"Just a guess. Otherwise you have to assume at some point the shooter let Bedford get between him and the door. Why do that?"

"Well, I'll leave you to it." Mac pushed his chair up against the desk to open a path to the door.

"Leaving so soon? You haven't wasted my whole morning yet."

"I'd like to stay and solve your case, but I have to get Elmer Johnson to buy my lunch. The autopsy tell you anything special?"

"Yeah. He's dead."

Mac arrived at the Running Fox Tavern as Elmer Johnson got out of his car. Elmer reminded Mac of a human question mark, habitually standing with knees slightly flexed, shoulders hunched, a half-smile, and a cocked left brow. He was about Rudy Wilking's age, but devoid of dye, his hair was completely white.

They went in together and sat at the polished mahogany bar. A buxom, matronly woman hurried over. She wore a white apron over her cotton dress and smelled of paprika and onion.

"Hello, Elmer. Goulash today. I recommend it."

"Hell, Josie, you always recommend your own cooking and I wind up with heartburn. Just give me one of them greasy hamburgers and a bottle of Heineken."

"I'll try the goulash," Mac said.

"Yes, sir. Anything to drink?"

"You don't have to 'sir' him," Elmer said. "His name's Mac McKenzie. Get on a friendly footing while you can. Once he's tasted the goulash, it'll be too late."

"Coffee for me," Mac said.

Departing with the order, Josie said, "Watch it, Elmer. I'll tell Mabel you're hanging out in saloons again."

When she disappeared through the swinging door to the kitchen, Elmer said, "She makes damn fine goulash. Mabel and me had some last night. What you're gettin' is leftovers."

"Always better the second day, my mother used to say."

"What's a McKenzie know about goulash?"

"So what's *her* name?" Mac asked, nodding his head toward the kitchen.

"Horvath. Wilking did all right when he hired her. In more ways than one."

"Okay, Elmer. Now tell me. Just what sort of mess did you get us into?"

"Don't know what you mean. All I did was make you a hell of a deal on a historic landmark, zoned for business. Sure to coin money."

"And parking?"

"Now, Mac. You been listenin' to Rudy Wilking. I know Taylor's been to see you, so you know that problem's well in hand."

"Yeah, I saw Taylor's mouth move, but I kept hearing Elmer Johnson's voice."

Elmer chuckled. "Poor country boy like me can't put anything past you city fellas. Sure, it's my idea. And it'll work slick as goose grease, too."

"What if you can't get the easements?"

"You ain't thinkin' of turning him down, are you?"

"No."

"Well, then the only one standing in the way is Wilking, and he won't fight it once he knows everybody else goes along." Elmer looked around the room. "But just between you and me, timing is everything on this deal. That boy didn't inherit a farm. He inherited a debt heavy enough to sink one of them aircraft carriers he used to sail on. And if he can't bring the bank some kind of guarantee by May first, they'll foreclose the whole shebang."

"Can he get things set by then?"

"You forget, he's got me helpin' him. And I got a real personal interest. I'm in hock for a string of shops I'm building on Twilly. I admit it's a shoestring operation. But once we sell the Village Board on this scheme, property values are goin' up, and the bank will be glad to throw some more cash my way."

"And the graveyard?"

"The lawyer's got that in hand. It'll work out just fine," Elmer said as Josie approached with their lunch. "Josie, where's the boss?"

"Rudy's in the kitchen making a nuisance of himself. We got schnitzel on the dinner menu, and he checks every piece of veal himself. Tonight'll be worse. He'll hang over my shoulder with every order."

"He have his fingers in the goulash too?" Elmer asked.

"Who can tell a Hungarian about goulash? No, he sticks to schnitzel and sauerbraten." She pushed her fingers through salt-and-pepper hair and leaned on the bar. "Listen, who was that nice couple in here last night? The ones you said hello to?"

"John Taylor and Karen Cannelli," Elmer said. "I was kind of surprised they knew each other."

"I'm surprised they're speaking to each other," Mac said.

Josie grinned and shook her head. "The way they were looking at each other, who needs talk?"

Mac waited for Josie to leave before, under prodding from Elmer, he explained the source of the Taylor-Cannelli feud, and his surprise that it had evaporated so quickly.

"Handsome young couple like that," Elmer said, "you know a little thing like principle ain't gonna stand in their way."

Mac chuckled. "You sound like my wife."

After lunch he walked to the parking lot with Elmer. Looking north to the old willows that marked the course of Running Fox Creek he asked, "Is there anything else I should know about that old firetrap you sold me?"

"That fine old example of American craftsmanship? Like what?"

"The creek is pretty high, and there's a lot of spring rain still to go."

"Never had a problem there that I know of. Twilly rises from Main all the way to your place, then drops off back down to the creek. So you should be good. This side of Main is another story."

"I notice the lot here is lower than the crown of the street. They get wet cellars?"

"Didn't use to. Most of the natural flood plain was north and east of the creek. But back in the fifties a developer got in there cheap, and before those sleeping beauties on the Village Board knew what was up, he'd filled in a lot of land and built a cracker box subdivision.

The water has to go somewhere, so it shifted south."

"I wonder if Metlaff's place floods."

"If he ever had plans for a game room in the basement, I'd guess he's given 'em up. Even the tavern has problems in bad years. You can tell this used to be high and dry, though. Otherwise the schoolhouse wouldn't be here. Those old farmers weren't no fools."

Looking at the ground at his feet, Mac asked, "Any idea what used to be here before somebody poured asphalt on it? I don't suppose they needed to park many cars back in eighteen whatever."

"Small local brewery I understand. Owned by the fella that built the tavern." Elmer got into his car and rolled down the window. "Went out of business when prohibition came in, and burned down in the twenties."

Mac leaned on the driver-side door. "How do you figure this Bedford thing, Elmer?"

"You ever meet Jerome?"

"No. Abby did, though."

"I can't figure anybody settin' out to do him in. He just wasn't interesting enough to make real enemies. You know what I mean? The only passion he ever stirred was exasperation." He grinned. "Course, he stirred something in Agnes Ketchall, but *passion* might be puttin' it a mite strong."

Mac straightened up as Elmer started the car, waved, and drove off, leaving Mac looking over the half-filled lot.

Most of the cars were clustered near the rear door of the Tavern, but two were parked at the back. Probably employees leaving the choice places to paying customers. He tried to visualize it as it had been on the night of Jerome Bedford's death.

There had been only a few cars. Were there any at the back of the lot? He wasn't certain, now, partly the result of the fog, partly lack of attention, partly time. One thing he was sure of: Taylor's car had not passed him as he walked home. Of course, Taylor had been delayed giving the time of day to someone.

The door behind Mac opened and Rudy Wilking came out. "Ah, Mac. A fine spring day, true?"

"Beautiful. I was just thinking about that foggy night when Bedford was killed. I notice your people park at the back. Were they able to help the police?"

"Unfortunately, no. I thought perhaps the police themselves were in a better position to bear witness."

Mac nodded. "I heard they were by here that night."

"Yes. I don't like to keep money on the premises, so I always take the day's receipts to the night depository right after closing. The police are kind enough to have a patrol car check my lot about that time, especially any cars that are left. Then they follow me to the bank."

"Can't ask for a better alibi than that," Mac said.

Rudy laughed. "I suppose you are right. Depending, of course, on precisely when poor Jerome died. Has that been established?"

"Haven't heard. Did the police notice anything?"

"Police are the same everywhere. They ask questions, they do not answer them."

"Do you park in the back?"

"No. I require others to do so, but privileges of rank. I reserve a place around the corner of the building, there. Near the kitchen entrance."

"Still plan on selling your lot to the village?"

"You see through me, then." He grinned. "Yes, I believe it would be a good solution for everyone concerned. You don't agree?"

"I suppose so. As long as there's no alternative."

"There is none. Why don't you and your good wife come for dinner tonight? The schnitzel is excellent, if I do say it myself."

Mac said he'd check with Abby, and when Rudy left, he walked across the lot onto the schoolhouse grounds.

The two driveways were separated by no more than three feet. Concrete bumpers on the tavern side prevented cars from damaging the scraggly privet hedge growing between them. He walked through one of the several gaps in the hedge and followed the drive to the schoolhouse door. A hasp held to the frame by one screw, but the staple was missing. He opened the door and stepped inside.

The large room was bare except for a cast-iron stove in one corner. It showed signs of rust and the stove pipe was missing. A sheet metal plate covered the opening to the chimney. There was a small chalk circle near the center of the room. He assumed it represented the approximate position of the murderer at the time the shot was fired.

Bedford was still present, in the form of a chalk outline near the door, his arms outstretched as though reaching for freedom and safety. What, in his dull, mildly eccentric life had foreshadowed this dramatic and tragic end?

There had been his hint of some mystery, no doubt exaggerated. . . . Nonsense. No one cared about an old graveyard.

Except Jack Taylor, of course.

Chapter 8

Abby saw Mac on his way to Stan's office and then put on a coat with large pockets and worn sleeves. It should have been clear from the beginning that nothing would get accomplished today. They had slept—or been abed—late, dawdled over grapefruit and coffee, stared at the blue sky and white clouds. Spring fever had them in its grip.

Then meeting Karen at the bakery and worrying that the romance, even though she had hoped for that very thing, was moving too quickly. Nonsense, really. Jack Taylor was exactly what he seemed and they made a perfect couple. She turned her back on stacks of catalogs and brochures, floor plans and estimates. It *was* Saturday, and everyone needs a weekend off. She picked up a sketch pad, several pencils, and the Sarahville history booklet.

At the creek, although the water level was fairly high, several rocks showed their tops, and the stream appeared fordable. Her jump for the bank from the last rock resulted in a muddy shoe.

The stepping stones suggested prior crossings at this point, but Abby found no trace of a path. She made her own, through last year's dried weeds, skirting various woody shrubs, until she arrived at the low hill topped by the Schneider family graveyard.

She circled the hilltop to get a general idea of the layout, then settled at the southeast corner facing the earliest graves. Toward the back of the cemetery, modern-looking granite stones set on concrete rose above thistle and milkweed. The early graves were marked with thin slabs of gray marble flecked with black. One of the stones, inscribed "Anna," had cracked across the middle and lay on its back.

She stood there for some time, absorbing the sad, abandoned spirit of the place, watching cloud shadows chase rapidly across the ground. Bits of quartz in the granite seemed to turn on and off, like small lights, as sun and shade alternated. What had Jerome Bedford found here? Or was it something buried not in the ground, but in some musty archive?

She felt a vague uneasiness as the thought slipped into her mind: Was Jerome dead because of what he found? More nonsense! There was no possible connection.

Abby shook off the feeling and made her first drawing, a close-up of Anna's marker, grass growing through the crack. The name and dates chiseled into the marble were worn and difficult to read. She rubbed them with charcoal to make them more legible. Careful copying of the German script took some time.

Then, working rapidly, she sketched a wider view, a row of stones and a few strokes to suggest the unkempt appearance of the graves. She moved to the southwest corner and repeated the process.

Not quite sure whether the scene warranted sketching from a third angle, she walked between the graves, reading the inscriptions, until she was at the north side and could see her house across the creek. Viewed from this perspective, she thought about a future footbridge and path. By the time she had drawn several varieties of bridge and an idea for a path-side display stand for her business, the sun had moved perceptibly westward.

Turning for a last look at the graveyard, she was

struck by its lack of symmetry, as seen from the back. On a fresh page of her sketch pad she set to work, recording the way the cemetery appeared to have grown haphazardly. Dissatisfied with the view, she moved to another location. Although unkempt, the general outline of the cemetery could be seen: It was an approximate rectangle, roughly half again as wide as it was deep. She realized the layout was not haphazard at all. There were ten marked graves and, she estimated, room for ten or eleven more.

There should have been room for at least three more graves, except that the southeastern corner had been cut off. The graveyard was overgrown, but the corner growth was ranker, and older, than the rest; several staghorn sumacs and a silver maple sapling rose above the general tangle.

Abby sketched what she could see from this angle and then moved up for a closer look at the overgrown corner.

Placing her sketch pad on the kitchen table, Abby pointed to the last drawing she had made. "The outline is clear, once you push through all this growth. The ground has sunk and it makes an almost perfect rectangle." She straightened up and pushed her hair back behind her ear. "Mac, there's another grave up there, hidden in the underbrush."

"Okay, so there's a grave in a graveyard. What's the big surprise?"

"Don't be dense. First, why was care withheld from that one grave, long before the general neglect set in?"

"Good point, but—"

"There's more." Abby produced the Sarahville history booklet and thumbed its pages. "See, here's a list of the people buried up there. I matched them all with their markers. Nobody left over."

"The list was probably made by reading the tombstones, and since you tell me this grave doesn't have one . . ."

Abby turned to another page in her sketchbook. "Look at this plan of the cemetery." Each grave was located and marked with the name and dates of birth and death. "The earliest stone is for Anna, wife of Jacob, the original homesteader. Jacob is buried to her right, her daughter Liesle to her left. Then Jacob Jr. inherited and he starts his own row. The same thing with succesive generations."

"Primogeniture," Mac said. "Hard on some of the family, but it keeps the property from being broken up."

"So why a grave in Jacob's row, but separated from the rest by unoccupied grave sites?"

"Jacob's bastard?"

Abby stared at her sketch for a moment. "I never thought of that. It would make sense, wouldn't it?" She looked at the history booklet again. "Do you suppose this is what Jerome found?"

"Maybe. But I'd restrain the urge to spring it on the local historians."

"Why?"

"Jack Taylor can no doubt prove he's the only surviving relative of the residents in those marked graves, but until this one is identified he's not going to move those graves anywhere."

"Damn. You're right." Abby slumped into a chair. "That means no parking lot." She frowned. "While I was on the hill, I began to sympathize with Karen. I hated the idea of digging up those graves. Especially Anna. And flattening the hill. A picture flashed through my mind of all that land covered with gravel baking in the summer sun, cars, exhaust fumes." She sighed. "But now that it seems it will never happen . . ." She drew a sheet from the bottom of the stack and pointed to a rustic covered bridge and a flower-bordered path leading to the Twilly house. "Look here. It could be very good for business, couldn't it?"

"Can't have it both ways, though." Mac reached for the sketches and began leafing through them. "And if the parking lot doesn't materialize, Taylor loses the whole works."

"I know."

"May first is his deadline."

"And Karen will marry a penniless sailor, her business will fail for lack of parking, Jason will never go to college—Mac, you have to do something."

Mac passed one of the sketches over to Abby. "The last burial, before Henry Schneider's, was Hans. February 1946. Who was Hans?"

"That was Henry's—Heinrich, actually—his father. You can tell from the placement of the graves."

"Anyway," Mac said, "you're overdramatizing. They'll probably live in sin, her store will be bought by a big chain, making her a millionaire, and Jason would rather drive a fire engine anyway. Besides, it *is* a family graveyard. I don't think you can use those to bury the general public."

"But he'd have to prove that, wouldn't he? I mean, before he can move the graves?"

"Sure. I think so."

"So get your trench coat and go prove it."

"I don't have a trench coat. More important, if I had one I'd sell it along with my office furniture."

"How about making this McKenzie's last case?" When Mac refused to answer, Abby gathered up her drawings and placed them in a portfolio. "I suppose not. But if you *did* investigate this, how would you go about it?"

He thought for a moment. "Bochman's Funeral Home. His sign says he's been in business here since 1923. There's a good chance he buried some of the Schneiders. Might be a shortcut. Save a lot of checking of the public records."

"Bochman's, huh?"

Mac's face tightened. "Hold it. You're not getting into this."

"Why not? If you're determined to be a store clerk, why can't I be a supersleuth?"

"Not a chance. Did it occur to you no one knows why Bedford was killed? And the only unusual thing in his life at the time was connected with the graveyard? Probably this grave?"

The unease Abby had felt on the hilltop returned, but she said, "Nonsense! What harm can a few questions do? I'll just—"

"Absolutely not! Stay out of this."

Sunday morning was overcast but springlike temperatures continued. Abby waited until she heard Mac, in the cellar, sawing boards for shelving. Then she left, taking care that the screen door didn't slam behind her.

Bochman's Funeral Home looked like a suburban ranch-style house, except for its size, the double-door front entrance, and a parking lot in the rear. The owner, August Bochman, was a large man who always looked as though a barber had removed a hot towel from his face just before he entered the room. A memory of her father smelling of witch hazel on a Saturday morning flashed through Abby's mind.

Bochman rose and took her hand. "Miss Novack—I'm sorry—I mean Mrs. McKenzie. I haven't seen you since your sister passed away. Nothing untoward brings you here, I hope?"

"No, no." She took the seat in front of his desk and opened her purse. "I'm looking for some information about a burial that took place a long time ago, I'm not sure how long ago, and I don't know who—"

"Does this have to do with the Schneider family plot?"

"How could you possibly know?!"

Bochman smiled. "Just a guess, really. Am I right?"

"Well, yes, as a matter of fact." Abby didn't believe it was a guess, and had her doubts about ESP, but let it go in favor of telling her rehearsed story. "You see, we bought the old house—on Twilly?" She took a notebook and pencil from her purse. "So I got interested in local history. One thing led to another, and I joined the Historical Society. You know about them?"

Bochman nodded.

"I can see the graveyard from my window," Abby said. "Have you read the little booklet the Society put out?"

Bochman nodded again.

"Well, I happened to notice an extra grave, you know? And I thought maybe I'd try to contribute to the next edition."

"The gentleman in that grave is Jacob Goldfarb," Bochman said. "The son of one of the Schneider girls."

"Then he *is* a Schneider? More or less?"

"Oh yes. You can't open a family cemetery to the general public."

"No, I suppose not." Abby wrote down the name *Jacob Goldfarb*. "So besides the Schneiders, there were Goldfarbs living on the farm?"

"Not that I know of."

"Then how did this Goldfarb come to be buried there?"

"Well, he had no other living relatives—"

"Oh, good!" As Bochman's eyebrow rose Abby quickly added, "I mean, it's good he had someone here, at least." And no relatives to be awkward about his removal to a new site. "When was he buried?"

"September twenty-third, 1946."

Abby made a note of the date, then tapped her teeth with the eraser end of the pencil. "That's amazing. Do you remember the burial date of all your—clients?— that well? As a matter of fact, you're not old enough to have been here when he was buried."

"No. My memory is pretty good, but not that good.

74

Dad buried Mr. Goldfarb. But as it happens, I recently looked up the record."

Abby's elation was beginning to fade. "How can you be sure there are no other relatives?"

"Henry Schneider made the arrangements and is listed as next of kin. Dad wrote 'next and only' in the margin. I assume he had Henry's word for it."

"And you looked at the record just recently. Why is that?"

"Jerome Bedford." Bochman laughed. "Mr. Bedford asked me about that grave, in almost the same terms as you just used. That's the secret of my mind reading. I just jumped to the conclusion that you were interested in the same thing he was."

"You heard—?"

"Yes. Shocking. Poor Mr. Bedford was quite excited by his discovery. I gather he never got to announce it?"

"No. He hinted that he had something to tell, but didn't say what it was." Abby looked down at her notes. "I'm new at this and I'm sure there are a dozen questions I should ask. I just don't know what they are."

"The cause of death?"

"Yes, I suppose so."

"Accident."

"Automobile?"

Bochman shook his head. "No. People don't realize, but farming is one of the most dangerous occupations. In this case, some mishap with a tractor."

"If there were no Goldfarbs on the Schneider farm, how did Jacob Goldfarb come to die here? Where did he live?"

"Somewhere in Nebraska, I believe. He was visiting, I suppose, and perhaps decided to help with the harvest."

"So, case closed." Abby looked around the kitchen table. Karen grinned, obviously pleased. Mac, poker-faced, was watching Jack Taylor. "And all is well, right?" Abby asked. "Right, Mac?"

Taylor summoned up a small smile. "I appreciate your interest, Abby, but if you hadn't told anyone about the grave, there wouldn't be a problem in the first place. I swore an affidavit I'm the only one with a family interest. One grave more or less don't matter."

"Jack! You could be a little grateful," Karen said. "Suppose somebody else found the grave at the last minute? The bank might just go ahead and foreclose before you could straighten it out."

"I didn't mean . . ."

Abby saw a flicker of irritation cross Mac's face as he spoke. "Did you know about that grave, Jack?"

"It's a surprise to me. I didn't know there was a—Goldfarb?—in the family."

"But you had to include a list with your affidavit?" Taylor nodded.

"And when the graves are moved, you think you can just slip through an extra corpse?"

"By then the deal with the bank will be set."

"You expect the bank to buy this deal without twelve pages of contingency clauses?" Mac shook his head, his eyes locked on Taylor's. "Like backing out if you can't get the graves moved within a reasonable period of time? And you expect the court to let you go ahead when the gravedigger turns up an unnamed body? You're damn lucky Abby found it first and took the trouble to look into it."

"I guess I didn't think of all that. Sorry, Abby. But I can have Metlaff add Goldfarb to the list, right?"

"Get Metlaff's advice on that," Mac said. "My guess is it won't be that easy. Better trace this Goldfarb a bit further. Which Schneider was his mother? Are there relatives on his father's side that have an interest? Those are the questions a court will ask."

"Won't the same questions come up on all the graves?" Abby asked.

"I'm not a lawyer, but I imagine the circumstances are different. The others lived on the farm and Taylor can claim complete knowledge. Maybe stick a legal notice in one of those weekly newspapers that nobody reads, asking any unknown relatives to come forward."

"Damn! Time's running out." Taylor stood up and took his pea coat from the back of his chair. "I better get moving while we still have a fighting chance."

"Mac?" Abby touched his arm.

Karen, who had been frowning, smiled. "Of course. You're a detective. You can investigate Goldfarb."

"Detective!" Taylor said. "You're a—"

"No way!" Mac shook his head. "It's not my kind of case, number one. And I've quit the business. Let Metlaff handle it."

And there, despite Abby's occasional appeals, the matter rested until Monday afternoon.

Mac, noting the station wagon's lack of enthusiasm for quick acceleration, decided to clean and regap the sparkplugs. If that didn't work, he'd have to commit his fortune to a mechanic. He was pulling the third plug when a car turned into the driveway. He glanced up, identified the car as Elmer Johnson's, and ducked back under the hood.

"Don't like to keep a man from his work," Elmer said, "but we need a little professional advice."

Mac gave the socket wrench a final twist. "Who's 'we'?" He backed out from under the hood and found himself facing Elmer and Jack Taylor. "Oh, it's you, Jack. Which one of you is paying for this advice?"

"This is his idea," Taylor said, jerking a thumb in Elmer's direction. "Send *him* the bill."

Mac laid a sparkplug on the fender. Taylor's expression might have been described as grim, or obstinate, Mac wasn't sure which. "Is this going to be a long dis-cussion?"

"No time at all," Elmer said. "I just want you to tell this young fella how easy it is to put that extra guest in the graveyard to rest. Jack, here, is ready to chuck the whole project over a little technicality."

"Little technicality!" Taylor said. "By the time I prove I can move the grave, the bank'll own my skivvies. And what if there *are* a bunch of Goldfarbs out there someplace?"

Mac put down the socket wrench and wiped his hands on an oil-stained cloth. "You could be right."

"See," Taylor said. "It's a waste of time."

Elmer raised his right brow level with the habitually raised left. "Not so fast. You ain't telling me it's hopeless, are you, Mac?"

"I'm just saying there's no guarantee. You still have almost a month—"

"Nineteen days," Taylor said. "What can we do in nineteen days?"

"Unless there's an army of Goldfarbs, and they're scattered all over the world, that should be enough time. Get Metlaff to tell you how far you have to go. I mean, do thirty-second cousins twice removed count? There's probably some reasonable limit. Maybe spouse, siblings, direct descendants. If so, and if Goldfarb was an unmarried only child . . ."

"See?" Elmer said. "Might not be a problem at all."

"And what if we can't find out in time?"

"I'd guess Metlaff will show the court you made a good faith effort. Then he'd present Bochman's contemporaneous note, which says no relatives except Henry Schneider."

"There you go," Elmer said. "When can you start, Mac?"

"Metlaff will get somebody."

"I know you ain't takin' any cases for a while," Elmer said. "But I'd feel a whole lot better if you'd take just this one. Like you said, it wouldn't take too long."

Mac looked at Taylor, whose expression was now darker than before. Definitely obstinate. "I'm permanently out of the business," Mac said. "Talk to Metlaff. The sooner the better. He can get somebody on it."

"Well, okay," Elmer said. "Come on, Jack. Let's do it. The day ain't gettin' any younger, and neither am I."

"He's *my* lawyer," Taylor said. "I'll talk to him."

"Sure you don't want me along?"

"I've got some personal matters to take up with him," Jack said. "Just drop me off at my car and I'll take care of it."

Obviously reluctant, Elmer said, "Well—okay. But you be sure and call me right after."

Mac, frowning, watched them leave. Taylor had not struck him as a man who would throw in his hand before the last card was dealt. Something had changed drastically since yesterday. But what?

Chapter 9

Abby agreed with Mac that it was a beautiful Tuesday morning, but pointed out that it was still mid-April, and insisted that he wear a jacket against the uncertainty of the weather.

"Just to the lumberyard in Bartlett?" Mac asked. "You'll make some man a wonderful mother, you know that?"

Abby had several things to say in response, but she noticed Stan Pawlowski's car stopping on the drive. Pointing, she said, "Stan's in an awful hurry this morning."

Stan crossed the screened porch, entered the kitchen, and wasted no time on preliminaries. "What's all this about an extra grave?"

"How did you hear about that?" Mac asked.

"Julie told me."

Abby avoided Mac's accusing eye. "I know. I wasn't supposed to say anything. But Julie won't tell anyone. Well, except Stan, naturally."

"Why does that grave interest the great detective?" Mac asked.

"Tell me if I got any of this wrong," Stan said. "Taylor wants to move the Schneider graves to make room for a parking lot. If he can't, he loses everything and has to re-up in the Navy or pump gas at Lou's Service

Station. Okay so far?"

"Sort of," Abby agreed.

"Finding the extra grave can put a monkey wrench in the whole deal. Right?"

Abby shook her head. "No. It's a Schneider—close enough anyway. He just has to verify there aren't any other relatives."

"If he can. You agree that Jerome Bedford found this same grave."

"We don't know that," Abby said.

"But probably true," Mac said.

Stan nodded. "That means Bedford was a threat to Taylor's future."

"I know what you're thinking," Abby said. "But it's ridiculous. We talked to Jack. He thought he could just add one more to the list of graves. No problem. It wasn't till Mac started spreading gloom—"

"When he was here yesterday he had changed one hundred and eighty," Mac said. "He—"

"You didn't tell me he was here," Abby said.

"Didn't I?" Knowing Abby would urge him to investigate, as Elmer wanted, Mac had elected not to mention the visit. "Guess I was busy with the car and forgot. Elmer brought him over. Jack wanted to drop the parking lot project. Said it was a waste of time now that Goldfarb surfaced. Elmer wanted me to talk him out of it."

"Did you?" Abby asked.

"It's his decision. I just told him to have the lawyer look into it before he makes up his mind."

Stan took out a pocket notebook and scribbled briefly. "Maybe he's getting worried. Maybe he thinks dropping his project will cut the connection between him and Bedford."

"You don't *have* a connection," Abby said. "They never met."

"As far as we know. If I find a point of contact . . . In the meantime, keep this to yourself." Stan looked directly at Abby. "Right?"

"I won't mention it to Jack Taylor," Abby said.

"Or Karen Cannelli. Right?"

Abby's mouth tightened and she said nothing.

"Take what you can get, Stan," Mac said.

After Stan left, Mac placed a finger against Abby's lips as she was about to speak. "No," he said.

"But Mac—"

"No. Murder is police business. Stan's a smart cop. If Taylor's clean, he'll be okay."

Abby frowned. "That's not the point. If Jack Taylor's guilty, and I don't believe it for a minute, I'll be as pleased as anyone to see him put away. And I trust Stan, I really do. But what about Karen?"

"Tell her to stay clear of him until the dust settles."

"You know very well she won't do that."

"Then she's a damn fool."

Abby started for the stairs. "If women weren't damn fools, guys like you would all be bachelors!"

Abby went directly to the upstairs phone and called Karen. "Listen. You have to get over here right away. The police think Jack's mixed up in Jerome's death and—"

Karen gasped. "You must be joking! He didn't know Jerome. And why would—"

"No time," Abby interrupted. "It's because of the extra grave. Jerome found it and it may scuttle Jack's plans. They're about to jump to a conclusion, and you have to convince Mac to help." Abby interpreted the lack of response as shock. "Karen? You have to catch Mac before he leaves the house."

"Can't you—"

"Karen, Mac is stubborn as a mule. It's guilt, you see—"

"Guilt?"

"I'll explain later. Just get here." Abby started to hang up, then added a final word. "Bring Jason. He can't resist mother *and* child."

Abby sat for a moment. Guilt. That's what it was. He could recite a long list of reasons for quitting, ranging from being tired of worrying about clients' problems to the need to get the store off to a good start. Abby shook her head and moved slowly to the stairs. She believed none of his reasons.

Ann, Mac's first wife, had spent their marriage following him from one military post to another. Then he retired, promised a new life. They moved to Sarahville, near the Chicago of their origins. But his detective practice (he could call himself a management consultant all he liked) demanded irregular hours and frequent travel. And Ann had to create community ties without his help, or for that matter, his interest.

A year later Ann was dead.

Now Mac was determined that Abby would have his full attention and support. She quickened her pace, worried he would leave before Karen arrived. Mac sell basket weaving kits? Sooner or later he'd hate her for it.

"Another thing," she said to Mac, as though there had been no lapse in their discussion. "If the bank finds out he's under suspicion, they won't take a chance on his plan. He'll be wiped out whether he's guilty or not."

"What do you expect me to do about that?"

"It wouldn't hurt you to help. Maybe he could be cleared before the bank hears."

"As small as the Sarahville Cop Shop is, Stan still has a lot more resources than I have."

The doorbell rang before Abby could answer. She ran to let Karen in and hurried back to catch Mac grabbing his jacket and heading for the back door.

"Sit, Mac," Abby said.

He turned and smiled. "Hello, Karen. And how are you, Jason?"

"Uncle Jack bought me a sailor hat," Jason said.

Karen looked drawn and pale, a deep line etched between her eyes. "Mac, you've got to help him, please."

"Karen, I just explained to Abby—"

83

Jason dug a shoelace from his pocket. "Want to see me tie a knot?"

"And now you can explain it to *her*," Abby said. "I tried to, on the phone just now, but it was too confusing."

Mac sighed, defeated. "Listen. I'll look into this business of Jacob Goldfarb. Maybe once that's settled, Jack can close a deal with the bank before they learn what's going on. But that's absolutely all. The rest is police business."

Karen looked far from satisfied. "But—"

Abby patted her arm and said, "Come see the needlework kits I ordered, while Mac and Jason tie knots." As they moved toward the front of the house Mac heard her murmur, "Don't worry. Once he starts, he doesn't know how to quit."

"The hell I don't!" Mac muttered.

Karen stayed long enough to hear a full explanation of the police theory, and to absorb Abby's repeated assurances that Mac would make it all come out right in the end. By the time mother and child left, Abby, despite her expressed optimism, was torn between worry about Karen and hope that this turn of events might eventually change Mac's mind about quitting. She began straightening the mess in the parlor-to-be-showroom.

Then Mac came in, frowning, and Abby abandoned her attempt to shift a carton of books on the art of quilting. "Mac, can you give me a hand with this?" she asked.

He looked startled, as if he hadn't been aware she was there. "What?"

"You worried, Mac?"

He shook his head, but his frown had returned.

"You look ready to bite someone."

Mac grinned and made a grab for Abby. "Just what I had in mind."

Abby laughed, holding him at arm's length. "Don't change the subject. We can get back to that later."

Mac lifted the carton Abby had been struggling with and placed it against the parlor wall. "Why this sudden urge for neatness?"

"You haven't forgotten the Historical Society is coming today!"

"Yeah. I mean, yes, I forgot. I'm not going to be here."

"Forget about the lumber yard today. You have more important things to do now."

He leaned on the newel post. "When Taylor wanted to call off his project yesterday, I had the feeling something new had happened to cause his change of mind."

Abby pointed to another carton she wanted moved.

Mac started to lift the box and felt a twinge in his back. "What's in these things?"

"Books. They'll go in a display rack between the windows there. When I get a rack."

He slid the carton along the floor. "The guy's holding out."

"I could have done that myself," Abby said, sliding another carton over the polished oak flooring. "I didn't want to scratch the floor."

"He was heading for Metlaff's office when he left here. I'm going there now and see what I can find out."

"Will you be back before the tour of our house is over?"

"I've seen the house."

"But you haven't met the Society."

"What time do you pour lunch?"

"I don't. They insist on taking me to the Running Fox. You too. Can you?"

"I never pass up a free meal."

Glancing through the window, Abby said, "Here they come now."

"Leave introductions for later." He started for the kitchen. "I'll slip out the back."

Helen Rhine got out of her car, along with a short, chubby woman. By the time they reached the porch, Karen Cannelli drove up. A third car followed closely. Abby opened the door.

"I'd like you to meet Alice Hill," Helen said.

"Nice to meet you," Alice said, her voice pitched just below a dog whistle. "Real nice." Her smooth, round face lit with a cheerful smile.

Abby returned her smile and offered to take their coats.

Karen came through the door, steering another woman by the elbow. "Abby, this is Agnes Ketchall."

Agnes appeared to be about fifty, thin, a head taller than Karen, with dark hair pulled back from a high forehead. She wore wire-rimmed glasses. Her reply to Abby's greeting was indistinct.

"Is anyone else coming?" Abby asked.

"The Arlys," Helen answered. "But Horace said he and Jean might be a little late. My Al couldn't make it."

Abby swept her arm around, indicating the high-ceilinged parlor. "As you can see, this room is in the middle of being converted to a store. I'm afraid it's not a very comfortable place to wait. Why don't we go sit in the kitchen until the Arlys arrive? There's a fresh pot of coffee."

Helen Rhine darted across the room to the back wall, where an enlarged copy of the Twilly house photograph, oak framed, hung above the fireplace. "Is this the picture you got from Karen?" she asked. Helen and Alice read the caption with evident interest. Agnes Ketchall hung back, glanced once in their direction, then moved to the corner bay and gazed out of the window, her shoulders drooping.

Karen came to Abby's side and whispered, "Poor Agnes didn't hear about Jerome until she got back from Iowa. She's taken it hard."

"Were they especially close?"

Karen shrugged. "Talk to you later."

Alice Hill's shrill voice awoke an echo in the large room. "You're lucky to have open space like this all the way across the house. It's just perfect for a store. Just perfect."

"Mac—my husband—thinks this was originally two rooms separated by a hall surrounding the staircase. Something about the crown molding not matching."

"He's right," Helen Rhine said. "The woman who owned it in 1937 had the walls removed. She used this as a dance studio. Invested her husband's insurance in the remodeling, and was bankrupt by '39."

Karen grimaced. "Imagine that."

Abby touched Karen's arm. "This isn't '39. It's a good time for business start-ups."

The doorbell drew everyone's attention. "Oh, good," Alice said. "That must be H.A. and Jean. Now we can start."

Harold J. Metlaff, Esq., combined office and residence in a beautiful example of Midwestern gothic on the north side of Old Main. His lot was irregularly shaped owing to the curve of Running Fox Creek, which bordered it on two sides before entering a large culvert to flow beneath the street.

What had once been the parlor now contained his secretary, Mrs. Dancer, seated at an antique desk. She removed her glasses, letting them dangle from the cord around her neck, and smiled at Mac. "Go right in, Mr. McKenzie."

"Aren't you going to announce me?"

She shook her head. "You are expected."

Mac concealed his disappointment; the experience of watching Mrs. Dancer walk from her desk to the inner office almost compensated clients for the reality of dealing with her boss. He entered the former dining room, complete with crystal chandelier, which now served as a spacious office.

Metlaff, chewing his habitual cigar, raised his bald head from the file he was reading. Seeing Mac, he switched the cigar from left to right and lost his scowl, for him the equivalent of a smile. "Well, McKenzie. What sort of mess have you created that requires this urgent meeting?"

"Came to talk about John Taylor and the Schneider farm. Since this is for your other client's benefit, not mine, you can stop the meter."

"Just how are you concerned in the matter?"

"Didn't you hear about the extra grave in the family plot?"

It was evident from Metlaff's ferocious expression that he had not. "What are you talking about?"

Mac filled him in on Abby's discovery and Taylor's reaction to it. "Am I right about the consequences?" he asked.

"It seems I have *another* fool for a client. He should have told me as soon as he learned. He can't afford any delay in tracing this Goldfarb's descendants." Metlaff swiveled his chair around, favoring Mac with a view of the fringe of gray hair at the base of his smooth, freckled scalp. After a moment he turned back. "Can you take on the job?"

Mac saw no need to admit he intended to look into the case anyway. "Sure. Shouldn't take too long."

"Fine." Metlaff made out a check. "A small retainer. Not your usual. If Mr. Taylor should turn out to be a bankrupt, you will share the risk of nonpayment with me."

"Did Henry Schneider leave any personal papers that might help?"

"Not with me. When he entered the hospital with his last illness, he left a box of memorabilia with one Alma Linsdale. Taylor obtained it from her and found several birth and death certificates and a few other items of significance which he placed in my custody. None refer to Goldfarb."

Before Mac could frame his next question, Mrs. Dancer appeared. "You have a real estate closing in Arlington Heights this morning."

"I'll leave immediately." Metlaff threw the cold butt of his cigar in the waste basket. "But back to Mr. Taylor's problem," he said to Mac. "Knowledge of the matter is, so far, limited. Perhaps it can be kept from the bank long enough to settle the issue. You're certain no one else knows?"

"I'm certain."

A woman wearing wire-rimmed glasses caught Mac's undivided attention as he walked into the Running Fox Tavern's private dining room.

"Jerome found the grave!" she said.

Chapter 10

The woman in the wire-rimmed glasses was speaking to the Society members gathered at a small bar presided over by Rudy Wilking. "What did the rest of you ever find?" she asked.

Mac, unnoticed by the group, paused in the doorway to observe and listen.

"You didn't know he came to see me the night he was murdered, did you? Well, he did!"

Rudy was the first to react. "Have you told the police?"

She seemed puzzled or, judging by her voice, confused by too much drink. "Tell them what? That he found out whose grave it is?"

The other man in the group, other than Wilking, said, "So who was it? Come on, Agnes, don't keep us in suspense!"

The woman's bristling antagonism faded. "I don't know. But I'm going to find out." She looked around the group. "I'm going to finish what Jerome started. And when I'm ready, there'll be a new section in the history of Sarahville, dedicated to Jerome Bedford."

A buxom semiblond woman standing next to Abby said, "Well of course, Agnes. The next edition will have some sort of memorial tribute to Jerome. I'm sure we all agree."

"Have you seen this grave, Agnes?" Wilking asked.

"No. But Jerome told me exactly where to find it."

"Why don't we all go," the semiblonde said. "It sounds fascinating."

"Oh, no," wire-rims said. "I'll do this myself. You're not going to grab Jerome Bedford's credit."

Abby separated herself from the group and came to meet Mac.

"That settles Taylor's plans," Mac said to her.

"Maybe not. Maybe it'll only take you a day or two—"

"Not unless I find a shortcut."

"What kind of—"

Mac took Abby's arm and moved toward the group at the bar. "We'll talk later. Who are these people? Especially the big mouth with the glasses."

Karen Cannelli, face grim, stood separate from the others. As the McKenzies passed her, Abby murmured, "It'll be all right. You'll see."

Abby steered Mac toward the center of the group. "Everybody," she said. "I'd like you to meet my husband, Mac."

The semiblonde smiled and lifted her glass in greeting. "Hi. I'm Helen. Come have a drink."

"Helen Rhine," Abby said. "You remember I told you about her. Don't you, dear?"

"Sure," Mac said. "Chairman and librarian. I believe I've seen you at the library."

Helen nodded three times. "I *know* I've seen you there."

"And this is Alice Hillman," Abby said.

Alice giggled. "Pleased to meet you."

Abby turned next to the Arlys. "You remember Horace, don't you? This is his wife, Jean."

Horace extended his hand and said, "Call me H.A."

Jean Arly was in her mid-forties and had developed the leathery skin of someone who had spent too much time chasing a golf ball without a hat. The outdoor, athletic image was further emphasized by a slim, supple body. She wore a snug skirt to maximize her strong point and a loose-fitting sweater to de-emphasize a perceived lack.

Her eyes, a brilliant blue, had a tendency to squint. She smiled and held Mac's hand. "So nice to see a new face in this old group."

Abby took Mac's arm and turned him toward wire-rims. "And this is Agnes Ketchall."

Mac smiled, murmured, "Hello."

Agnes adjusted her glasses and stared at him.

A bit uneasy under the woman's wordless stare, Mac turned to the bar. "How are you, Rudy?"

"Very well, thank you. I had someone clean up the lot next to yours. Was it satisfactory?"

"Yes. Thanks. You're one of the historians here?"

"No. I have considered joining, but there is only so much time in a day."

"That's the truth," H.A. said. "I really shouldn't have come. This is my busy season."

"People wait till the last minute to do taxes," Jean Arly said, "then they expect H.A. to work night and day."

"You're an accountant?" Mac asked.

"Right."

Rudy handed Alice Hillman a sherry. "And a very good one." He took the empty glass from Agnes's hand and began mixing Kahlúa and cream. "He has handled my books for years."

"Can't let an endorsement like that go by," H.A. said, fishing a business card out of his vest pocket. "Have one."

"That's Abby's department," Mac said. "She just keeps me around to help with the sweeping up."

Helen Rhine, perched on a stool, placed her empty glass on the bar and lit a cigarette. "Abby tells me you're a consultant of some sort."

"That is not what I have heard," Rudy said. "Elmer Johnson told me you are what the television calls a private eye. Not true?"

Mac looked around at the group, whose interest in him had suddenly peaked, and sighed. "Elmer—bless him."

"Well," Abby said, "you'll just have to get over being shy."

Alice Hillman's voice rose and squeaked a bit. "Are you a private eye?"

Mac asked Rudy for bourbon and water. Turning back to the group, he said, "I used to consult on company security. And sometimes that overlapped, or so the state of Illinois claims, things a private detective does."

"Like a blanket overlaps a bed," Abby whispered.

Mac squeezed her hand. "So I have a license. As a convenience, so I can do a complete job. Or could—but I've given it up."

Abby smiled. "Well, actually that's not quite settled yet."

"Any other kind of consulting? When you're not detecting?" H.A. asked.

One more time, Mac thought. "I never did detecting. No divorce. No missing cats."

"According to Elmer—" Rudy began.

"Of course," Mac hastily added, "it's a little unusual, the license, so I suppose maybe companies tended to call me in more often when that's useful."

"According to Elmer," Rudy persisted, "you have been involved in investigations of various crimes. Including murder."

"Well, you know Elmer." Out of the corner of his eye, Mac saw Agnes drain her drink. Her glasses slid forward on her nose.

"Tell me," Rudy asked, "what is your opinion of the Bedford affair?"

"No idea," Mac said. "Anyway, that's police business."

"Do you think they'll catch him?" H.A. asked.

"Nobody saw or heard anything," Mac said. "Bedford didn't seem to have any enemies. No obvious motive. Unless they find some link in his background, or turn up the weapon, which doesn't seem likely, I'd say the chances of solving it get less as time passes."

Agnes pushed to the front of the group and stood directly in front of Mac. "So why don't *you* find out who killed him?"

"The police—"

"The police don't care." She turned around. "None of you care." Her voice rose. "You never liked Jerome!"

Alice Hillman looked shocked. "Agnes! We all liked Jerome. But what can we do? It's up to the police."

Agnes swung back to Mac. "What did they find in Jerome's apartment?" she demanded.

Surprised, Mac said, "His apartment? Nothing. What did you expect—"

"That's what I thought. Nothing!" She turned her head to the side and looked at Mac through narrowed eyes. "And why haven't they been to see me?"

"They've been waiting for you to get home," Mac said. "Why don't you go see Captain Pawlowski? I know he wanted to talk to you."

Agnes shook her head, and her glasses slid forward again. "Not until I've been to the graveyard."

"What's so important there?" Helen Rhine asked. "All graves look pretty much alike."

"That's where Jerome started."

"Are you suggesting that Jerome's murder had something to do with what he found?" Helen asked.

Rudy, coming out from behind the bar, said, "Surely not. Why would anyone care about the grave of an ancient Schneider? No. The more interesting question, it seems to me, is, why did he break into the schoolhouse?"

"Jerome would never!" Agnes said.

"Still, something brought him there," Rudy insisted.

Mac, having remained silent so as not to get back on the subject of his trade, couldn't resist a question. "If Bedford wanted to get in, couldn't he have gotten a key? He could have gone to the Parks people with some story about historical research."

"As a matter of fact, he could have gotten it from me," Helen said. "For a while, it looked like the schoolhouse would be torn down. The Park Department got lax. The old lock got rusty and was hanging open, so I replaced it at my own expense. I gave one key to the park's maintenance department, and I kept one."

"Even if the *murderer* had a key, surely it would be foolish to draw attention to that by using it, would it not?" Rudy asked. Helen turned on him sharply and opened her mouth. "No, no, dear lady," he said. "I'm not suggesting—believe me, it was just an idle remark." Sounding relieved, he said, "I see lunch is ready to be served, so if you will excuse me?"

Helen took a seat at the table next to Mac and tried, unsuccessfully, to get him to discuss his cases. He looked to Abby for rescue, but she ignored him.

Alice chattered, commenting on the food, her indecision about buying a new car or getting another year out of the old one, and why she was changing hairdressers.

The Arlys responded to all this without enthusiasm, and when dessert was served, H.A. remembered he had a lot of work to catch up on. Jean Arly started to get up, but when Helen offered her a lift home, she chose to stay to the end.

Agnes had eaten little. Now she waved aside the dessert, and rising, she leaned on the table edge. "Whoever got Jerome into that schoolhouse on a foggy night was somebody he knew well." She shoved her chair aside and walked a careful straight line to the door. She stopped and turned back. "He didn't *have* many friends." She scanned the table. "Outside of this group."

Lunch over, the McKenzies walked home to get their car. Abby hooked her arm through Mac's and said, "What did you make of all that?"

Mac shrugged. "Interesting group."

"They certainly found *you* interesting." When this brought no response, she said, "I notice it's always the big-chested women who are attracted to you."

Mac silently held the car door for Abby.

She slid in. "You have a book that's a week overdue. Would you like me to take it back for you?"

"No, I'll do it. Maybe I can negotiate a reduced fine." He pulled out into Main Street traffic without stopping for the sign.

"Mac!"

"Sorry."

"All right, Mac. What's bothering you?"

"That Agnes Ketchall needs a keeper. I hope Stan gets to her today."

"You think she's right? About Jerome identifying the grave and that being—"

"Probably not. But if she *is* right, then the sooner her story is on record, the safer she'll be."

They drove to three major shopping malls in neighboring villages trying, in vain, to find a pair of shoes acceptable to Abby. The way home took them down Schneider Road. As they approached the old farmhouse Abby said, "Look. There's a light on. Do you suppose it's Jack?"

"Let's find out." Mac turned in at the drive and stopped where a walk led to the front door. "I have a few questions anyway."

Despite the twilight, he could see the gleam of a chrome bumper just visible at the rear corner of the house. Another car that he recognized as Taylor's was parked on the grass at the front. The house was square, two-storied, and utilitarian. The only decorative note was some gingerbread over the narrow stoop.

The sound of the bell was clearly audible outside. Jack Taylor opened the door almost immediately. "I was just on my way down to the kitchen when you rang," he said. "Come on in."

"We noticed the light," Abby said. "Are you on an inspection tour?"

"I've moved in. No use paying motel prices when I own a perfectly good home."

"Thought you said it was beyond repair," Mac said.

Taylor laughed. "Did I say that? Well, it's not so bad. Sweep out the cobwebs and throw a little paint around. Probably livable."

"And Karen likes old houses," Abby added.

"That too." He flipped a wall switch, lighting the way to the kitchen. "I was about to put the coffeepot on. Won't take long."

They followed him through the hall into a large, high-ceilinged room containing a modern gas range and refrigerator. The stainless steel, double basin sink, Formica countertop, and maple cabinets all looked like fairly recent additions. "This room was a real disappointment to Karen," Taylor said. "She was hoping for a garbage burner and a pump sink, I guess."

Abby looked around the room. "I thought you said nothing had been done for the last twenty years."

"It looks like the old man shut down most of the house and just lived in the kitchen and a small bedroom off the upstairs hall. I'll probably do the same."

Abby sat at the oak table, an item that could have been there since the early twenties. Mac chose to remain standing and leaned back against the sink. "Why didn't you go to Metlaff? You promised Elmer."

"Well, it was getting late—"

"Not that late."

"And I got busy. Don't see that a day makes that much difference."

"Have you been to the graveyard at all?"

"Sure. One of the first things I did was walk the property with the plat map. And I was interested in the headstones. This is a whole side of my family I didn't know at all." He found a can opener in a drawer and started opening a can of Maxwell House. "It was kind of strange, looking at dates in the eighteen-forties and thinking what it must have been like here."

He poured coffee into a percolator basket without measuring, added water to the pot, and reassembled basket and stem. "The relatives I knew, my mother's side, are all gone. Even there, all I ever heard about family history only went back to when Grandpa moved to California from Cleveland. He was a grocer."

"What about your father?"

"Well, I knew *his* father originally came from some place in Illinois. And how he got his in World War I without ever seeing his son, my father. And then how *my* father died in World War II without ever seeing me." He lit the burner under the coffeepot. "I guess maybe that had something to do with picking a Navy career. They were both Navy."

"I've often wondered why anyone would want that kind of life," Abby said. "I asked Mac, but he just mumbled something about 'all them good bennies,' whoever they are."

Taylor laughed. "That's GI benefits, like cheap beer and cigarettes, or world travel, mostly to places where there's no shore leave."

"Free medical care for tropical diseases and work-related injuries, like bullet holes," Mac added.

"Good food and good company in pleasant surroundings," Taylor continued. "To tell the truth, I kind of miss it."

"Why did you leave?" Abby asked.

"When I inherited the farm, I figured I'd look into it after one more hitch. I'd be eligible to retire then. But Metlaff tells me I'm in deep—I mean, I'm going broke. So I get leave and come here to see what's what." He turned down the flame under the coffeepot as it started to boil. "I ran into Elmer Johnson and he explained how I could save everything. Metlaff agreed there was a chance." He got three mugs from the cabinet over the sink, one chipped, one without a handle. "So, I had a choice. Stick with the Navy and lose the works, or get out and gamble on this parking lot scheme."

"But nobody knew about Goldfarb," Mac said.

"Right. Looks bad, don't it?"

"Metlaff tells me you have a box of family papers."

Taylor nodded. "An old woman had 'em. Friend of Henry Schneider, I guess."

"Did she say why he gave them to her?"

"I didn't talk to her, I talked to her daughter. She didn't know much."

"Can I have a look?"

"Sure. It won't help with this Goldfarb business, though. Besides what I gave Metlaff, what's left are old pictures with no names or dates, a few school report cards. The usual junk every family has in the attic."

Abby laughed. "I'm surprised Karen hasn't made you donate it all to the society."

"Hey, great idea!" Taylor grinned. "That'd make me a few points."

"I'd like to see it first," Mac said.

"I'll get it."

"I see you picked up a second car," Abby said.

"Second? No. Just my VW. You saw it out front."

"Who belongs to the one out back?" Mac asked.

"Out back?" Taylor raised the shade and peered through the kitchen window. "I don't know."

"When did you get here?"

"I don't know. Maybe four?" He stepped out on the wide back porch, closely followed by the McKenzies.

"You didn't see it then?" Mac asked.

"No. I had some gear in the car, so I pulled up on the grass to carry it through the front door. Never went around back at all."

"That's Agnes Ketchall's car," Abby said.

"Who is Agnes—" Taylor began.

"It's the same make and color," she said. And she was coming here. But Mac, that was hours ago. What would she be doing up there all this time? It's too dark to still be—"

"Who is Agnes Ketchall?" Taylor asked.

"I'll get a flashlight," Mac said, already on the way to his car. By the time he got back, Jack Taylor had also gotten a flashlight.

Taylor turned to Abby and said, "You better wait here."

Abby just linked her arm through Mac's and the three of them started toward the graveyard, Taylor leading, Mac swinging his light left and right, not sure what he expected to find. The path soon narrowed and they had to continue single file.

Taylor stopped suddenly and Mac swept his light forward until both beams centered on the fur-coated form lying next to Jacob Schneider's tombstone.

"Agnes!" Abby started toward the figure on the ground but Mac held her arm.

"Don't muck up the ground." He moved forward cautiously, avoiding any spot that looked as though someone had recently passed. He knelt and felt for a pulse at her throat. The skin was cool to the touch. He moved the coat collar, which partially concealed her head. "It looks like she fell against the edge of this tombstone."

"Is she . . ."

"Yes, she is."

Chapter 11

The police chose a direct line of approach from the road to the cemetery. Their route through the field was outlined in yellow tape stretched between sawhorses. By avoiding the farmhouse path they would minimize disturbance of the ground where Agnes Ketchall had walked.

The place where Agnes had fallen was also marked with yellow tape. No one had been allowed inside the demarked area since the first examination and taking of photographs. Harsh worklights cast deep shadows behind the tombstones and brought each blade of grass into sharp relief.

Agnes had been removed.

"She'd been drinking," Stan said, picking burrs from his trouser leg. "Right?"

Mac looked at Anna Schneider's stone and thought someone should repair it and place it back on its base. He thrust his hands into his pockets and turned away. "Right."

"And she left the tavern in an excited state. Or angry?"

"Both, I guess. Mad at the police for not doing enough. More or less suggested Bedford had been killed by a Society member. Vengeful? You like that word?"

"Stay with words you understand. She was pissed?"

"And excited, too, like a kid on a big adventure. She was coming up here to solve a mystery and show everybody up." Mac turned and looked toward the overgrown corner that concealed the extra grave. "I wonder what she expected

101

to find out here."

"I've got the whole area cordoned off, and it'll stay that way until we've been over it in daylight. If there's anything here, we'll find it."

"Yeah, but will you know it when you see it? Remember the Great Pearl Robbery?"

Stan started to take a cigarette pack from his pocket, then shoved it back. "If I drop a butt here, Henderson's liable to scoop it up in an evidence bag."

"You won a phony string of pearls at the Italian carnival on Chicago Avenue," Mac said. "You meant to give it to Wanda, remember? It got ripped off from your school locker."

"So what's that got to do—"

"Wanda wore the necklace on your next date and you never knew the difference."

Sergeant Henderson, halfway down the path toward the farmhouse, rose from his stooped position, waved, and called, "Cap'n!"

"One string of phony pearls looks the same as another," Stan said as he started down the path.

Mac trailed along. "Until she told you Butch gave 'em to her."

"I busted him in the snot locker and he confessed."

"Not even a Miranda warning."

"Justice was swift in those days. What's up, Bob?"

"Maybe it's nothing," Henderson said, "but . . ." He pointed to a piece of deadwood that had dropped from a silver maple that overhung the path. "You can see that's been down quite a while. It sunk in a bit when the ground was soft." He reached out and lifted one end a careful six inches, revealing a scrap of badly weathered wood directly underneath. He returned the branch so that it matched the original indentation exactly.

"Looks like an ordinary piece of wood to me," Mac said.

"Yeah, it's a piece of wood." Henderson stood and, pressing both hands to the small of his back, stretched. "But Stan sent me out here this morning to look at what your wife found. There was an impression in the ground, twelve by eighteen, at the head of the grave. Like there might have been a marker. I took a cast and picked up wood fragments. This could be a piece of the marker."

"Any chance of a positive ID?" Stan asked.

"If it's from the bottom of the original, we can get a match on the cast. If not, we can get a probable by matching the wood species and the fungus that's been working on it."

Stan frowned. "Wood fragments. Why does that ring a bell?"

"Damn! I should have thought of that," Henderson exclaimed. "Bedford's apartment."

"Right!" Seeing Mac's puzzled look, Stan went on. "We went over Bedford's place, including a vacuum sweep. Bob found some particles of rotted wood in a drawer." Turning to Henderson, he said, "How soon will you know?"

"I'll get some pictures before I move anything. Maybe make a guess by, say, noon. Then we'll let the county lab have it, and you tell *me* when they'll get to it."

"I'll be down at the farmhouse if you find anything else," Stan said.

"We haven't finished between here and the house, Stan. You'll have to go back and use the work route."

Stan nodded. "Stick close, Mac. Let's not muck things up more than you have already."

Mac, following in Stan's footsteps, asked, "Tell me, Holmes, what do you make of this curious affair?"

"Never get ahead of your evidence, Watson."

"Very professional. I like wild guesses, myself. So Bedford found a wooden grave marker and took it to his place."

"Just for argument, why would he do that?"

"Bob said the wood was rotting. He probably figured the next big storm would finish the job. Or he worried about kids hauling it away. You said they come up here sometimes."

"You say the Ketchall woman knew what he was up to."

Stan stepped onto the pavement of Schneider Road and waited for Mac to come abreast. "Then she must have known he took the marker away. So what was she looking for?"

"She asked me if the police had found anything unusual in Bedford's place. I wasn't sure you weren't holding out—but I said no." They detoured around the evidence van parked on the shoulder and walked toward the Schneider driveway. "So she knew the marker was missing."

"She couldn't have thought it was back here," Stan said. "That wouldn't make any sense."

Mac wondered if it was possible that Bedford had returned the marker to the grave, then dismissed the idea. "Maybe Bedford told her he lost a piece of the marker carrying it out of here. Maybe he came back to look for it, but it had already been covered by deadwood. With the marker gone, she might figure that scrap was important. To corroborate her story."

"And now," Stan said, "for ten silver dollars and a lady in the balcony, why would anybody care? Except for Taylor?"

They turned into the drive, Mac shaking his head. "If you're thinking this was no accident, and that Taylor . . . There's no motive, Stan. We already know about the grave, and who's in it. What's left to conceal?"

"Maybe nothing. The odds are, cause of death was hitting her head on the tombstone. Combination of rough ground, high heels, and too much booze. But don't bet on it. Two down in one small group bothers me."

"Me too."

They walked the rest of the driveway in silence, and entered the farmhouse through the back door. Mac was surprised to see Karen Cannelli sitting at the table with Jack Taylor. He glanced at Abby, who was leaning back against the kitchen counter. She shook her head. He thought Karen blushed, but the light was not very good and he couldn't be sure.

Stan pulled out a chair and sat opposite Taylor. "I'd like

to ask you a few questions, Mr. Taylor. What time did you arrive here?"

"About four." Taylor glanced at Karen, and she nodded.

"Would you describe your actions for me?"

Now Mac was sure Karen blushed. Stan must have noticed too. He said, "Just in general terms."

"We drove up to the front of the house, right on the grass. The car's still there. I had some stuff to carry upstairs and that's the shortest way."

"Did you see anyone around?"

"No. No one."

Stan turned to Karen. "How about you, Mrs. Cannelli? See anyone?"

"No." She turned her cigarette pack over and one fell out. "We went straight in. We didn't look around at all."

Mac watched her pick up the cigarette and light it. Her hand trembled.

"Straight in? I thought you had things to unload?"

"Well, sure," Taylor said. "I unlocked the door first and propped it open. Then I went back for my gear."

"And you helped, Mrs. Cannelli?"

"No. Jack said he didn't need any help."

"You didn't happen to look out of the window?"

Karen shook her head. Jack said, "We were busy—moving in—you know."

"No trips to the kitchen?" He looked at them both. "No?"

"Jack and I were together the whole time," Karen volunteered. She hesitated. "Well, I mean Jack was carrying things upstairs. But he was only gone a couple of minutes each time. Two or three times."

"When the McKenzies arrived, they noticed the car parked behind the house. But neither of you—"

"I wondered about that too," Jack said. "So I went out and checked. You can see my tire tracks where I turned off on the grass, and if you stand there you'll see the bumper hardly shows." He started to rise. "I'll show you."

"That's all right," Stan said. "I'll have someone check it

later."

Taylor sat back and ran a hand through his hair. "When you do, then walk on up to where Mac parked on the drive and you'll see the line of sight changes. The bumper's more visible."

"Did you know Miss Ketchall?"

"Never heard of her."

"But of course Mrs. Cannelli knew her. Did you expect to see her here, Mrs. Cannelli?"

"She left the Running Fox around two. I wouldn't expect her to still be here." She looked as though she were waiting for the next question, but Stan just sat quietly, nodding as if to himself. Karen stubbed out her cigarette and reached for the package. Jack Taylor placed his hand on hers, stopping the movement. She said, "All these questions—Jack said it was just an accident."

"Very likely. But a death has to be investigated. Especially with no witnesses." Stan got up. "Thank you for your cooperation." He motioned for Mac to follow him and, about to open the back door, asked, "Can I have your phone number here, Mr. Taylor? In case anything comes up."

"Sorry," Jack said. "The phone won't be connected until tomorrow. I'll call your office."

Stan nodded and left, followed by Mac. They stopped on the porch, and Stan said, "Why do you suppose he went to all the trouble of checking the sight lines?"

"Good question."

"I didn't ask if they were together the whole time. Why did Karen Cannelli feel she had to explain that point?"

"Because they weren't?"

"Why do you suppose Karen Cannelli didn't tell Taylor all about Agnes Ketchall's scene at the lunch? And about her coming here? Especially since his property was involved?"

"I suspect they had other things on their minds."

Stan grinned. "Is that what they call it now? 'Other things'? I guess they could have been filling his sock drawer from four to almost seven, if he had one hell of a bunch of socks. Last question. Why didn't she come downstairs when you and Abby got here?"

Now Mac grinned. "I can think of a few good reasons. How about taking me in for questioning? I'd really appreciate it."

"What for? You ain't been any help so far."

"I want an excuse to stay out all night. As soon as Abby gets ahold of me, she'll try to get me to work on this case."

"Why? You getting underfoot at home?"

"She'll be worried about what Karen's getting into. And she thinks if I take this on, I'll change my mind about giving up my license." Mac was about to go back into the house when he noticed a bobbing flashlight coming down the hill. He decided to wait.

The light reached the clay and gravel yard behind the house and the figure behind it turned out to be Sergeant Bob Henderson. "Thought you'd want to know about this right away, Stan," he said, carefully holding out a clear plastic bag containing a scrap of wood. The scrap was about three by four inches, and thicker at one end than the other. "This end seems to be the full thickness of the piece, so it should match up with part of the cast I took. You can see it has some letters cut in, probably with a carving chisel. Very neat job." Henderson turned the package. "The end here is square, so it's an edge. These letters must be at the end of a word. Probably a German word, like on those other tombstones."

Stan examined the scrap, Mac looking over his shoulder. The letters *cht* were quite clear. "You know any German words that end that way, Mac?"

"The only German I know is *Schnitzel, Schnaps, und Fraulein*. I'd guess it's the end of a name."

"How do you make 'Goldfarb' out of that? Stan asked.

Chapter 12

Mac, watching Abby stack breakfast dishes in the sink, heard them strike the stainless steel basin with unnecessary force. He noted, with a mixture of affection and exasperation, the stubborn set of her mouth. He poured another cup of coffee and said, "All right. Let's get it over with."

"I have nothing further to say." Abby started the water flowing. "I know how much you want to quit the detective business." She put her left hand into the stream and adjusted the temperature with her right. "And how you'd love helping the ladies select patterns and yarn colors." She took Mac's cup, still full, and dropped it into the water. "And that's more important than Jason and Karen's future." She added soap. "I mean, they're not *your* responsibility."

"I can *see* you have nothing further to say. Stop fidgeting and sit. We'll talk about it."

Abby sat, drummed the tabletop with the fingers of her right hand, and said, "So talk."

Mac got a fresh cup. "Karen can protect Jason's future by staying away from Taylor until Stan gets this sorted out."

"You know damn well she won't do that. What did you think they were doing yesterday? Playing gin?"

Mac sighed. "What do you expect from me anyway? If he's guilty, he's guilty. I can't change that."

"No, but—"

"Leave it to Stan."

"Sarahville has barely enough police to direct traffic at Founders Day. Stan wants a case for a jury. He can't afford to look past his main suspect."

"Right now, only suspect."

"I want a case for Karen. Yes or no. Up or down."

Mac reached out and took her hand. "And you're convinced it'll be thumbs up. Because if it's not, you'll feel guilty for getting Karen involved."

"I thought you liked Jack."

"Abby, think. If Agnes Ketchall's death was not an accident—"

"But if it was—"

"If it's *not*, then two murders are linked to that grave. Even if Agnes was an accident, the Bedford killing is linked. There's no doubt about that anymore."

Abby sat forward. "You didn't tell me that."

"You weren't in the mood last night."

Abby snatched her hand away. "I wasn't . . . ? I did everything but pour water on you to keep you awake!"

"Well, I was tired. Much better to have these little discussions when we're fresh and can think straight."

Abby went back to the sink and plunged her hands into the suds. "You just wanted to avoid a fight!"

"Why are women always so aggressive?" He came up behind her and put his arms around her waist. "What do you have against the quiet life? Why—"

"Why can't a woman be more like a man?" She turned and put her wet hands on his chest. "I'll tell you, Higgins. If we were, nothing would ever get done!"

Mac picked up the dish towel and blotted his shirt. "You want to hear the evidence or not?" Without waiting, he went on, "Bedford must have kept notes on what he was

109

doing. Makes sense, right?"

"I suppose—"

"None were found in his apartment. We know he had the grave marker at one time. Matching wood particles were found at his place. Where is the marker now?"

"Okay. You don't have to beat it into the ground." Abby took the towel from him and dried her hands. "The killer went to Bedford's apartment and removed anything having to do with the grave."

"And as far as we know, Jack's the only one with a direct interest in the grave."

"Wait a minute. Lots of people have an interest, including us. We all want the parking problem solved."

"If the parking turns out to be in Rudy's lot, you'll manage to scratch out a living. If Jack's plan worked, you'd scratch out a slightly better living. The same is true for everybody else. Where's the motive in that?"

"Except for Elmer," Abby said. "Without that parking lot, he'll have to drop his plans and write off the money he's already put in."

Mac sat down and raised his cup. "You've got a point. Not that I believe it, but . . ." He put down the cup without drinking. "You've got a point."

"See?" Abby smiled for the first time. "Jack's *not* the only suspect."

Mac shook his head. "It won't wash. Elmer wasn't at the lunch with Agnes."

"If she died accidentally, that's a blind alley. He could still have killed Jerome. Has Stan checked his alibi?"

Mac shrugged. "I doubt it. But I'll ask. Of course, if Agnes *was* murdered, and I think she was, we're back to Jack anyway."

"Mac, the grave's been found. We know who's in it. There's nothing left to hide. So why would Jack kill Agnes?"

"I said the same thing to Stan last night." Mac swallowed coffee and shuddered. It was cold. "But—then the wood scrap turned up. No use reading too much into it,

110

but it doesn't exactly square with a grave for a guy named Goldfarb. And—what motive did Taylor have for lying? What motive did Karen have for lying?"

"How do you know they lied?"

"You heard. Did you believe them?"

Abby silently traced circles on the tablecloth. Then, "No. They separated for a while. Karen lied about that. And I think Jack knew the car was there." She propped her head in her hands and closed her eyes.

Mac sighed. He had vowed to be there when Abby needed him. He just hadn't expected that what she'd need was a gumshoe. "Tell you what. I'm looking into the Goldfarb thing anyway." And the puzzle had him hooked. Maybe one more case wouldn't hurt. "Maybe something will turn up. Meanwhile, talk to Karen. Maybe she'll tell you the truth. Or at least make her think twice about getting committed while the jury's out."

It was Abby's turn to sigh. "I think she got *committed* yesterday. But I'll try." She returned to the sink. "What are you going to do, exactly?"

"First, I'm going to talk to a few people locally. Maybe I can pick up a lead that'll speed things up. If not, then it's time to slog through a lot of record checking."

"Maybe I can help. I could talk to the ladies of the Historical Society."

"Better leave it to me. These interviews take quite a bit of experience.'"

Abby admired Jean Arly's early American furnishings and the pewter tankards on her mantle. She expressed particular delight at a fine example of the quilting art hanging on the wall.

Jean Arly's sun-darkened face lit with obvious pleasure. "I took up quilting to keep me occupied when the snow falls. I remember, as a child, watching my grandmother. You never know where a childhood interest will

111

crop up."

"I'd have guessed you'd be more interested in winter sports than needlework," Abby said as she settled on a wing-backed loveseat.

"No, thank you. I'm strictly a warm weather person. But you can't spend all your time on the beach, or so H.A. keeps telling me. I'd spend the whole winter in Mexico playing golf, if it was up to me."

"I know what you mean," Abby said. "After living in California for many years, coming back to a Midwest winter was quite a shock."

"Spring is no treat either," Jean said. "Mud and flood. Not too bad yet, but all it takes is a little more rain on this saturated ground . . ."

Abby wondered how to get off the subject of weather and on to the purpose of her visit.

Jean Arly solved the problem. "I can't get over what happened to Agnes Ketchall." Her voice carried no special emotion. "It must have been awful for you, finding her like that."

"Yes it was," Abby nodded. "A terrible shock. Do you suppose she really knew what Jerome Bedford found in the graveyard?"

Jean shrugged. "I suppose she knew *something*. They *were* close. But it's hard to say with those two. They were always a bit — let's say imaginative."

"Then you don't think Jerome found anything of real importance?"

"At least nothing as important as he'd have had you believe." Jean moved from the sofa to a Salem rocker near the window. "It's pretty clear our list of the Schneiders buried in the family plot is incomplete. But in the end, what does it amount to?"

Not exactly a dedicated local historian, Abby thought. "I guess it was important to Jerome."

"Everything involving Jerome was important to Jerome."

Abby smiled. "I only met him the one time, but he did

112

seem a bit self-important."

"I'd heard you were at the last meeting he attended. We don't miss many, but H.A. was desperately ill all that week. A particularly vicious brand of flu this year. Came down with it the day of the meeting. Did it miss you?"

"Yes, thank God."

"Self-important. I'd say that's a pretty good description of Jerome." Jean leaned back and began to rock gently. "Oh, he was decent enough in his own way. I mean—not mean or anything. Just exasperating."

"Do you know anything specific about the grave he supposedly found?"

"No. And I'm not sure I want to. After what happened to Agnes, I think the whole business is bad luck."

"Didn't the police question you? According to them, it may be more than just bad luck."

Jean stopped rocking. "It was an accident. The fool woman drank to much and then went teetering up the hill in high heels."

Abby nodded agreement. "I'm sure you're right." She ran her hand over the top of a cherry wood end table. "I love the way this room is furnished. This is an antique, isn't it?"

Jean inclined her head and resumed rocking.

"Is that why you joined the Society? An interest in antiques?"

Laughing, Jean said, "No, I can't claim any special knowledge. I just like the way they look. Jim Farrell advised me on what to get and sold me some."

"Then why did you join?"

"That was H.A.'s doing. He believes in community involvement."

"Good for business, too, I expect," Abby said. "Have you ever heard the name, Goldfarb?"

Startled, Jean repeated, "Goldfarb?"

"It seems the grave Jerome found belongs to a Jacob Goldfarb."

"Not a Schneider?"

"A nephew of Henry Schneider's."

Jean shook her head. "Never heard of him."

Mac climbed the outside back stairs of the square, two-story brick building. There had been a blacksmith shop on this site right up until 1932. The blacksmith at that time still used it occasionally for custom wrought iron work, but derived most of his income as a farrier working from the back of a truck. When the shop burned down, he sold the site to a farmer who wanted a retirement home, complete with Greek revival porch pillars. The residence was carved up in 1950 to accommodate several businesses.

The outer office on the second floor rear was empty, but the door to the inner office was open. Horace Arly, his long, bony face split in a wide grin, waved Mac in.

"McKenzie! Have a seat. Coffee? Got some right here."

Mac sat in the client chair. "No thanks, H.A. I'm about coffeed out. I came by because everybody tells me you're the man who knows everything around here."

"Is that what they say? Well, not everything." H.A. folded the weekly *Crier* with its pages of legal notices, and pushed it aside. "One way you keep tabs is by reading these things." He patted the paper. "For instance, Alice Hillman's husband has a 'doing business under an assumed name' notice in here. HouseCheck, Inc. He's a construction engineer with an architectural firm in Chicago."

"Meaning?"

"He must be moonlighting as an independent home inspector."

"I suppose doing the books for local businesses, not to mention your tax work—"

"Strictly confidential." His swivel chair creaked and tilted at a dangerous angle as he leaned back.

"Sure. It's the same with my business." Mac moved his

114

chair closer and leaned on the desk. "Of course, if I can confirm what I know from other sources . . ."

"So you want to know about Jacob Goldfarb. Right?"

Mac concealed his surprise at being anticipated. "I see people are right about you. How did you know?"

H.A. chuckled. "No big mystery. Taylor needs to know if he can move the graves. His lawyer is Metlaff. You do jobs for Metlaff sometimes. Stands to reason if you're fishing for information, that's what it's about."

"I'd swap jobs with you, but I can't balance a checkbook. How did you know about the parking lot deal?"

Still grinning, H.A. laid a finger alongside his generous nose. Can't reveal my source. You know accountants have to be pretty good detectives sometimes."

"But how did you know the name was Goldfarb?"

"I was working on Rudy's books the day Jerome came in. Heard him ask."

"So you pretty well knew what Jerome's big secret was."

"Just that it had to do with this Goldfarb. And I think everybody knew it had to do with the Schneider graveyard. Anyway, that was before my time."

"The Goldfarb funeral, you mean?"

"Around the end of the war, wasn't it? I didn't move out here from Chicago until 1949. Right out of college." H.A.'s eyes seemed to focus on the far distant past. "Went to work for a guy who handled most of the farm accounts around here. Shrewd old buzzard. Learned a lot from him." He tilted forward and rested his arms on the desk. "When he retired in 1952, I bought the practice."

Mac leaned back and shook his head in disappointment. "Guess you can't help me then. Unless . . . Did you handle Schneider's taxes?"

"Yes, but—"

"I just wondered if he ever mentioned Goldfarb."

"Not a word."

"Damn! I was counting on you, H.A."

"Sorry." Horace started to doodle on a pad of paper

next to the phone. "I *did* hear your client may be in trouble with your friend, Pawlowski."

With some effort Mac managed to keep his face impassive. "Where did you hear that?"

Horace shrugged. "I hear things. Is it true?"

"I suppose the police are interested in everybody at this stage."

"Okay, so you can't talk. But the fact is, Taylor's the only one they're really looking at."

"How about you?" Mac asked. "You think Taylor's involved?"

Horace shrugged again. "Not up to me to point fingers." He laid down his pencil. "Nobody else gave a damn about Jerome and his graveyard. But that grave screws Taylor."

"While we're on the subject, what did you think of Agnes Ketchall's little speech at the lunch?"

"Agnes?" Horace's wide grin reappeared. "The woman was a hysteric. Nothing she said would surprise me."

Mac adopted a thoughtful expression. "I suppose so. Still . . . Seems like too much of a coincidence, her death so soon after Bedford's. And after what she said."

"Nothing in it, McKenzie. What did she say? She was going to find out who was buried in the Schneider graveyard." H.A. laughed. "So what? We know who it was. And who cares?"

"Agnes Ketchall came pretty close to saying one of you at the lunch pulled the trigger on Bedford."

"Crap. Where's the motive? No, the only one worried about Agnes Ketchall right now is Rudy Wilking."

"Rudy?!"

"He served the booze. He should have stopped her from driving. And booze contributed to her accident. One of those Iowa relatives of Agnes's ties up with a lawyer, Rudy could have a mess on his hands." H.A. took a letter opener from the desk drawer and began cleaning his fingernails. "I tried to talk Rudy into more liability insurance a while back. Could have gotten him a good deal. Now he wishes he'd listened to me."

H.A. pointed at Mac with the letter opener. "Agnes had an accident. And nobody had a motive to kill Jerome — except Taylor."

Chapter 13

Breakfast service at the Running Fox had dwindled to one man at a corner table determined to finish the entire morning paper on free coffee refills. Mac went into the deserted barroom and on back to the kitchen. Josie was standing at the open side door smoking a cigarette. Despite a fan running in the range hood and the open door, there was still a faint aroma of bacon in the air.

"Good morning. Is Rudy around?"

Josie flipped her cigarette butt through the door and then closed it. "He's out buying produce." She looked at a pendant watch hanging from a gold chain. "Should be back soon. Want to wait?"

"Have you worked here long?"

"About twenty years. Seems longer."

"Twenty years. That's not long enough. I don't know why I even asked. You're too young to go back thirty."

"Thank *you,* sir. Thirty years ago I was a waitress in Elgin. You haven't joined that hysterical society, have you?"

Mac laughed. "What made you think that?"

"Jerome Bedford came in one day looking for who might have been around thirty years ago. Weird. Said he was writing a book, or something."

"What did you tell him?"

She shrugged. "What could I tell him? I got back to my kitchen and let Rudy talk to him."

"The name *Goldfarb* mean anything to you?"

"Have some coffee? On the house. Goldfarb? No, I don't think so."

"Did Bedford ask about anybody by name?"

"Maybe Rudy . . ." She glanced out the window and opened the door. "Here he comes now."

Rudy Wilking, carrying a basket of lettuce, stopped on the threshhold. "Well. Mac. Good morning." He hesitated briefly. "Let me get the rest of this in and then you can tell me what brings you here."

Mac had the impression Rudy considered him an unwelcome distraction on a busy day. "I'll give you a hand." He placed his cup on the butcher's block. Rudy carried the lettuce to the sink and Mac brought in a box of tomatoes from the Ford pickup parked in the service drive. "I just stopped by to get some information." He returned for a box of green peppers, the last of the produce. "Josie tells me Bedford came around asking questions too."

Mac's help seemed to restore Rudy's usual cordiality. "Then you must be referring to Goldfarb. That is the only time Bedford was ever here. I don't think we were his kind of place. He referred to my tavern as a saloon."

"But you knew Bedford, didn't you?"

"It was the first, and only, time I actually met him. However, he was known to me by reputation. I take it he was a rather peculiar gentleman in some ways."

Mac nodded. "What did he ask you?"

119

Rudy thought a moment. "He wanted to know if I had heard of one Jacob Goldfarb. He said the man was here in the fall of 1946. But you see, I was just then in the process of buying this place and was not yet well acquainted. I was not very helpful, I'm afraid."

"He didn't say why he was asking?"

"Part of his historical research." Rudy smiled briefly. "The matter takes on an entirely different connotation now, of course."

"What connotation do you put on it?"

"Well, after Agnes Ketchall's dramatics yesterday—"

"Poor Agnes," Josie said. "Wasn't that awful?"

"Yes, a tragic accident," Rudy said. "One would naturally suspect that the grave Bedford had discovered belonged to this Goldfarb, whoever he might be."

Mac reached for his cup, but Josie beat him to it. "That's getting cold. Let me get fresh."

"And I would further guess that you are seeking information about Goldfarb on behalf of young Taylor, so that he can establish his right to move the graveyard."

Mac's eyebrows rose. "How long have you known about that?"

Rudy smiled. "For some time, actually."

"Why should it be a secret, anyway?" Josie asked.

"You too? Apparently it *wasn't* much of a secret, then."

"True," Rudy said. "Horace—H.A. as he prefers to be known—told me. I don't know how he found out."

"I just asked him," Mac said. "He wouldn't say."

"H.A. has his sources. Perhaps at the bank. I don't ask. Tell me, am I right about Goldfarb?"

"Looks like he's the extra grave. He was Henry Schneider's nephew."

"So, then it is a member of the Schneider family, and young Taylor should have no problem with his

120

parking lot plans. Well, that means the Village will not be interested in my lot."

"Disappointed?"

"I have mixed emotions. There are certain advantages to selling, but on the other hand, a beer garden back there *is* an attractive idea." Rudy smoothed the hair over his right temple. "As a matter of fact, the first necessary step will be taken in about a week."

Josie said, "We'll be closed for a couple of days while they do the digging."

"You're going to pour a patio slab? Before you're sure about the lot?"

"No. Not a slab," Rudy said. "I am having an old subcellar unearthed and filled in. I have meant to do it for some time. It extends beyond the limits of this building into the lot, and it is a nuisance."

"Nuisance is right," Josie said. "I hate to go in the cellar. I'm always expecting a rat to come out of it."

Rudy looked pained. "No rodents, I assure you. I take care there should be none. But it floods in heavy rain, and I have absolutely no use for it. Besides, it is becoming dangerous and may collapse, leaving me with a large hole and a larger lawsuit, should someone be injured."

Mac decided to get the discussion back on track. "So I guess you can't help me with Goldfarb. Know anyone else that might?"

"I should have thought you would check—what are they called?—vital records. What does asking questions, locally like this, accomplish?"

Mac wasn't about to explain that a wood scrap, with the letters *cht* carved on it, had raised doubts in his mind. "Checking public records can be slow. I'm looking for a shortcut. Tell me. What sort of a place was Sarahville back then? Everybody know everybody?"

Rudy laughed. "I would say so. There were only a few hundred residents. And it was not the sort of place that would attract summer visitors. Strictly a farming community."

"Not too good for business."

"The Running Fox was a favorite gathering place for the locals. Actually, I believe it was livelier back in prohibition days. This was a speakeasy and a brothel, you know."

Josie said, "I think he made that up just to give the place color."

"No, it is true, I've been assured. There is even a rumor that this is the very place where Al Capone contracted his fatal disease. There is, of course, no way to confirm that."

Mac laughed. "You should put up one of those bronze markers. 'Al Capone got his here.' "

Rudy chuckled. "Not the sort of reputation I cultivate. I like it known as a family tavern."

"Did Schneider come here much?"

"Oh yes. Father and son. Both of them on Fridays for the fish fry, and Henry more often."

"Father and son?"

"Yes. Hans Schneider and his son Henry—actually his name was Heinrich, but everyone except his father called him Henry."

"So you got to know them pretty well."

"Henry, yes. His father only a short time. Then he died. Pneumonia."

"Well, thanks for the coffee," Mac said. "What's on the menu tonight?"

Josie said, "Your choice of barbecued ribs or spareribs and sauerkraut. The soup is barley."

Mac stepped through the door of the Feed and Farm Implement store and waited a moment for his eyes to adjust to the dimness. The place had an interesting odor compounded of furniture polish, dust, and just a hint of mildew.

A counter at the back had a row of tin bins across its front, all painted red and gold, each marked with the name of a coffee variety. He noted Farrell's disheveled red hair rising just above the counter top, and approached to find Farrell sitting in a battered oak swivel chair, eyes closed, a heavy book with a dark brown dust cover in his lap.

Mac knocked on the counter. "Having a slow day?"

Farrell opened one eye and grinned. He opened the other eye and held up the book. It was titled *Despatches of Sir Douglas Haig.* "Exciting stuff."

"You must be a World War I buff to wade through that."

"One and two. I just found the book and some other stuff in the attic," he said, indicating a box near his feet.

"Found it? Don't you know what's in your own store?"

"I bought the place a couple of years ago. There was so much junk on the floor I didn't do a very thorough check of the upstairs against the inventory. Now that I've made some room down here, I decided it was time."

"Looks like you got sidetracked."

"Yeah. When I saw this military stuff, I brought out some I'd bought a while back to see if there was enough for a separate display. Or maybe I'll take it out to Union, next time they have a collectors show, and set up a table."

Mac indicated a cigar box, lid held closed with a rubber band, sitting on the counter. "Mind?"

"Help yourself. We'll dicker price later."

Mac opened the box. It was filled with brightly colored bits of cloth and tarnished metal. "Much of a market for military patches?"

"It's a steady market. German patches bring more,

especially the Nazi stuff."

"You bought this place two years ago? Then I guess you can't help me. I'm looking for people who might know something about a Jacob Goldfarb. Goes back thirty years."

"Before my time, buddy. What's the story, or can't you tell me?"

"It's pretty much an open secret. Agnes Ketchall spilled the beans about an extra grave, which turns out to be Jacob Goldfarb, old Henry Schneider's nephew."

"Damn shame about Agnes. And so soon after Jerome. Makes you wonder, doesn't it?"

"Wonder what?"

"You're supposed to be the detective; don't you wonder? Agnes and Jerome were close, too. Well, she made that clear over at the tavern yesterday, didn't she?"

"Here's a Twentieth Air Force patch. Worth much?"

"Not much."

"I wondered, because I've got a couple." Mac dropped the cloth circle back in the box. "Not exactly a Hollywood-style romance, those two."

"Like they say, eye of the beholder. They must have had some great conversations. Every bitchy little remark out of Jerome got a giggle out of Agnes."

"Jerome didn't exactly endear himself to people, did he?"

"Oh, he wasn't such a bad guy, once you got used to him. People didn't take him seriously, which was part of the problem. More than anything else he wanted to be taken seriously."

"And Agnes did? Take him seriously?"

Farrell nodded. "Two of a kind. Both lost their mothers, and their purpose in life, fairly recently. About a year apart."

"Purpose in life. How do you mean?"

"Well, you know—Momma looked after her own se-

124

curity by dominating her son; he took care of her, and never made a move without her okay."

Mac nodded. "Momma's boy."

"Agnes had a similar deal but she seemed to resent it, where Jerome accepted it." Farrell scratched his head, then smoothed his hair back. "But resent it or not, without Momma, Agnes was at a loose end."

"You're quite an amateur psychologist."

Laughing, Farrell said, "That's what this business does for you. I was just a kid, sixteen, when I started as a helper to an old bandit. Papa John they called him. He took me all over the countryside, Wisconsin, Michigan, Indiana, talking farmer's wives out of the junk in their attics. Later I worked flea markets from coast to coast. It's a liberal education, believe me."

Farrell paused, head tilted to one side. "I learned to study people. And I wonder what it is about Jerome and Agnes that got them killed. Now you come along asking questions about the grave."

"I'm checking it out for the current owner of the property, that's all."

Farrell's smile struck Mac as a bit sly. "Jack Taylor, you mean."

Mac sighed. "Does everybody know?"

"Well, it's pretty obvious him and Karen got the hots for each other. So naturally, everybody wants to know who he is. Can't have our gal taking up with some lowlife, right? Turns out H.A. knows all about him."

"What's the verdict amongst the ladies?"

"They think he's the greatest thing since Paul Newman." Farrell laughed. "In spite of that, I guess he's all right."

"I suppose you heard about the parking lot idea too."

"Yeah. Sounds great to me." Farrell took a business card from his shirt pocket and used it for a bookmark, placing Sir Douglas on the counter. "When will he start moving the graves?"

"I thought you were in favor of historic preservation."

"That's what Jerome said, but business is business."

Startled, Mac said, "You mean Jerome Bedford knew about Taylor and the parking lot?"

"No, no. Jerome heard I bought some stuff from Henry Schneider, and after Henry died he thought I should contribute it to the Society."

"What would they do with it?"

"We'd like to set up a small museum someday, if we can ever talk the village into letting us have the old schoolhouse."

Mac, examining a First Infantry patch, said "If I can't find out who this Goldfarb's survivors are, Taylor may not be able to go ahead."

"Shouldn't be any trouble tracing them, should there?"

"Not in the long run, but there isn't much time. That's why I've been looking for a shortcut, like someone who knows the facts and can give an affidavit. Otherwise I've got to start where he came from, which is Nebraska."

Farrell stood up and stretched. "I'd hate to see Taylor give up the idea. I like it a lot better than Rudy's solution. You collect military patches?"

"No, they're just interesting to look at. Since you can't help me, was the former owner of this junk shop around thirty years ago?"

"Yeah, but he's dead. I bought from the estate."

Mac stirred the contents of the little box with his finger. Both Rudy and Josie knew Bedford was asking about Goldfarb. Bedford must have asked others about him as well. Everybody suspected Bedford was on to something regarding the graveyard. So it was no trick to connect the two. And apparently everybody knew about Taylor and the parking lot. The question was, did Taylor know everyone was so well informed? If he did, there was no point in killing Bedford. He'd have to kill off the entire Historical Society. At a minimum.

Mac drew a small gilt badge from the box. "What's this one?"

Farrell took it from Mac and held it up to the light. It was a steering wheel surrounded by a laurel wreath. "German. A military driver with some sort of meritorious service."

"Maybe he never missed a scheduled oil change."

"I don't know." Farrell set it aside. "Worth more than those U.S. patches, though. Want to see some more?"

"Maybe some other time. As long as I'm here, do you have any stained glass? I'm looking for a fan light."

Farrell chuckled. "I've got just what you're looking for. And I guarantee it'll fit."

Farrell led the way through a mazelike path between several oak iceboxes, a mahogany hall tree, numerous tin advertising signs, and assorted junk, to the west wall. Sunlight, filtered through two grimy windows, fell on the wide planks of the floor. A large window depicting an anonymous saint in stained glass leaned against the wall.

"That came out of an abandoned church that burned down over near Marengo. There's only one small piece missing."

"Nice. But not a fan light."

Farrell carefully moved the church window to one side, revealing oak-framed stained glass patterned to resemble green leaves and purple grapes. Mac thought it was remarkably ugly.

"How do you know it'll fit?"

"Because it came from your house, that's why. The guy who owned the Twilly house, before Johnson got it, said he hated this thing. Replaced it with the pebbled glass that's in there now."

Sure that Abby would change her mind once she saw it, Mac said, "I'll have my wife take a look at it. You can talk price with her."

Chapter 14

At eleven o'clock on Wednesday the only sound in the township library was a faint squeak from the wheels of a book cart being pushed between the stacks. Helen Rhine sat behind the reference desk reading the *Chicago Tribune*.

"Hi, Helen," Abby said. "Busy?"

"Don't I wish!" Helen folded her paper. She waved toward the visitors chair. "It's so nice to hear a human voice."

"Doesn't anyone in Sarahville read?" Abby sat down and put her purse on the floor.

"Oh, it's pretty lively in the evening, but daytime is deadly." Swiveling her chair to face Abby, Helen struggled briefly with the hem of her skirt. "I've thought about working the late shift, but Al won't hear of it. Insists on my company and then ignores me for television."

"They're all alike," Abby said. "No use fighting it."

Helen's eyebrows rose in mock astonishment. "I'm surprised to hear that from a newlywed like you."

Abby laughed. "Not even *that* can compete with Monday night football, and now it's baseball coming up."

"At least, with a detective for a husband, when he does talk the conversation should be interesting. I heard all I ever want to hear about drill presses and milling machines years ago."

"When it comes to his cases, Mac can give the sphinx a run for its money."

"Really? I hoped you could tell me what's going on. I know he's a friend of that Captain Pawlowski."

"You mean about Agnes?"

"Well—yes. But that was an accident. I was thinking more of Jerome."

"Did the police question you?"

Helen's laugh lacked the warmth of humor. "After a lifetime without so much as a parking ticket, I'm beginning to feel like one of the usual suspects. They came around twice about Jerome, and now about Agnes." She shook her head slowly. "At first I thought it was to find out how drunk Agnes was. But some of their questions were pretty peculiar." She paused, looked away, and asked, "They don't think it was an accident, do they?"

Abby shifted in her chair. How much information should she give, in hope of getting more? "Do *you* think it was an accident?"

Helen glanced toward the woman reshelving books at the far end of the room. "No, I guess I don't. That would be too much of a coincidence, wouldn't it?"

"But why would anyone want to kill two harmless people like Jerome Bedford and Agnes Ketchall?"

"I don't know, but I can tell you what has everyone worried sick, whether they admit it or not." She rolled her chair closer to Abby. "You heard Agnes at the luncheon. Suppose she was right? Suppose she was killed to shut her up?" She leaned back and shook her head in disbelief. "Then I think about what that means. These are people I've known for years. They have their faults, don't we all. But one of them a murderer?" She shook her head again.

Abby waited, but Helen seemed to have exhausted her urge to talk. "What you say about Agnes is possible, I

130

suppose. But that leaves the question of why kill Jerome."

Helen looked surprised. "Because of the grave, of course."

"The grave?"

"Jerome thought it was such a secret! And being Jerome, he was going to milk it for attention. I suppose that's why we didn't give him the satisfaction of being curious, although we were, actually."

"Just what exactly *did* you all know?"

"We all heard Jerome's heavy-handed hinting. And then Agnes. She couldn't resist a few hints of her own, just to let us know she was in on it." Helen sighed. "It's really sad, when you think of it. Jerome and Agnes. I've always had trouble trying to visualize—well, you know."

Abby leaned forward. "But Jerome and Agnes both seemed to believe . . . You mean all of you knew all about the big secret?"

"Like I said, from the hints, adding it all up, you'd have to be dense not to know Jerome found something in the graveyard. Then, one day, my Al went up there and had a look for himself. He found the grave and asked the rest of us to keep quiet. Let Jerome have his little triumph. Well, it was only fair. Jerome *did* find it first."

"I still don't see how any of that is motive for murder," Abby said.

"Obviously Jerome, in his persistent way, found out who is buried there."

"And?"

"And suppose the burial was unauthorized? Suppose it's a murder victim?"

Abby smiled and relaxed in her chair. "One thing I *can* tell you. The burial was handled by Bochman's. Does the name *Goldfarb* mean anything to you?"

"Goldfarb?"

Abby nodded.

"I know Jerome was asking questions about a Goldfarb."

Mac arrived in Elk Grove Village about noon, assured by calling ahead that Al Rhine would not be out to lunch.

The Elk Grove industrial area consisted of modern brick structures, each with a strip of grass and shrubbery across the front. The buildings ranged in size from multiple-tenant strips, where each company was alloted space not much larger than a storefront, to block-long warehouses with high-bay loading docks and a rail siding. Rhine Tool and Die was on a corner, one of a row of six identical buildings housing small manufacturers.

Al Rhine's office was big enough to accommodate a drawing table in addition to his desk and a conference table. A large window in one wall looked out on the shop floor. Sleeves rolled, tieless, and with an oil stain on his index finger, Al was obviously a hands-on businessman.

"So, what are you up to, McKenzie?" Al asked. "Taking up Agnes Ketchall's challenge?"

"You heard about that?"

"My wife was there. You didn't take her seriously, did you?"

"Ketchall? Should I?"

Al gave a short laugh. "Seems like the police do. You know they asked Helen for an alibi?"

"Did they ask you for one?"

"Me?" He appeared surprised. "I wasn't at the lunch that day. They just asked me what time she got home."

"That's right, you weren't there." But that didn't prove he hadn't intercepted Agnes at the graveyard. All it would have taken was a phone call from Helen. Was there a call? Mac decided to push his luck a little. "I just thought your wife's phone call—"

"How did—Christ, don't tell the police that. She just

132

wanted to know when I'd be home, that's all."

Mac shrugged. "My only interest is in the grave. I'm checking it out for Jack Taylor. I suppose you heard about that? Seems like everybody has."

"Sure." Al, grinning, slumped down in his chair and folded his hands. "I don't know why people bother with secrets in Sarahville. They don't keep worth a damn."

"Seems like some secrets keep pretty good," Mac said. "I've been trying to get a line on Jacob Goldfarb and so far I've got zilch."

Al shifted in his chair and glanced through the window. "If that's what you came for, I'm not going to ruin your record. It's zilch here too."

"You heard about Goldfarb?"

"I knew Jerome was on to something in the Schneider graveyard, and . . ." He leaned toward the window, then sat back again.

"So I've been told." Mac leaned forward and tried to hold Al's eyes, which kept switching to the window. "But Jerome planned a dramatic announcement, right? Not much drama if everybody knew."

"He couldn't resist little remarks to heighten the suspense. After a while, knowing Jerome, it wasn't hard to figure. And then he started asking questions about a Jacob Goldfarb. Word got around."

"So what about Goldfarb? What do you know about him?"

Al laughed. "Zilch, like I said. Who is he, anyway?"

"According to Bochman the undertaker, he's buried in the Schneider graveyard. Appears to be a Schneider on his mother's side."

Al shook his head. "You know, Helen and I were speculating the other day. How maybe Jerome got killed because he found out something? Particularly after Agnes — but that can't be. I mean, you just said the grave's a matter of public record. Just because folks forgot about it doesn't make it a secret. Right?"

"Right. Unless there's something else. Any idea what it might be? Any other hints from Jerome? Or Agnes?"

Al swiveled his chair to the window and remained silent for a moment. Then he swung back and picked up the phone. He punched the intercom line and a bell rang out on the shop floor. Al spoke to the phone. "Why isn't the milling machine running?" He raised his eyes to the ceiling. "So you're a man short. Jesus, Charlie, did you forget how to run it? Or do you want me to come out and do it myself?" He put down the phone and shook his head. "I'll be glad when the place is sold. People just don't work like they used to."

"I've noticed that," Mac said. "What about Jerome? Could he have found something else? Besides the Goldfarb grave?"

"If he did, I don't have any idea."

"Have you always lived in Sarahville?"

"I apprenticed at the Douglas plant. During the war. Met Helen—she worked in the office. When we got married we moved in with her folks, in Sarahville. You know how housing was—couldn't get an apartment without a little cash under the table, and we were broke."

"Then you were in Sarahville around the time Goldfarb was buried."

Al shrugged. "Could be. I wasn't paying much attention to local events in those days."

"From apprentice to owning your own company. You did pretty well."

Al looked around his office and grinned. "Yeah, not bad for a kid from back of the stockyards." He sighed. "But it's time to hang it up. Move where it's warm. These winters get harder every year."

"Hasn't been a very productive morning, has it?" Abby asked.

"Oh, I don't know. I found your fan light."

"I better get over there this afternoon. Before it's gone."

"Not much danger of that. Let's have lunch. I have a long afternoon ahead."

"I'll get out the lunch meat. You start the coffee." Abby opened the refrigerator. "Aside from the fan light, I don't see much progress."

"A few interesting points," Mac said. "We now know several people knew about the extra grave. And the name *Goldfarb*. And could easily connect the name with the grave."

"Which makes the grave a pretty unlikely murder motive," Abby said. "Where do you go from here? On Goldfarb, that is."

"Metlaff is getting a copy of the death certificate. I need to hear Bochman's story firsthand, but—did you get a chance to talk to Karen?"

Abby put liverwurst, salami, and rye bread on the table. "I called, but she was out. I left a message with the babysitter."

"Surprised she didn't dump Jason here. Do you think you can talk to Alma Hinsdale for me? I don't want to leave it too long."

"The woman who had Henry Schneider's personal papers?"

"Right." Mac swept spilled coffee grounds off the counter into his palm and dumped them in the sink.

"Not before tomorrow. Don't wash those down the drain. You'll clog the pipes. What should I ask her?"

Mac turned on the water. "Actually, coffee grounds are good for the drains. Abrasive. Scrapes off the crud." He turned off the water and plugged in the pot. "She might remember the Goldfarb funeral, and what was said at the time."

"Okay, but when the sink backs up, *you* deal with it. What will you be doing tomorrow?"

"Guess I better do some phoning to Nebraska, since I don't see any shortcut developing. I'll try to hook up with a local PI out there and hope Taylor can pay the freight."

"How do I find Alma Linsdale?"

"She's living with her daughter, somewhere in Lake County, according to Metlaff." Mac took a notebook from his pocket and tore out a leaf. This is the daughter's phone number. She'll give you directions."

"What will I say? That I'm investigating a murder?"

"You're from the SHS doing research on the Schneider graveyard." Mac placed one hand on her shoulder. "And that's absolutely *all* you're checking on."

When Abby failed to respond, he drew her closer. "I hate to point it out, but there *is* something else that was known to more than one person. Despite what Taylor thought, his identity and his parking scheme were not a well-kept secret."

"I know. Horace 'call me H.A.' Arly knew and told at least some people."

"Which means Bedford could have known. If you were after information on the Schneider graves, and knew the last surviving Schneider was in town, who would *you* have made an appointment to meet on that foggy night?"

Chapter 15

Abby watched Jason skate across the waxed parlor floor in his stockinged feet. A few dust motes raised by this game glistened in the late afternoon sunlight. "I'm glad you could come by, Karen. We have to talk."

Karen cupped her hand under her cigarette to avoid dropping the ash, and looked around for an ashtray. Abby got one from under the counter at the back of the room.

"This is new, isn't it?" Karen asked, resting her hand on the counter.

"Like it? I understand it came from a drygoods store. It's at least as old as the house. Older, I think."

"It's just what the place needs." Karen examined the finish, consisting of a milky patina over assorted nicks, scratches, and burns.

"It needs refinishing, of course. But look what's leaning against the wall behind it."

"The fanlight! Where on earth did you find that?"

"Mac found it at Farrell's. Now if I can just get him to put it — Jason! Don't climb on the counter. You'll hurt yourself, honey."

Karen removed him bodily and said, "Go play in the yard, Jason."

"I shouldn't complain," Abby said. "The poor man is busy as it is, between water heaters, the Goldfarb business —"

Jason ran toward the door, dropped on his seat, and slid until his foot struck the wall. He jumped up and grabbed the doorknob.

"Stop!" Karen shook her head in exasperation. "Put your shoes on, Jason. You can't play outside in your stocking feet."

"Is it muddy?" the boy asked.

"It's too cold."

"Let's go to the kitchen," Abby suggested. "He can play in the back yard and we can keep an eye on him."

They waited while Jason struggled with his shoes, then Karen finished tying them and escorted him through the house and out the back door.

Abby put cups on the table and placed the coffeepot and an ashtray within reach. "Mac's out working on Goldfarb."

Karen paused while lighting another cigarette. "Has he made any progress?"

"Not really. I want him to look into the whole business of Jerome and Agnes, not just Goldfarb. So far he says no, but—"

"Jason!" Karen darted to the door. "Stay away from the creek!"

"—I think he'll do it in spite of himself."

"Why should he?"

"He hates loose ends, and I've a feeling there'll be plenty of those where the grave is concerned."

"I mean, you said he doesn't want to be a detective, didn't you?"

"He said it. I don't believe it."

"But he's doing this because you pushed him into it," Karen said. "He said this isn't his kind of case."

Abby shook her head. "Don't you worry about that. Mac likes to keep up that low-key, detached front, but he's just as concerned about you and Jason as I am." She smiled. "If he ever got the kind of case he *says* he wants, I don't think he'd know what to do with it."

Karen kept her eyes fixed on Jason, who kept edging

closer to the creek.

"Karen, you *do* understand, don't you, that Jack is the chief suspect in Jerome's death?"

"Yes." Karen ground out her cigarette and avoided Abby's eyes. "I know." She reached for the coffeepot. Her hand trembled.

"Don't you think it would be a good idea if you—and Jason—saw less of Jack? Until things are a little clearer? If not for your sake, then for Jason's?"

The afternoon sun was unkind, piercing the makeup with which Karen had tried to conceal the dark circles under her eyes. She blinked back tears. "Oh, Abby! I don't know what to do." She rummaged in her purse. "I'm sure Jack hasn't done anything. But if . . ." Abby got a box of tissues from the counter and placed it at Karen's elbow. "Jason is too young to remember his father." She wiped at her nose and stuffed the tissue up her left sleeve. "Jack took Jason to Busse Woods to feed the elk. Jason talked about nothing else for two days."

Abby touched Karen's hand. "I don't believe Jack is guilty. But suppose he has to stand trial? No matter how hard we try, children pick things up. They don't understand, they get confused, frightened. At the very least, Jason will sense how *you* feel."

Karen looked miserable. She nodded. "My Aunt Florence is taking Jason for a week. Maybe by then—"

"When?"

"This evening."

"Maybe you should go too."

Karen raised her chin and her mouth firmed. "I am *not* going to run out on Jack!"

"No, I suppose not." Abby sighed. "All right. But if we're going to help, you have to be honest with us."

Karen darted to the back door. "Jason!" The boy looked over his shoulder and reluctantly withdrew his foot from the water. "You come in here this minute!"

"Karen," Abby said, "nobody believes you and Jack

139

were together the whole time yesterday. Jack was gone for a while, wasn't he?"

"Not for long, really."

Exasperated, Abby said, "He was gone long enough that the two of you thought it was worth lying about!"

"All right!" Karen lit a cigarette. "Half an hour, that's all."

Jason appeared at the door. He managed to lower his head, as though studying the floor, and at the same time turn his eyes up toward his mother. "I slipped."

"Get those shoes and socks off, young man."

Abby produced a towel, and Jason managed to pull his shoelace into a knot. Karen sat him on a chair, pulled off his shoes and socks, and used the towel vigorously.

"Why do I have to go to Aunty Florns?"

"Aunt Florence," Karen corrected.

"Aunt Florns."

"Because I'm going to be real busy for a while. I thought you liked Aunt Florence?"

"Huh-uh. Uncle Jack could take me fishing. He said!"

Abby brought a box of crayons and a coloring book from the parlor. "I just got a carton of these sets for the store," she said. "They'll give the kids something to pester Momma for while Momma picks out yarn."

Karen's laugh was a bit forced.

Abby installed Jason on the floor in one corner of the kitchen, and then nodded to Karen. "Now tell me the whole story. Don't leave anything out."

Karen started her story haltingly. Jack had told her he was moving and she offered to help him after the SHS lunch. An afternoon at the Schneider farmhouse seemed a perfect opportunity for them to be alone. She got a babysitter for Jason. They arrived at the farmhouse in the late afternoon with Jack's luggage, essentially everything he owned, crammed into the trunk of his car. On the drive she told him about Agnes, and her plan to visit the gravesite.

"How did he react to that?" Abby asked.

"He was irritated, naturally. He was afraid the story would be all over town. The bank would be sure to hear about it. He said if he had known that's why she was there—"

"He saw her?"

"Earlier. She pulled up in back of the house and he went out to see what she wanted. She asked if she could visit the graveyard and he said okay."

"She didn't tell him why?"

"No. He said, if she was still there . . . Well, he was irritated."

Abby leaned forward. "Karen, I have to hear the whole thing. He said what?"

"It's not important. Just one of those things people say when . . ." Karen withdrew a cigarette from her pack, then stuffed it back in. "He said, 'If she's still there, I may dig another grave, just for her.' It was just a joke, sort of. I told him she might help. Maybe she knew about Goldfarb's family."

"Did that satisfy him?"

"I guess so. He dropped the subject. And then we got to the farm and he pulled up on the grass, just like we said."

Abby lifted the coffeepot, but Karen shook her head and lit a cigarette.

"I was really surprised when we went in. I guess I expected cobwebs and dark shadows. I mean, the place hadn't been lived in for over a year. The floor actually shone." Karen smiled. "He said, 'They don't call us swabbies for nothing.' "

They took Jack's duffel bag and a couple of cartons upstairs to the bedroom Jack intended to use. "He'd cleaned that room too," Karen said. "There really wasn't anything for me to do."

Karen suddenly blushed, and Abby said, "I'm sure you managed to keep busy. And after that?"

Karen cleared her throat. "About six-fifteen Jack decided to make coffee. I guess I—I dozed a bit. About six-forty I began to wonder why he wasn't back. That's when I heard him running, taking two steps at a time."

Karen shielded her eyes with her hand and stared at the tablecloth. "He said you and Mac were coming up the drive. And then he said, 'Listen, if anyone asks, we've been together the whole time. Okay? I'll explain later.' Before I could answer he ran down the stairs to let you in."

"And did he explain later?" Abby asked.

"When Jack was in the kitchen, he noticed the car was still there," Karen said. "He went out to look for Agnes."

"So when we got there," Abby said, "he already knew she was dead."

Karen tried to light a cigarette, but didn't seem to have the strength to tear the match from the matchbook. She laid cigarette and matches on the table. "Yes. We knew the police suspected him of Jerome's murder. What would they think now?"

"Karen, the autopsy may show Agnes died before the time he left you. Then he's in the clear."

"What if she died before he picked me up that afternoon?"

"Where was he?"

"At the farm. All day."

Mac dropped in on Bochman's Funeral Home at 6 P.M., reasoning that family and mourners would likely be at supper, leaving the owner free to talk. He found that business was slow that Wednesday and all three parlors were unoccupied. August Bochman, Jr., accepted Mac's explanation for taking an interest in Jacob Goldfarb without question, and invited him into the office, seeming glad of the company.

Mac declined to sit in a chair drawn up to a coffee

table in one corner of the office. "A little back problem. That looks like one of those overcomfortable chairs you have to struggle to get out of." He took a straight-backed chair in front of the desk.

"The Goldfarb grave," Bochman said. "Well. I was just out of the Army, and in college, at the time of the burial, so I can't tell you anything firsthand. But looking up the record for Bedford, and then later discussing it with your wife, some of the stories Dad told me came back." Bochman laughed. "You've no idea some of the bizarre things that happen in our profession. Many of which can't be told to a nonprofessional audience. Can I get you some coffee?"

"No, thanks. Would it be possible for me to see your father?"

"Dad's gone."

"Sorry."

Bochman shrugged. "He was eighty-five and in fairly good health. Died in his sleep. I hope to be as lucky."

"Me too," Mac said. "But you do remember his talking about Goldfarb, right?"

"Our family has buried Schneiders since the early twenties. Not just in the farm plot. In the churchyard too, and in Chicago, the girls generally buried with their husbands. Well, my father always had some reservations about the Goldfarb funeral."

Mac leaned forward. "What sort of reservations, Mr. Bochman?"

"Call me Augie. Everybody does. Well, you must remember this was a much smaller community at the end of the war. The postwar housing boom was just starting, and we were still able to say we knew everyone. And Dad was very familiar with the Schneider family history."

"Goldfarb didn't fit what he knew?"

"Camilla Schneider, Henry's sister, had married Irving Goldfarb, a Jew. You can imagine it caused quite a sensation at the time. He did say that while the

143

Schneiders weren't pleased, they behaved decently at first. Then they learned Goldfarb was not only a Jew, but a devout Jew who intended his children to be raised accordingly. After that they never spoke about her again. So, on the face of it, it was plausible that she should have a son that no one locally had heard about. What was less plausible was that Henry Schneider should welcome him into his home."

Mac shrugged. "People change. Maybe he regretted losing contact with his sister. Maybe he wanted to make it up to his nephew."

Augie Bochman seemed to be thinking it over. He finally nodded. "Anyway, Dad suggested having a rabbi officiate, but Henry wouldn't hear of it. Said Goldfarb had gone off to college and become an atheist." Augie laughed. "According to Henry, that's what happens if you go to college."

Mac smiled. "Did your father think Henry Schneider balked at a rabbi officiating in his family graveyard and made up a lie to avoid saying so?"

"No, that's not it." Augie hesitated. "When I told Bedford it was Jacob Goldfarb buried there, he was obviously surprised and asked me several times if I was sure. I showed him the records and his eyes lit up. 'Isn't *this* a gorgeous little mystery,' he said." Augie paused. "It *is* an intriguing mystery, although I don't know why *Bedford* thought so."

Mac waited patiently.

"But now that Henry is dead, we'll probably never know the truth. You see," Bochman said, "Goldfarb, or whoever he is, wasn't circumcised."

Chapter 16

"I'm glad I didn't know the latest Goldfarb development when Karen was here," Abby said. "She's on the verge of coming unglued as it is." She opened the refrigerator.

Mac peered over Abby's shoulder. "Let me have one of those candy bars."

Abby handed him a Baby Ruth and took one for herself. "What do you think it means?"

"Looks empty. What do we do for supper?" He unwrapped the candy. "What do I think *what* means?"

"That business of the uncircumcised Goldfarb."

"A very wise Polish police person once told me, 'Never get ahead of your evidence.' An ancient proverb from his native land."

"Stan was born on Division Street."

"Division Street is well known for its proverbs. Like, *zimnie piwo,* 'warm heart.'" He thought a moment. "Of course, that's since been changed to *cerveza fria.*"

"You're avoiding the question. What does it *mean?*"

"It means 'cold—'"

Abby reached up and grabbed Mac's ear. "Goldfarb!"

"Okay!" Mac sat down and drew her onto his lap. "No need for violence. Three possibilities. One, a boy with a traditional Jewish father somehow escaped the knife. Two, Bochman's got it wrong and Goldfarb Senior was Norwegian. Or three, Goldfarb is not holding down a slot in the Schneider family plot."

She leaned back against his shoulder, her own fears confirmed. "That ends Jack's career as a real estate tycoon, I guess." She sighed. "Well, at least that rules out Jack. He had no motive to kill Agnes Ketchall."

"We don't know for sure Agnes was murdered."

"You know she was." Life was one coincidence after another, but she simply didn't believe in this one. "So now you'll either find Goldfarb alive and well, or dead and buried in Lincoln, Nebraska. Or maybe Camilla never had a son." She thought about that for a moment and found no flaw in the logic. "So why kill her? Whatever Agnes knew wouldn't change the outcome for Jack."

"You're moving a little fast. Jack's motive for the Bedford killing was a little weak before. Now—"

"Weak? I thought you said—"

"I said he had the only *known* motive, not a *good* motive. If Jack thought the body in the ground was Goldfarb, he still had a shot at making his fortune—either by finding there are no relatives or by getting their permission to move the grave. Maybe all the way to Nebraska. Murder's a pretty extreme business tactic. Especially when there's a chance it isn't needed."

"So . . ."

"So if he killed Bedford, it was because Bedford told him the body in the ground was *not* Goldfarb."

"Okay. I see that. And Agnes knew, or was about to find out, it wasn't Goldfarb?"

"Maybe. Or maybe . . ." Mac tried to put his candy wrapper through an imaginary hoop and missed the trash can. "Taylor denies ever meeting Bedford. What if Agnes knew otherwise?"

Abby's gloomy reception of this idea was evident on her face. "I *really* believe Jack is innocent, Mac. But if he's not, the sooner we know, the better. Karen has to be protected, in spite of herself."

"Maybe we're being too pessimistic. Things may look

better after we've eaten." Mac kissed her gently. "Speaking of which . . ."

"I guess we eat out. There's nothing here."

"Can't. Got a line on a PI in Lincoln and left a message this afternoon. He's supposed to call back. See if we can strike a deal." Abby received a gentle shove and stood up. "Try the deli. How about smoked fish and potato salad?"

She got her coat and, ready to leave by the back door, said, "Mac, are you sorry I got you involved in this?"

He smiled reassuringly. "No. Not really." He appeared a bit embarrassed. "I've been thinking. Maybe you're right about the store—all that." He cleared his throat. "And I'd hate to see Jason's mother in a mess."

Abby's felt a sudden sense of relief. Smiling, she said, "Then I'm not going to worry. You'll work it all out."

"There's still a lot we don't know," Mac cautioned. "I hope Alma Linsdale will shed a little light."

Abby walked across the yard and climbed the berm separating Twilly from the shopping strip on Harper. She entered the back door of Jeanine's Sewing Center, a shortcut she'd learned of while discussing mutually beneficial business referrals with Jeanine Schwitzer. She waved to Jeanine and smiled.

Stepping out of the front door into the Harper-side parking lot, she nearly ran into Alice Hillman. "Alice! I was just thinking of you," Abby lied.

Alice giggled. "Should it make my ears burn?"

Abby laughed and wondered if this sweet-tempered innocent would ever grow out of girlish mannerisms. "Well, we didn't have much chance to get acquainted at the luncheon. I was thinking, 'I really must ask Alice Hillman over for coffee one afternoon!' "

"Thank you, but we only have one car, and Bobby has that during the day. Otherwise I'd love to." Her fair brow wrinkled slightly. "It's really a pain, not having a car. Bobby keeps saying we'll get another one, but I don't think he likes for me to drive."

There might well be good reason for that, Abby thought.

Alice giggled again. "The truth is, I'm a much better driver than he is. I'd never let him know that, though."

"Where do you live, Alice?"

"Over in the Spring Grove subdivision, on the other side of the creek."

"That's where Jean Arly lives. How about if I invite her too, and you can ride with her?"

Alice's eyes narrowed. Her hesitation in answering was marked. "Tell you what," she said. "Why don't you have coffee with me? Not this week. Let's see—how about a week from tomorrow? About two?"

"Fine. I'll be there," Abby said, wondering what the source of friction was with Jean Arly. Judging their sidewalk conversation was about to end, and not wanting to lose the opportunity, she asked, "By the way, have you ever come across the name *Goldfarb?*"

"Sure. That's the man Jerome was asking about. Of course he didn't ask me. I could have told him he was barking up the wrong tree."

"Really? How do you know that?"

"I was brought up in Sarahville, you know? When I was a kid, before things got so built up, we used to play in the Schneider graveyard. We'd sit on the tombstones and tell ghost stories." She moved closer to Abby. "I'd never have said anything while Jerome was alive, but I always knew about that extra grave."

Startled, Abby said, "For heaven's sake, why not tell Jerome?"

Alice pursed her lips and shook her head. "Poor Jerome. He didn't have much of a life, really. Why should I rain on his parade?"

"Do you know who's buried there?"

Alice shrugged. "I remember there was a marker, and

a name. I've racked my brain, but I'm pretty sure the name wasn't Goldfarb." She looked over her shoulder and moved a step closer. "I'll tell you another thing. If you ask me, poking his nose into that grave is what got Jerome killed. Agnes too. And don't tell me Agnes had an accident."

Abby felt a sudden chill. "Alice, I wouldn't tell anyone but the police what you know."

"Why not?"

"If you're right—about why Jerome was killed—you might be in danger."

Alice unsnapped the top of her purse and held it up to Abby. Nestled between a wad of tissue and a leather key case, reflecting the neon light of Jeanine's Sewing Center, was a small automatic with pearl handgrips.

"Alice! Are you sure you know how to use that thing?"

Giggling, Alice said, "I won a trophy on the combat course last year. That was with my three fifty-seven, but it's too heavy to carry around." Snapping the purse shut, she said, "Well, I have to go. Bobby'll be getting worried about me."

Abby returned with a six-pack of Hamms and a cold supper. Mac popped the tops on two cans, and Abby brought glasses to the table. He ignored them.

"Your Nebraska call come through?" she asked. "No? Then let me tell you about Alice Hillman and the steel under all that padding."

The next morning, when Abby called Alma Linsdale's daughter, she made the mistake of doing it in Karen's presence. Abby hung up to face a determined woman.

"Now that Jason is staying with my aunt, I have plenty of free time. And you said yourself I should see less of Jack. If I just sit around, I'll probably kill my-

149

self with these things," Karen said, lighting her third cigarette in the last half hour.

Abby sighed, and nodded.

The weather remained good, and a drive in the spring air was appealing. They drove north on Interstate 294, exiting westbound on Half Day Road in Lake County. The rest of the trip consisted of exploring side roads, some of which were little more than private drives, and in asking directions from people who had no idea what they were talking about.

Abby was about to give up when Karen spotted a mailbox at the side of the road labeled "Muntner." Alma's daughter.

The gravel driveway penetrated a tangle of osage orange and crabapple to reveal a front yard dominated by a large cottonwood. The house was a two-story frame with a narrow stoop. Abby mounted three stairs and pressed the bell. A pleasant-looking woman in her forties, wearing jeans and an apron, opened the door.

"Have any trouble finding the place? It's always so difficult giving directions, don't you find? I'm okay with left and right, but north and south, east and west, just confuse me."

"No trouble at all," Abby lied.

"Well, good. Mother's looking forward to talking with you. I told her about the Historical Society and all."

Mrs. Muntner led the way through the house to an enclosed porch flooded with the morning sun. A frail, white-haired woman sat in a comfortable chair, a heavy sweater draped around her shoulders, the sleeves hanging free.

The woman smiled and raised a hand in greeting. "You must be the history lady. Come in. Sit down. Bea, let's have some tea, dear."

Abby introduced herself and Karen. They made small talk about the leaves just beginning to show, and the relative mildness of the past winter. Abby and Karen

150

agreed with Mrs. Linsdale that the climate was changing because of the atomic bomb.

By then tea had arrived and Abby felt ready to get to the point. "Mrs. Linsdale, I understand you were a good friend of the Schneider family."

"Well, I wouldn't say that, dear."

Abby and Karen looked at each other. Was their trip for nothing?

"But I understood Henry Schneider entrusted you with all his personal papers," Abby said. "We just assumed—"

"Oh, Henry." Mrs. Linsdale smiled and sipped her tea. "Yes, Henry. I never did get along with his father though. Terrible man. Always swearing in German. I don't know much German, but I know cursing when I hear it."

Abby laughed. "It does have a distinctive sound in any language, doesn't it? Well, it's Henry we're interested in anyway. Can you tell us about him?"

"Henry Schneider was a hardworking farmer in season, but a real hell-raiser in the winter." She turned and looked out over the yard, where a forsythia was beginning to show a hint of yellow. "He never married."

"Was there any special reason he didn't marry?" Karen asked.

Mrs. Linsdale didn't seem to hear. "Folks called him Henry, but his name was Heinrich. They kept to a lot of the old customs around here. Even church services were in German up till 1935. Did you know that?" She sighed. "A hardheaded Dutchman."

Abby wasn't sure whether the Dutchman referred to was Henry, his father, or the local pastor. "Do you remember anything about a Jacob Goldfarb?"

"Goldfarb? No, I—oh, Goldfarb. What about him?"

"How did he come to be buried on the Schneider farm?"

Mrs. Linsdale looked out at the yard again, and Abby began to wonder if she was dozing off. Then she turned back. "No harm in telling it now, I suppose, Henry being gone and all.

"Henry had a farmhand. Albrecht, his name was. Joseph Albrecht. Turned up back in '44 or maybe '45, I don't recollect. Kept to himself. Folks around here never saw much of him."

"Around here?" Abby asked.

"Did I say here? Around Sarahville, I meant. I used to go over to the Schneider farm to buy eggs—we had a grocery store. Where the Barn is now—Main and Harper. You know where I mean? That was back in the thirties." Mrs. Linsdale sipped her tea and leaned back. "I got to know Henry then. Funny how things happen."

Silence stretched to the point that Abby felt impelled to speak. "You say it's funny . . . ?"

"I was married in those days and Max didn't much like the Schneiders. We started buying eggs over at Woolram's and I didn't see Henry for a long time, except to run into on the street now and then."

"But he thought of you as a close friend, even after all those years," Abby said.

"Funny how things happen. Max left me the store to run when he died, and then after a while the old man, Hans died, and I started buying Schneider eggs again, it being closer and all."

Mrs. Linsdale reached for the teapot then, flexing her fingers, thought better of it. "Would you get that, dear?" Abby poured, and Mrs. Linsdale continued. "So I saw him once or twice. Albrecht, I mean. Him and Henry always talked German."

"How do you spell *Albrecht?*" Abby asked.

"Now some folks around here mixed up German and English, sometimes in the same sentence." This time Abby didn't ask where "here" was. "But then, Joseph Albrecht had a real kraut accent, which Henry didn't have any, except sometimes the way he strung his words together sounded a little foreign, you know what I mean? It bein' the war and all . . ."

152

Alma Linsdale's voice had faded and she seemed lost in a private world of memories. "Can you spell *Albrecht* for me?" Abby asked again, hoping to get her back on track.

"I remember the day he died. Harvest season. He was workin' the south field—it's all houses now—and expecting rain. So he'd work as long as he had daylight. You understand?"

"You mean the hired hand?" Karen asked.

"But it got dark and he wasn't back, so Henry went lookin'. He found the tractor run up against a tree. It dug itself into the ground before it ran out of gas. Henry followed the tracks back a ways and found Albrecht. Far as anybody could tell it was some kind of freak accident. Like he got down off the tractor for some reason and it slipped back in gear. I don't know."

Feeling a chill despite the sun streaming in, Mrs. Linsdale drew her sweater close around her. "I went to see Henry that night. Seems old Hans, Henry's father, and Albrecht got to be real good friends, maybe because it gave Hans a chance to talk German, which he couldn't hardly do anymore around here, the old crowd mostly dying off. So, instead of lettin' the county bury him, Henry put Albrecht in the family plot. Henry swore the man was a nephew and winked at me. Wasn't no skin off my nose."

Abby nodded. "What about Albrecht's family?"

"Albrecht was a Jew who got out when Hitler came in, didn't have a pot to pee in and no friends or relations." She nodded to herself. "Barely talked English—kept to himself, except for . . . It was just Henry, me, and the undertaker at the funeral."

Abby sighed. "So Jacob Goldfarb is really Joseph Albrecht, Jewish refugee."

"I asked Henry if he shouldn't have one of them rabbis come out and do whatever it is they do. Henry said he didn't figure a rabbi would come do it in a Christian cemetery. Might even make him dig up the casket and move it."

Abby said, "I see. So that's why Henry told Bochman—"

"A-L-B-R-E-C-H-T," Mrs. Linsdale spelled.

Abby smiled. "Thank you. And after all these years, this is the first time you've told the whole story."

Alma Linsdale looked confused. "Did I say that? Must have slipped my mind. I told that strange young man."

"Who was that?" Karen asked.

"Had a small mustache, hardly worth keepin'. Kept asking me was I sure the name was Albrecht. Like I didn't have all my marbles no more. I wouldn't likely forget Joseph Albrecht."

On the way home Abby said, "Henry Schneider gave her all his personal papers, and she was the only one at the Goldfarb, or Albrecht, funeral. How close do you suppose they were?"

"There's a picture of Henry and his sister, Camilla, in the Society collection," Karen said. "Strong family resemblance between brother and sister."

"What did you expect?"

"Mrs. Muntner looks a lot like Camilla."

Chapter 17

Abby dropped Karen at the Winslow Apartments and headed home, followed all the way by an unmarked police car. She parked in front of her garage and got out to greet Stan Pawlowski. "If you'd put on your siren, Officer, I'd let you pass. Or are you giving me a ticket?"

"You had a safe driver award all sewed up, until I saw you roll that stop sign on Wilson and Harper." Stan held the porch door for her. "Where's your old man?"

"In his office, probably. Let's go up. I want to see both your faces when I tell you what I found."

Stan paused at the refrigerator long enough to liberate a beer and followed Abby up the stairs.

Abby looked around the office in surprise. What had this morning looked like a storage shed had been transformed into the semblance of a workplace. Boxes had been removed from in front of file cabinets, the desk had been half-cleared of miscellaneous junk and, most surprising, his State license hung on the wall. Abby raised an eyebrow at that but Mac, leafing through several pages of notes at his desk, avoided her stare.

Abby found an uncluttered corner and perched on the desk, inviting Stan to take the visitor's chair.

"Looks like you've been busy," she said to Mac. She tried to keep any hint of the surprise she was about to spring from creeping into her voice. "Any news from Nebraska?"

Mac's tone matched the gloom on his face. "Too damn much news. The PI I made a deal with is good. And fast. He's uncovered a nest of Western Goldfarbs. Not only Nebraska but Wyoming and Utah. One of them's a state representative." He threw down his pencil. "I don't see any point in going on with this."

Grinning in spite of herself, Abby said, "You're right about that, Hawkshaw."

"So what did you find out from Alma Linsdale?"

Abby nodded toward Stan. "Think we should talk in front of the fuzz?"

"Why not? He's an honest cop and you already bribed him with a beer."

"Yeah," Stan said as he pulled the tab on his can of Hamms. "Once I'm bought, I stay bought."

Abby launched into her account, sparing them no twist or turn on her journey through Lake County. The surprise on their faces as the story unfolded was most satisfying. For good measure she added Karen's remark about the resemblance of Alma's daughter to Camilla Schneider.

"You did great, kid," Mac said. He turned his legal pad to a fresh page and made a note. "You say Alma Linsdale was confused, or forgetful, once or twice. How accurate do you think she was?"

"I believed her."

Stan nodded. "My grandmother was eighty-nine when she died. Had trouble remembering what she had for lunch, but she could tell you every detail of the boat trip from Poland."

"Why didn't Karen come back with you?" Mac asked.

"She had a headache." At Mac's snort of disbelief

Abby said, "Yes, I know. She's probably on her way to see Jack." Then hearing Stan mutter under his breath, she continued, "Well, why not. This affects him more than anyone. He has a right to know."

Stan shrugged, resigned or disgusted, she wasn't sure. "Well, Linsdale's story ties in with the scrap of wood we found," he said. "Clears up that point."

"Not to mention Alice Hillman, who also remembered a different name on the marker," Abby added.

"Yeah. Thanks for the tip. I talked to her, but didn't get any more than you did."

"Stan, maybe I should have . . ." Abby hesitated, torn between a general belief that people shouldn't carry guns, and concern for Alice's safety.

"What she means is," Mac said, "Alice packs a piece in her purse."

Laughing, Stan said, "Can you beat it? Giggles like a kid, screeches like an owl, and a face like a kewpie. But she can light a match at twenty-five yards with a cannon she can barely lift. Her old man was a hardcore gun nut and collector. Raised his kids accordingly."

"A collector?" Mac asked. "Anything in the collection that throws nine-millimeter Parabellums?"

"Word from the county is, it's a Luger." Stan finished his beer, threw the can into the waste basket, and tipped his chair back on two legs. "Getting back to this Albrecht, hard to believe Henry Schneider went to all that trouble just to save the county the cost of planting his hired hand. But I guess stranger things have happened."

"You going to look into this Albrecht business?" Mac asked.

"Better you should waste your client's money, than I should waste the taxpayers'."

Abby, incredulous at Stan's reaction to her story, made no secret of how she felt. "You're not suspicious about Albrecht's accident? You're not curious

157

about his background?" Warming to her subject, she stood and leaned over the desk. "You don't want to know the connection between Albrecht's grave and the murder of Jerome Bedford? Too busy chasing speeders?"

Stan held up a placating hand. "Let's see if I can sort out those questions. Yes, I'm curious about Albrecht, and as soon as your old man here figures it out he'll tell me. The cause of death? Why doubt the coroner's verdict? Anyway, I've got enough crime on my hands. I don't need to go back thirty years looking for a case which probably doesn't exist."

"Okay, but you must believe Jerome's murder is connected."

"Make that Jerome and Agnes," Stan said. "The autopsy showed she was suffocated while unconscious from a blow on the head."

Abby turned pale. "God, that's awful."

"What time?" Mac asked.

"We know she left the tavern at quarter after two. She was dead no later than four."

"And everybody was out of the tavern by three," Mac said.

Stan nodded. "Horace Arly was the first to leave. He walked to his office and worked there alone until three-thirty when he had an appointment with a client. Mrs. Rhine played taxi, dropping Alice Hillman and Jean Arly at their homes between three-fifteen and three-thirty. Rhine then stops for gas and arrives home about four, where she finds Mr. Rhine who had left work early."

"You slipped up there, Sherlock." Mac's smile was a bit smug, Abby thought. "Should have asked Al Rhine for his alibi."

"Why? He wasn't at the lunch."

"No, but his wife phoned him. He probably heard all about what happened. Are the other alibis confirmed?"

"We're working on it," Stan said.

Abby said, "See? There are other possibilities besides Jack. And you can't ignore the man in the grave."

"Maybe the murders are connected to the grave," Stan said. "But that don't mean they have to be connected to the person *in* the grave. Taylor wanted to keep anything from lousing up his little development plan. So he'd want to keep it quiet no matter who it was."

"But he couldn't," Abby said. "Once they start moving graves it would come out anyway.

"So he was dumb." Stan lit a cigarette, then belatedly looked for an ashtray. Finding none, he fished his beer can out of the waste basket. "Probably thought once the bank was committed they'd give him extra time to straighten it out. But you screwed it up by poking around in the weeds up there." His face tightened and he stared directly at Abby. "If he had known that before you spread the word too far to stop . . ."

"Nonsense!" Abby said, but she couldn't control a slight shiver.

"Then you come up with Goldfarb, and—"

Abby waved her hand impatiently. "I've been through all that with Mac. I still say Alma Linsdale's story about Albrecht changes things."

"Makes it worse for Taylor," Stan said, "if he knew for sure the body was a hired hand and not a relative." He shook his head. "No, my main problem is, as far as I can prove, Taylor and Bedford never met. To make this work, Taylor had to know what Bedford found and what he intended to do about it."

Abby had come home elated by her detecting and the further mystery she had uncovered. She now realized that, as far as Karen was concerned, matters had become worse. She turned to Mac in frustration. "And there sits my husband, looking smug, because he told me practically the same thing you did." Her irritation mounting, she turned on Stan. "You're going to be sorry you didn't follow up on Albrecht. There are all kinds of possibilities there."

"I've got other cases and not enough people to work 'em. Which is where Sam Spade here comes in. He's getting paid to check on that, and I look forward to a full report. If there *is* anything to report."

"As soon as you make a serious move toward Taylor," Mac said, "Metlaff's going to hire me for the defense. That'll cut down on what I can tell you."

Stan got to his feet, grinning. "As long as you don't suppress evidence of a felony."

Abby slumped into the chair and watched Stan depart. When Mac came over and took her hand, she snatched it back. "Sometimes that man infuriates me.

"No use getting mad at Stan. He's just objective, which you're not. I admit Taylor is a likable guy, and I worry about Karen and Jason. But did it occur to you that Taylor wasn't really keen on me investigating the grave?"

"Maybe you *should* be a ribbon clerk," Abby said. "This private eye paranoia is interfering with your social development. Also, did it escape your notice that Mr. Albrecht, Jewish refugee, is still mysteriously uncircumcised?"

Mac patted her hand. "You're emotionally involved. Better leave it to a professional."

"And just what is the great professional going to do?"

"First, I'm going to call off this Great Plains bloodhound before his bill gets any higher. Then, a relaxing evening with a beautiful woman."

Abby felt she had been patronized long enough. "Unless you have someone *else* in mind, forget it. We have a case to work on."

"Tomorrow. We'll question the suspects then. Tonight we make peace."

Mac paused on the screened porch, looked across the backyard to the creek, then beyond to the gentle slope crowned with Schneider gravestones. He held the screen door for Abby and, letting it slam behind him, took her hand.

"It's a beautiful morning for a walk," Abby said. They crossed the gravel drive. "How are you at spading gardens? I can hardly wait to get some color back here." They walked slowly down the sloping yard. "The creek looks higher today." The rocks were wet and slippery, some an inch or two under water, but she moved nimbly from stone to stone. "Watch your step," she warned as Mac, following, plunged his left foot ankle deep in the creek.

He cursed briefly, but sincerely.

Abby laughed and took his hand again. "Does that mean you've broken your morning silence?"

He grinned a bit sheepishly. "Good thing I'm wearing boots instead of shoes."

"What's been going on in the silent recesses behind those eyebrows?"

"My sinus cavities?"

"Let's go back to silence, shall we?"

They started up the slope toward the graveyard. "I've been thinking," Mac said, "about Goldfarb and Albrecht — sounds like a law firm, doesn't it? — and how that all came about."

"I thought Alma Linsdale cleared it up pretty well," Abby said.

"Then maybe you can explain it to me."

"Sure, Chief. Henry Schneider befriended his hired hand, probably because of the language —"

"Were they friends?"

"Safe assumption. Considering what Henry did later. And natural, because, as I was about to say, of the language thing."

161

"Go on."

"Henry learned all about Albrecht's life—"

"Not all."

"Well, he thought he knew." Abby swung around and halted Mac with a finger poked to his chest. "Who's doing this, anyway? Albrecht had no family, and Henry didn't feel right about letting him go to a pauper's grave. Falsifying official records didn't bother him. Who cares about bureaucrats and politicians?"

Mac swung her around and urged her up the hill with a slap to the behind. "How did you get that? Hold a seance and talk to him?"

"Young man, if you're going to be a success at your trade, you'll have to learn to put yourself in the subject's shoes. Henry was an independent farmer of the old school, a rugged individualist, a man—"

"I get the picture."

"But it was unseemly to let Albrecht lie unnoted in his grave. I mean, in that case he might as well have let the county do it. So he made a marker. That explains the scrap of wood with the letters *cht* on it."

"Wanted the world to know, right? So he let the weeds grow, not to mention a tree or two."

"So he was ambivalent. Didn't want to attract notice. And being a private graveyard, there wouldn't be any visitors."

"Until Jerome Bedford."

"You have to give Henry Schneider credit," she said. "Given the times, the family background, that business of his sister—"

"His—"

"Camilla. Marrying out of the faith—way out. Enough bad feeling to cut her off from the family. Still, Henry befriended this man who—"

"Who certainly was *not* Jewish," Mac said.

"Henry thought he was, don't you think? Albrecht probably said he was a refugee to get sympathy.

Maybe he was wanted by the police. Or by his wife and six kids."

They reached the graveyard and paused to look back at their home. "I really love that house, Mac."

He admitted it looked good from this vantage point. The gabled attic, the conical top of the turret, the sharply etched appearance of the blue trim against white siding. Curling roof shingles, rot under the threshold, skimpy insulation, all invisible. Not to mention the plumbing. He turned and they moved on through the rows of headstones. "If Henry believed Albrecht's story, why not have a rabbi officiate?" he asked. "You believe that atheist business? Or that he was worried a rabbi wouldn't allow the burial?"

"I don't know. It's not impossible." Abby bent to examine a headstone, her soft brown hair sliding forward along her right cheek. "Hans Schneider, born September 23, 1869, died February 2, 1946. He was born just after the Civil War and died just after World War Two." She straightened and shoved the lock of hair back behind her ear. "It always surprises me — how much history one life can cover."

Mac looked toward the undergrowth that concealed the Albrecht grave. "There was a time when people were born, married, had children, grandchildren, and the world looked the same when they died as it had when they were born." He followed the path created by police feet and looked down at the rectangular depression. "Yet people today claim to be bored. How do you suppose they manage that?"

"If you have no sense of the past, you have no sense of change," Abby said. "I guess that's why I like Olde Sarahville and old houses. Keeps my link with the past from breaking under the strain of progress."

Mac came back to Abby's side. "The Civil War, assorted hostilities and two World Wars. I guess that's progress, of a sort. Albrecht died in September '46.

163

We don't know when he was born, and no one's mentioned his age."

Hands linked again, they took the path to the farmhouse. "Is there something about consecrated ground that would make it a problem for a rabbi to conduct a funeral here?" Abby asked. "Either in the rabbi's mind, or in Henry's?"

"I don't know. But I'm going to check on it."

Karen answered Mac's knock at the back door of the farmhouse and silently waved them in. Abby reminded him to wipe his feet.

"Old Coordinated here stepped in the creek," she said.

"Don't worry about it. I have to mop this floor anyway."

Mac glanced at Abby to see if she had noted Karen's proprietary attitude toward the house, but her smile gave nothing away. "Where's Jack?" he asked.

"He's in the parlor with that policeman friend of yours."

Abby, eyebrow raised, nudged him. "Mac?"

"Yeah. I'll see." He started for the front of the house, and after a moment's hesitation, Abby followed. He looked back as they entered the parlor and found Karen on Abby's heels.

"Good morning, Officer," Mac said. "Is this a private third degree, or can anybody join in?"

Stan stood in front of the small fireplace. He nodded. "I was just asking Mr. Taylor if he owned a gun. He says no."

Taylor sat on an old horsehair sofa, legs crossed, arms folded, face impassive. Karen immediately went to him and sat down, arm against arm. She folded her hands in her lap, and affected a stony gaze.

Turning back to Taylor, Stan said, "Are you sure about that answer?"

"I'm sure."

"So if one of your former shipmates said you *did* own a gun, that would not be correct."

"Depends. I had one, but that was a couple of years ago. I don't have it anymore."

"Tell me about it."

"It was a Luger. Made in 1934."

"Can you tell me anything else about it?"

"I'm not an expert. I know the Colt Model 1911a; I did enough shore patrol."

"You recall the caliber?"

"It was seven point six five millimeter. Aren't they all?"

"You have no special interest in firearms. Why did you get a Luger?"

Taylor shrugged. "A shipmate bought it in Hong Kong. Said something about the proof mark and when it was made. Said it was in mint condition, which even I could see was true. Anyway, he claimed it would bring a high price from a collector stateside. When it came time to take it aboard ship, he got cold feet. So I gave him what he paid and smuggled it home."

"And who did you sell it to?"

"I didn't. By the time I figured out how to go about finding a collector, and how to put it up for sale, I shipped out again. When I got back, the gun had disappeared."

"You reported it stolen?"

"No." For the first time Taylor looked unsure.

"Why not?"

"Well, I wasn't sure . . ." He paused, rubbed his chin. "Did I break any laws in this deal? I know damn well I broke Navy regs."

"And you're sure about the caliber?"

"Yeah, seven six five. Ain't that what Lugers are?"

"Thank you for your help, Mr. Taylor." Stan left the parlor and from the hall called, "Mac?"

"Be right back," Mac said as he followed Stan.

Abby patted Karen's shoulder reassuringly. "Me too," she said, and followed Mac.

Stan stopped in the shade of the front stoop and waited for the McKenzies to join him. "What brings you two here this morning?" he asked.

"I'm working Goldfarb's—I mean Albrecht's—grave. Taylor said I could look through the family album," Mac said. "Why?"

"When Nick and Nora horn in, I like to know how things stand." Stan leaned against the railing. "You're not working the Bedford killing then? The lawyer didn't decide it was time for defense?"

"No, I—"

"Yes he is." Abby's lips drew up in a gentle, left of center smile. "He just doesn't know it yet."

Mac spoke patiently. "Look. Taylor is not my client, except in the limited matter of tracing relatives. He—"

"Relatives are moot," Stan pointed out. "That all went down the drain when Albrecht popped up."

"Okay, but you wanted me to look into it. As for Taylor, he's shown no sign of wanting me to do anything more, and if he did, I wouldn't take it on. Murder is police business."

"Nice of you to say so," Stan said.

"*If* Taylor is charged or warned, and *if* Metlaff defends him, and *if* Metlaff feels he needs investigation to prepare a defense, *then* I'll think about it."

"Don't worry, Stan. You know Mac. He couldn't stop now if he tried," Abby said.

Mac shook his head in exasperation. "Pay no attention to her. How did you get on to Taylor's gun?"

"I haven't been sitting around with my finger . . ." Stan glanced at Abby. "Leave no stone—that's the secret of successful detective work. Write that down. Might help you move up from amateur status."

"Yes sir, Captain. I've made a note: When the case

isn't going anywhere, clutch at straws."

"You got it. His last duty station was San Diego. I asked for local help, and they came up with a statement by this shipmate. About the Luger, and how Taylor came to have it. He didn't say anything about it being stolen though. And he didn't know the caliber."

"They're not all the same?" Abby asked.

"The military model is nine-millimeter, but you can get them both ways. Bedford was shot with a nine-millimeter."

"He could be telling the truth," Abby said. "His gun could have been a seven whatever."

Stan nodded. "But Lugers aren't that common around here. I'll want to be sure about the caliber."

"Quite a few came back as souveniers," Mac said. "And you could buy them new at one time." He paused, considered the probability. "But it *is* more of a collector's item." He sat on the top step, leaned his head against the railing, and half closed his eyes against the sun. "The gun was a long shot. What did you have in mind when you went to the San Diego police? I don't suppose they were thrilled about doing your legwork."

"I doubt if I'd have gotten anything, but I've got a connection in homicide out there. I did him a favor once. So I asked him to check at the Naval Base. See if he could talk to a few people who knew Taylor and what they remembered he said when he inherited this place. Did he know the bank had more stake in it than he had? Did he talk about how he was going to handle it? Did he have any other heavy debts? Asking about the gun was an afterthought, and it's the only thing that paid off."

"But it really doesn't prove anything," Abby said.

"Every little bit helps." Stan frowned and looked up at the porch gingerbread. "You might suggest to Metlaff — well, it might not hurt to do a little checking on Taylor's behalf."

Startled, Mac said, "Why?"

"You need the work. I hate to see a man live off his wife."

"Come on, Stan. Why would you want a private snoop butting in?"

"I'm following up on Taylor because he's the logical suspect. I've got enough so that if I find any link between Bedford and Taylor, I'll have to take it to the State's Attorney. He'll decide if it's enough to indict."

"And you're not sure," Mac said.

"The extra grave gives Taylor a motive. And as it stands, it don't matter to my case who's buried in it," Stan said. He paused to take a pack of cigarettes from his shirt pocket. "I don't have any reason *not* to be sure." He fished a cigarette from the pack and lit it. "You may not believe it, but the Sarahville cop shop ain't the biggest one around." Nodding toward the graveyard, he said, "I don't have the time or manpower to go into this grave business. I'd hate to find out later that it *did* make a difference."

Mac nodded and watched as Stan left. Abby grinned at him, and then laughed when he told her to shut up. He followed her inside to the kitchen, where Karen sat at the table, alone.

"Now where is he?" Mac asked.

"He's getting the box of Schneider papers you wanted to see." Karen emptied an overflowing ashtray into a paper grocery bag. The top of the bag had been folded over into a neat cuff, so that it would act as a trash can. She sat down again and toyed briefly with a cigarette package until Abby joined her at the table. Then she lit a cigarette, laid it in the ashtray, and seemed to forget it. "You might as well know. I'm staying here for the time being. At least until Jason comes home."

Abby nodded. "It's your decision. As long as you understand. Nothing's happened to change things as far as the police are concerned. Jack is still the only one with a motive. And this gun business has made matters worse."

"I've gotten used to the idea that women have no sense about some things," Mac said. "But Jack ought to know better."

"Know better about what?" Taylor asked as he came through the door carrying a Campbell's Chicken Soup carton.

"Better than to involve Karen in your troubles."

"Can't argue with that. Can't argue with her, either. She's here and she won't budge." Taylor put the carton on the table. "Help yourself."

Mac sat down and pulled the box closer to him. "I wanted to talk to you yesterday, after Abby and Karen got back from Alma Linsdale's. Couldn't reach you."

"Karen told me all about it. I needed time to think. I didn't answer the phone."

Mac began emptying the carton, bringing forth a bundle of envelopes, photographs, and several newspaper clippings. Abby got up and stood looking over his shoulder.

"I've talked Jack into giving some of that material to the Society," Karen said.

Mac shook his head. "Not now. After I've had a look, if you don't object, I'll give it to Metlaff until this business is decided one way or another. I'll give you a receipt for it."

He glanced at the clippings first. Most of them mentioned one or another Schneider in some matter of local interest: a blue ribbon won at the state fair, birth and death announcements, Hans Schneider speaks out at a Zoning Board meeting.

A few were of less parochial interest: the front page of the *Tribune* headlining victory in Europe and the infamous edition announcing that Dewey was president. There were two entire sections of the *Crier*,

169

a weekly that subsisted on legal advertising: one headlined a story about the expansion of O'Hare Airport and its impact on suburban noise levels; the other covered the firing of MacArthur by Truman. The latter stirred Mac's memories of Korea and he turned the page, only to find news was limited to the front page and its obverse. The balance of the section contained legal notices of village bids and a list of abandoned assets left with the State.

And one clipping, datelined Pasadena, May 12, 1943, announced that John Taylor had been killed in action. "Looks like somebody kept the Midwest Schneiders up on what was happening to the West Coast Taylors."

Taylor nodded. "I was surprised to see that. My grandmother must have sent it to Hans Schneider when Dad died. She never mentioned any contact with him."

Abby started going through the photographs. There were only eight of them, half obviously very old, mounted in heavy cardboard frames bearing the name of the photographer and an Elgin address. "Do you know who any of these people are?"

"No idea."

"That picture of Henry and Camilla, Karen. Where did you get it?"

"I told you Jerome interviewed Henry Schneider. I gather he was allowed to look through some of the family material. Maybe this box. Anyway, he said one photograph was in duplicate and Henry agreed to let him take the extra on condition it be displayed in our museum. That's when we still hoped to get the old schoolhouse someday. It was in one of those cardboard frames."

"How did you know who they were?" Abby asked.

"Henry told Jerome."

"If this is the box Bedford saw," Mac said, "then the other copy of the picture should be in here."

"I've gone through that stuff. It isn't there."

"Then there must be another box."

"It's not in the house," Jack said. "I've been through it, attic to cellar."

"I know Jim Farrell bought some Schneider stuff, but I can't imagine Henry would sell family pictures."

"Farrell mentioned buying something," Mac said. "But you're right, Henry wouldn't sell family pictures." Mac turned his attention to the letters. "These are in German. I wonder if it's worth getting them translated."

He riffled through the envelopes. Most had local return addresses. One had no return address, but was postmarked Pasadena 1943. He looked inside. "Empty. That clipping about your father probably came in this, Jack."

"None from Alma Linsdale," Abby said. "I'm disappointed."

Mac picked up another envelope and looked inside. "Empty. Addressed to somebody named Uhlmann in Munich, Germany." He turned it over in his hands. "No return address. The stamp hasn't been cancelled, so it was never mailed."

"Let me see that," Jack asked.

"Mean anything to you?"

Taylor turned the envelope over, stared at the blank back for a moment. "No. Didn't think anything of it when I checked this stuff either. What do *you* make of it?"

"Somebody wrote a letter, then failed to mail it. But why destroy the letter and save the envelope?"

"For the address?" Abby asked.

Next, Mac picked up a blank envelope. He withdrew a photostat of a birth certificate. He studied it carefully, then paraphrased what he had read. "Joseph Albrecht, born July 18, 1902, Cass County, Michigan." He turned to Taylor. "You knew this was here."

Taylor, expressionless, said nothing.

"Okay. It wouldn't mean anything to you at first. But that scrap of wood with the *cht* on it, that didn't suggest anything? You weren't curious about why the Schneider family papers included a stranger's birth certificate?"

Getting no response from Taylor, Mac went on. "When Karen came back with Alma Linsdale's story about Albrecht—why didn't you mention it then? Why keep it to yourself?"

"If I meant to keep it to myself, I'd have taken the birth certificate out of the box before I gave it to you."

Abby glanced at Karen, who was looking happier each minute. "Karen, if we're going to help, Jack has to tell us the whole story."

"Jack, I think you should," Karen said.

Taylor looked at Mac. "And you'll keep it to yourself?"

"As much as I can. I can't conceal evidence from the police."

Still impassive, Taylor said, "Then that's that, isn't it?"

"If that's the way you want it, then that's that." Mac got up and threw the letters and photographs back in the box. "Abby had me convinced, finally and against my better judgment, to get into this case. But I'm not fool enough to have a client who won't tell me the truth. I'll drop this stuff off with Metlaff and then I'm through."

Abby touched his arm. "Mac, maybe Jack's too bull-headed to know he needs help, but what about Karen?"

"Okay. Here's free advice. Tell Metlaff everything. And I mean *everything*. He can promise confidentiality; I can't. If he asks me to take it on, I may. Or I may not."

The tension was evident in Karen's eyes. "Metlaff

172

will ask you to help us. I'm sure of it. Please say yes when he asks."

"I'll tell you one thing." He gestured toward the hill. "I'm going to find out who is in that grave."

Taylor frowned. "Joseph Albrecht is in the grave. Alma Linsdale says so. You saw his birth certificate."

Mac picked up the carton and headed for the door. "Whoever it is, it certainly isn't Joseph Albrecht."

Chapter 18

The McKenzies returned from their meeting with Karen and Taylor to hear the phone ring as Abby turned the key in the back door. In accordance with a well-known law of nature, the ringing stopped as soon as the door opened. Mac followed Abby inside and put the carton of Schneider memorabilia on the kitchen table.

"Care to guess who that was?" Mac asked.

"Metlaff? He'd call you as soon as he heard from Jack, don't you think?"

"I'd bet my Captain Midnight wings on it."

"Captain Midnight wings? That must be one of those things I'm too young to remember."

Mac put his arm around her shoulders. "I intend to have this marriage last, so I won't challenge that statement."

Abby turned and raised her face to his. "Mac, you are going to help them, aren't you? All that steely-eyed anger, that was for effect, wasn't it?"

"Some. But he *is* beginning to annoy me. He admits he knows more than he's telling. And you notice the idea of my checking on the grave hasn't filled him with wholehearted enthusiasm."

"I know. But there might be other reasons besides guilty knowledge."

"The odds are against it."

Abby leaned her head against his chest.

He lifted her chin and kissed her. "But after what Stan said, and with your nagging, I can't very well drop it, can I?"

The phone rang. It was Elmer, a hint of anxiety in his voice. "I'm at the Running Fox Tavern. I'll be right over."

"No, we'll come there. Ten minutes."

Sounds from the Running Fox dining room indicated a full house for the Friday "All You Can Eat Fish Fry," which was offered to both lunch and dinner patrons. Mac counted himself lucky that there was a vacant stool at the bar for Abby. He prevailed upon a man wearing a John Deere cap to move left one so that she could sit next to Elmer Johnson.

"Been sittin' here nursin' a beer, till a table opens up," Elmer said. "Glad you came so's I don't lose my place on the list. We need to talk. Why don't we do it over lunch? Bar's too public."

"Sounds good." Abby smiled in greeting.

"I'd appreciate the company."

"When did you last talk to Taylor?" Mac asked.

"The day we came to see you. He was supposed to tell me what the lawyer said, but I ain't heard word one. Got me a might anxious."

"Well, I'm not going to make you feel any better."

The dining room waitress called Elmer's name and he led the way to the table. "Can we get this parking lot scheme off the ground or not?" Elmer asked.

"Your partner has really kept you in the dark. I'd say that project is dead."

Elmer's left eyebrow was habitually raised as if he were questioning life and all the world. His right eyebrow now joined the left in a look of astonishment. "Damn! Why?"

Mac quickly brought him up to date. "Taylor hasn't

175

told you any of this?"

"Sure not. You know, unless I can figure another angle real quick, I might need to start workin' for a living. And I ain't done that in a long time." Elmer sat opposite the McKenzies. "This means I can't get financing to pick up my option. Damn shame. I already had two tenants committed."

"Karen Canelli being one of them." Abby said. "What happens to her?"

"My option ends June thirty." He shrugged. "After that, the deal's off."

They studied their menus in silence, the McKenzies finally deciding on the fish fry. Elmer announced that the news had spoiled his appetite and settled for pie and coffee.

"When Taylor first wanted to give up the plan, did he tell you any more than he told me?" Mac asked.

"No. Just seemed real discouraged, like the fight had gone out of him." Elmer toyed with his water glass. "Didn't make sense. I mean, I admit the Goldfarb grave spelled trouble. But it was too early to tell how much trouble. If you could get on it fast enough, we might've still been okay."

"Looking back, do you think he might have known it wasn't Goldfarb?" Abby asked.

"That could be. When we first discussed this deal, he was all for it. No sign that he could see a roadblock ahead. And when Goldfarb turned up, he was like me — worried, but still figured we could pull it out. Then something happened to change his mind. I don't know what."

Mac noticed Rudy Wilking making his way through the room, pausing at each table for a smiling word or two. He wore a blue cardigan and matching tie, and as he approached, Mac thought a bit of gray was beginning to show at the temples. Either he was letting it grow out, or was overdue for a touch-up.

Rudy came to their table and rested his hand on

176

Elmer's shoulder. "I understand you are passing up the fish today, Elmer. Not feeling well?"

"I've felt better." Elmer looked around the room. "Don't look like you'll miss my business."

"Fridays are always good," Rudy said. "And how about the McKenzies? Will you be here Monday?"

"Why Monday?" Abby asked.

"You have not heard? The Society is to meet here. In a weak moment I agreed to talk on the history of the tavern. There is to be a tour, my talk, and then lunch. Aside from my own efforts, it should be an enjoyable event."

Mac looked doubtful, thinking he wouldn't have time to spare. Before he could answer, Horace Arly appeared at Rudy's side.

Smiling all around, H.A. said. "Afternoon, folks. Sorry to butt in, Rudy. The contractor's here about the subcellar."

"Good. I wish to discuss his estimate." Addressing the group, Rudy said, "We start excavating Saturday, then finish Monday. That is why it is an ideal time for our gathering. The tavern will be closed. So—can I count on seeing you here?"

"I'm looking forward to it," Abby said.

"You may have to go alone," Mac said. "I'll be tied up on Taylor's problem."

"How are you progressing in your research regarding the gentleman buried on the hill?" Rudy asked.

"Not much progress."

Elmer, looking surprised at this noncommittal answer, began, "You said—"

"I'll check what records I can find," Mac interrupted. He was relieved when Elmer followed his lead.

"Those family Bibles with the family tree in front used to be real popular," Elmer said. "Be surprised if the Schneiders didn't keep one. If Taylor don't have it, he might have given it to Karen Cannelli for the Society. Her and Taylor bein' so cozy, and all."

177

Abby shook her head. "No Bible, just a box full of stuff. She's already talked Jack into—"

"Here comes the food," Mac said. "And not a minute too soon. I'm about starved."

"Enjoy your lunch," Rudy said. "I must deal with my contractor. Are you staying, H.A.?"

"No, I just need to pick up some numbers I forgot yesterday. Nice seeing you folks again." He followed Rudy out of the dining room.

"You seem to be in an interrupting mood today," Abby said.

"Makes sense not to spread this Albrecht business around," Elmer said. "I almost spilled the beans."

"Besides, private detectives are supposed to listen, not talk, Watson."

Abby turned to Elmer. "I think he just told me to shut up."

Returning home full of fish, they climbed the stairs to Mac's office. They had taken to calling it, fancifully, the tower room because it included the second-floor turret on the northeast corner of the house. Mac had placed his swivel chair inside the turret so that he could turn and see the length of Twilly Place and out onto Main.

Abby shoved aside a stack of magazines and junk mail and perched on the edge of his desk. "How did you wind up with the office with a view?"

He laid his hand on her knee. "And a very nice view it is, too."

"How did I get stuck next to the kitchen looking out on a driveway?" Abby lifted Mac's attache case and set it down beside her. "It occurs to me I've neglected my wifely duty to show a proper interest in my husband's business," she said, opening the case. "I haven't even gone through your pockets yet."

"They're usually empty."

Abby held up two ties, one in two shades of gray, the other blue with a thin red stripe.

"One for wakes, one for weddings," he said.

"And both could stand cleaning." She took up a small leather case, unzipped it, and held up a small spoon-shaped object. "What's this?"

"Lock pick."

"Really? Can you do that?"

"If the lock's simple and I have all the time in the world."

"I guess that's why we're not rich. Where did you learn your nefarious but inadequate skill?"

"A little school the government ran for us nefarious types."

"So you could steal the secret plans and save the free world?"

"Nobody likes a smart mouth." Mac rose and kissed hers.

They were interrupted by the doorbell. "I'll get it," Abby said. "You start going through that box again. Time marches on."

Mac had hardly begun on the papers when Abby returned followed by Stan Pawlowski.

"What brings you here on company time," Mac asked.

"Company business. What did you find out from Taylor after I left the farm?"

"We found out that we still don't know who is buried in the mystery grave."

"Not Albrecht?"

"He called himself Albrecht. But his birth certificate says he was born in Cass County, Michigan. Ever hear of a Michigander who couldn't talk English?"

"Well —"

"Not counting Detroit."

Stan settled back in Mac's visitor's chair and stared at the ceiling. "Where's the certificate?"

Mac fished it from the box and handed it to Stan.

"Going to check it?"

"I guess so." He nodded toward the box. "What's the rest of that stuff?"

"Pictures, clippings, old letters. Metlaff will have custody, but I want to take another look first."

"Something tells me you're in for more than checking on the grave," Stan said, nodding toward the license on the wall. "Looks like the old firm is open for business."

"He was getting bored with me and the store," Abby said.

Mac shook his head. "Never with you, dear."

"There speaks a wise and married man," Stan said as he got up and stretched. "It's been fun, but duty calls. I'll let you know about Albrecht." About to leave, he turned back. "By the way, I'm on my way to the farm. Bob Henderson is over there with a search warrant. Just in case the gun is still around."

"Always a pleasure to see you, Abby," Metlaff said. His scowl deepened. "What foolishness has your husband been up to now?"

"Always a pleasure to see you too, counselor," Mac said. "We just dropped in to tell you Taylor is now a suspect of record in the Bedford killing. The police are searching his place for the gun."

Metlaff slapped his hand against his desk causing his souvenier ashtray to bounce. "And of course it didn't occur to him to call."

"Right. Under the circumstance, anything you'd like me to do?"

"Just what you've been doing, but more of it and faster. What do you have so far?"

Mac summarized what had occurred since they last talked, including his conclusions regarding the nameless decedent.

"Good," Metlaff said. "A few weeks ago I would have considered that news disastrous. Now I find it hopeful. The more confusion that exists regarding the grave and the role it may play in this, the more smoke I can raise if it comes to trial." He looked at Abby. His scowl disappeared. "And you conducted the interrogation of Linsdale?"

Abby cleared her throat. "Well, Mac was busy. I wasn't sure what questions to ask and—"

"You did very well." Metlaff turned to Mac. "Have you taken on a partner?"

"He calls himself McKenzie and Associates," Abby said. "It's about time he had one, don't you think? An associate, I mean."

Mac sighed. "She's convinced I promised to 'love, honor, and tolerate interference from shopkeepers.' "

Metlaff went so far as to allow the corners of his mouth to lift a millimeter. The smile lasted a millisecond. "She could function as an operative under your agency license, I suppose."

"You're not helping," Mac said.

"And I've meant to ask. Who *are* your associates?"

"I've got some people I call on. Specialists. If I need one, he helps out as an independent contractor."

"In your wife's case," Metlaff said, "there are tax and other advantages to making her a part-time employee."

"I don't need a part-timer. Especially not—"

"Also, she might serve to curb your more extravagant impulses."

Abby grinned. "Do I get a badge, boss?"

Chapter 19

Leaving Metlaff's office, Abby and Mac paused on the porch and watched the sun drop behind a false horizon of cumulous clouds. Sarahville entered twilight two hours ahead of schedule.

Mac put his hands in the pockets of his windbreaker. "I guess we should have driven. Cold?"

"I'm fine." Abby held his arm as they began the walk home. "I know you'll do what you can for Karen. And Jack. But do you think he's guilty? Are we just going through the motions?"

He shook his head. "Maybe not. I've given it more thought, and I'm losing faith in the police theory."

"Good. Why?"

"Taylor's attitude, for one thing. Remember when you first dug up Goldfarb? He—"

"Mac!"

"—thought he could just add him to the list and go ahead with moving his private cemetery."

"Until you pointed out that Goldfarb couldn't be buried. Sorry."

Mac placed his hand over Abby's to warm it. "Now that I know him better, I can see he's not dumb. He reacted out of surprise. Given time, he'd realize that wouldn't work. But in any case, he was optimistic about it, because Goldfarb was related to the Schneiders. There was at least a chance to salvage things."

"His surprise," Abby said, "proves he didn't know about the grave—"

"It doesn't prove a damn thing. He could have been putting on an act. The point is, whether he knew or didn't know, cautious optimism was the appropriate response. Not murder."

"His motive was weak," Abby said. "You told me that. But once Goldfarb became Albrecht, the threat to his scheme became greater."

"At that point failure became certain. If he knew about Albrecht, then he knew the Goldfarb ID wouldn't hold up. Goldfarb, or his burial, would be found at some other place. As far as I can see, given that a strange grave existed, his scheme was doomed to fail from the beginning."

"In which case," Abby said, "there is no logical reason for him to kill anyone."

"Exactly. But then a time came when he *was* ready to throw in his hand. Remember when Elmer dragged him in to talk to me?"

Abby nodded. "I don't think he was ever convinced to go ahead. Otherwise he'd have gone to Metlaff as he promised. He just ran out of arguments and gave up in disgust."

"What caused the switch?"

"I see what you're getting at. He must have found out about Albrecht before we did. But by then Bedford was dead, so that still doesn't give him a motive." They were opposite Twilly Place and Mac was about to cross over. Abby held him back. "Let's walk a bit." They continued as far as the schoolhouse. Abby steered him into the driveway. "But if you follow that reasoning," she said, "there was no point in not telling us about Albrecht. It would have explained his turnabout, and Elmer would probably have agreed with him. So, he must have some other reason for not talking."

"Sure. Taylor knows the truth but hoped I'd buy Albrecht as the end of the line. That's why he gave me the birth certificate. To convince me that Albrecht existed."

"A native-born American that could hardly speak the language. He must have known that wouldn't fly."

"Probably didn't know we knew about the language problem. Or he didn't."

They stopped in front of the schoolhouse, the old building's windows boarded up and its paint peeling. Abby shivered. "Why did Jerome come here?"

"Enticed or brought."

"Karen knew Albrecht—whoever—spoke German. Surely she told Jack everything Alma Linsdale told us." They turned and retraced their steps. "I think she's holding out too. Jack must have told her what he won't tell us, don't you think?"

They stopped where Jerome Bedford's car had been found. "The murders must have been to conceal the identity of the body," Abby said. "I mean, what other reason could there be?"

"I can't think of any. The existence of the grave was no secret, just forgotten. And everyone I talked to knew about Jack's so-called secret plan. The killer must have known the grave would be rediscovered sooner or later."

"So who was he?" Abby asked. "Apparently Henry Schneider knew, and put the true name on a grave marker. Otherwise, why was the marker stolen from Bedford's apartment? Also, Bedford was surprised when Bochmann identified the man as Goldfarb, and according to Mrs. Linsdale, he asked several times whether she was sure about the name *Albrecht*. Obviously he had someone else in mind."

"Not bad for a shopkeeper," Mac said. "Of course,

without the birth certificate we might have settled for Albrecht." He looked across the tavern parking lot. "If that *was* Bedford who asked Taylor for the time, why drive the few feet from there to here? Why not walk?"

"What's that?" Abby asked, pointing to a large yellow machine parked at the back of the tavern. "It looks like a giant scorpion with its tail curled over its back."

"It's a front-end loader and backhoe. The wide part at the front is the loader. You scoop up dirt, or whatever, and dump it into a truck. Damned if I can see any resemblance to a scorpion."

"That's because you lack an artist's imagination. It even has legs folded up against the sides."

"Those are stabilizers. When the backhoe—that's the claw at the end of the boom your overheated imagination thinks looks like a tail—when that's working, you spread the stabilizers out to the side so it won't tip or move forward."

"I prefer to think of it as a scorpion," Abby said.

"You stretch out the boom, uncurl the claw—shovel actually—and take a bite out of the ground. The whole thing is pulled back toward the cab, like using a hoe."

"That's really more than I care to know on the subject. Let's get back to the mysterious Albrecht."

"It's great for small excavating jobs. Maybe we could take it and dig up the grave. Our corpse might have a drivers license in his pocket that shows his real name."

"Mac! That's terrible!"

"Okay. No digging," he agreed. "You know, given enough time, and some reason to pursue it, that story of being a Jewish refugee would have fallen," he said. "Immigration records—"

"Unless he entered illegally."

Mac turned and guided Abby down the drive toward the street. "But even without the circumcision clue, Albrecht's identification as Jewish would be questionable." Spurred by her questioning look, he said, "If you were Jewish, where would you go? To a German farming community, or an urban Jewish community? Sarahville or—"

"Wait!" Abby stopped and turned to Mac. "If the Nazis wanted to get you, any Jewish blood in your background was enough. Albrecht could have been raised as German, no Jewish connections at all, except a distant ancestor. So Albrecht *could* have been a refugee, here illegally and hiding from Immigration behind a phony birth certificate."

"I don't think he'd have to hide, if that's all there was to it. I wonder if that story was concocted by Henry Schneider."

"He knew Albrecht's real background and for some reason went along?" They crossed Olde Main and arrived in front of Farrell's store. "Okay. Then burying him in the family plot avoided having the county look for relatives. The less investigation the better."

"Right. Henry identified the body as his relative, Jacob Goldfarb. No one locally could contradict him."

"Why not just invent a relative?"

After a moment of silence Mac said, "Probably uncertain about the proof he'd need. Maybe he had documents or correspondence relating to Goldfarb. Actually, as long as no one raised any questions, Henry's word was good enough."

"But why claim Albrecht was a Jew?"

"For Alma Linsdale's benefit. She knew it was Albrecht that he buried, and would wonder why it was done without clergy. Having already invented a Jew turned atheist for Bochman's benefit, he stuck with that, except the relative became a refugee. You might say it was a matter of economy—why tell a new lie, when an old one with a twist will do."

They climbed the two worn steps to Farrell's porch and stood looking through the window at a pine pie safe. "Which leaves us where we started," Abby said. "Whose body?"

Mac stepped back from the window and leaned against a porch post. "What do we know for sure? He arrived in Sarahville in early 1945, late 1944. He died September twenty-third, 1946. He kept to himself, avoided the locals. He had a false ID, complete with birth certificate. He had a strong German accent. What does that suggest? Remember, we're talking about the closing days of World War II."

Abby turned abruptly toward him. "A spy?"

"The birth certificate suggests that. But if so, he was poorly chosen and poorly placed. No language skills to fit in. And what use could he be as a farmhand in Sarahville?"

"Weren't prisoners of war held in the U.S.?"

"An escaped POW? In that case, where did the birth certificate come from?"

"I don't know. How is that sort of thing usually done?"

"An agent would have professionally forged documents. But another way is to take a name from a child's tombstone and request the certificate by mail. Then apply for other documents, driver's license—in those days ration books—social security number . . ."

"A POW could do that, couldn't he?"

"With only a basic knowledge of the language? Would he understand U.S. practices? Know how?"

"Maybe, if he had someone to advise him. Like Henry Schneider?"

Mac left his leaning post and kissed Abby's forehead. "Very good. I've got a friend who's a military historian. I'll call him Monday, ask how many POWs got away." Mac opened the door to Farrell's store. "In the meantime, I've got one or two questions for our antique dealer."

187

A woman bearing a package wrapped in newspaper, and wearing a smile of satisfaction, passed them in the doorway. Farrell was hanging a tin sign, featuring the Gold Dust Twins, with the help of a hammer and nail. He stopped when they entered. "Hi, folks. How did you make out with the fanlight?"

"It's still leaning against the wall," Abby said. "Know where I can find a good handyman?"

"I can get the job done for you."

"No, but thanks anyway," Mac said. "There's no hurry." Seeing Abby was about to protest, he hurried on. "I hear Henry Schneider sold you some stuff."

"Matter of fact, I think you heard it from me."

"What exactly did you buy?"

Farrell scratched his chin. "Sounds like you're still grave digging."

"You could say that."

"Well, hand me a shovel. Let's see. Henry Schneider called about a month before he died. Said he was trying to get rid of some clutter. I had a pretty good idea he was hard up. It wasn't so much clearing out clutter as raising cash."

"Did you get to go through the whole house?" Abby asked.

"Pretty much. He excluded his bedroom and a few other items." Farrell's eyes gleamed. "I'd have given my right arm for the clock in the parlor, but he wouldn't part with it."

"Anything besides furniture?" Mac asked.

"A box full of *Godey's Lady's Book*s. I grabbed at those. And a box Henry said was junk and asked me to haul away."

"Just threw it in on the deal?"

"Right. I went through it back here at the shop and found a few things worth keeping. Didn't want to cheat the old man, so I called him back and offered a ten spot."

"Remember what all was in the box?"

"The only things of any interest were a button hook, two unused postcards from 1897, a German military patch—I think you saw that last time you were here—and a piece of Depression glass that's getting some play from collectors."

"Yeah, I think I do remember the patch. Still have it?"

Farrell's shrewd eyes narrowed. "Yeah."

"I thought I might take up collecting. How much?"

Farrell shook his head. "You ain't the collecting type."

"I've been after him to get a hobby," Abby said. "And he already has Captain Midnight wings."

"And an Orphan Annie shaker mug. But military patches sound more my style. Ex-Air Force, you know. Did I tell you that?"

"Why not Air Force insignia then?"

"Are you trying to talk me out of buying? I thought foreign would be more fun."

Farrell produced an envelope, the one Mac had seen on his last visit, from under the counter. He spilled the contents and selected a gilt patch depicting a steering wheel. He passed it to Mac. "Keep it, with my compliments. And for the record, I don't believe a word you said."

Mac sighed. "In that case, can I ask you to keep this under your hat?"

"Keeping secrets is an antique dealer's way of life."

"Then I might as well ask, did Henry Schneider know this was in the box you bought?"

Farrell grinned. "I thought we'd get to that. I told him exactly what I was paying for and that the rest was worthless. I believed at the time he was disturbed about the patch."

"Very disturbed?"

"Not a lot. Said he had forgotten it was in there. I offered to return it. He hesitated awhile, then said no, it didn't really matter anymore."

Back on the walk outside Farrell's store, Abby said, "I'm sure learning a lot from you, chief. Like how to ask questions without arousing the witness's suspicions."

"I suppose you could have done better?"

"Not with Farrell. Antique dealers have the same cynical outlook as detectives. Speaking of which, I'm still waiting for my first assignment, boss."

"Your assignment is to mind the store."

Abby looked up and down Olde Main Street, in the heart of what should have been busy shopping area. A man was walking a dog and two women were getting into a car. "Not exactly like downtown, is it? We've already got capital tied up in stock, and I don't think it's a good idea to buy more until the parking problems are resolved. I'm thinking of postponing the opening until next fall. What do you think?"

"You're the business lady."

They turned down Twilly Place toward home. "So I need the work, boss."

"You signed us up for this Tavern Tour on Monday. That'll be a good chance to see just how subtle *your* questioning techniques are."

"You're not going to wait around for Monday, are you? We have the whole weekend ahead of us."

Mac unlocked their front door and turned on the hall light against the early gloom. "Right now, I'm going to take Schneider's stuff over to Stan and try to convince him not to move too fast on Taylor. I'm not sure Metlaff would approve, but—"

"The hell with Metlaff," Abby said. "I don't want our client to spend time in jail while a lawyer tries to habeas his corpus. It would upset Karen."

"*Our* client?"

"Call first. Stan might have gone home early for a change." As Mac reached for the phone, she said, "It

190

just occurred to me. If there are tax advantages to hiring me as your part-time Watson, as Metlaff says, why shouldn't the reverse be true?"

"Meaning?"

"I can hire you as a part-time clerk. Between cases you can sell knitting needles."

Stan was indeed in. He sat with his feet propped up on his bottom desk drawer and listened patiently, through two and a half cigarettes, to Mac's analyses of the case.

"I'm not saying it ain't possible," he said. "But suppose—what are we going to call this decedent anyway?"

"Might as well stick with Albrecht for the time being."

"Right. Suppose Albrecht was a POW. Why is that a motive for murder?"

Mac shrugged. "Suppose he's not a POW. Suppose—"

"How about a Nazi war criminal?"

"He turned up too early. The rats weren't leaving the rotting hulk yet." Mac tried to extend his legs to a more comfortable position and kicked the desk. "I think he was a German agent."

"Easy on the furniture," Stan said. "I'm on a seven-year waiting list for new stuff." He planted his elbows on the desk blotter and folded his hands. "I get you. This guy gets landed by submarine on the Jersey coast at high tide. Makes his way cross-country using sign language. Not much English, remember. Finally he reaches his goal, Sarahville, Illinois, where he sets about stealing the secret of greater output from laying hens. That about it?"

"O'Hare used to be the Douglas plant, remember? Not so far away."

"If they sent a guy who couldn't speak decent English, they must have been pretty hard up."

"I'll tell you what I think happened." Mac leaned forward and punctuated his points with a forefinger. "There were *two* enemy agents—one with brains, the other strictly muscle. The Schneider farm was good cover for the muscle. The brains carved out a nice niche in a false identity. The war ended—but going home to a country gone down the tubes—not too attractive. Maybe he has a position worth murder to keep."

Stan coughed and lit another cigarette. "And maybe it's all moonshine."

"The theory covers the facts. And better than Taylor does."

"Let's say I buy the idea. At least part of it. That means Henry Schneider, and maybe Hans Schneider, too, harbored an enemy in time of war. Taylor finds out. Doesn't want the family name disgraced. That's been enough motive for murder in other cases."

Mac silently watched Stan's cigarette smoke rise in the still air and hang in a cloud over his head. "Hans?"

"Yeah. He was still alive while this Albrecht was on the farm, right?"

Mac took an envelope from the Schneider box. "This was addressed, but never mailed. Nothing inside. Can you get a line on this Mrs. Uhlmann? What would it take to check her out in Germany?"

"East or West?"

"West."

"Can do, but not easy. FBI has an agent at each embassy to handle liaison with foreign cops and Interpol. But I have to give a reason."

"Tell 'em you had a hunch. That should go over big with the FBI."

They discussed, debated, and speculated over what

192

Abby had taken to calling, over Mac's objection, the Case of the Grave Murders. "If it's anything, it's the Taylor case," he said. "You have an overly romantic imagination unbecoming to an apprentice detective."

"And you," she replied, "have the soul of a shopkeeper."

"Speaking of shopkeeping, are you serious about not opening until fall?"

Abby, preparing for bed, placed her earrings on the dresser. "I think we should conserve capital until there's a better chance of drawing people into this cul-de-sac. We can live with the parking problem, but . . ." She paused in the act of taking off her shoes. "Speaking of parking, did it occur to you that maybe Wilking's solution could have had a less obvious motive? It would have stopped Taylor from moving the graves and uncovering—sorry—discovering the Albrecht grave."

"Do we have any apple pie left?"

"I keep trying to think of you as Sam Spade, and you keep trying to turn into Nero Wolfe."

"Okay. No pie, but eggs, bacon, and hash browns for breakfast."

"You know where we keep the cholesterol and skillet. I'm having grapefruit and coffee. What about Wilking?"

"I'm thinking." He did so while emptying his pockets onto the dresser. He ignored Abby's impatient "Well?," entered the bathroom, and announced the result of his thinking as he emerged. "He's the right age. But to avoid opening up—sorry—bringing attention to the grave, he'd have had to move faster."

Abby began to brush her hair. "To forestall Jack?"

"Once Taylor's plan was out in the open, attention would focus on the graveyard. The risk of discovery would increase. And yet Wilking was being coy, just when an early push might have made Jack drop the whole scheme."

"Why would Jack do that? His plan is so much better than Wilking's—"

"Look at it from the Village Board point of view. Wilking could set the price low enough, zero if he wanted, to undercut Taylor. Moving graves is not cheap, and there's paving, a footbridge. . . . And Wilking's lot is available, Taylor's is uncertain. The bank's deadline for acceptance—a long fight on the Board would scuttle Taylor's ship."

Abby put down her brush. "It's as though Wilking expected his plan to be an alternative when Taylor failed. At that point he could jack up the price for his lot. So he'd *want* the grave found, if he knew about it." Abby plumped her pillow and got into bed. "I see what you mean by age though. The mystery man has to be a contemporary of Albrecht's—"

"We don't know how old Albrecht was, not for sure. The birth certificate would make him forty-four. All we can say about the other agent is he'd be eligible to serve in the war."

"You made a good case for the mystery man being the brains. Albrecht's superior. Wouldn't he be older?"

"More likely younger. That driver's patch means Albrecht was a noncom. The man in charge would be an officer. Much older and he'd be pushing a desk instead of operating in the field." Mac got into bed and turned off the bedside lamp. "Comparative age is irrelevant where rank is concerned. A fact brought to my attention several times before I retired." He turned toward Abby. "The concept is also well-known to most married men. Right, boss?"

"So our suspects are limited to—"

Mac, drifting off, said, "Only two worth thinking about."

"But which ones?"

"You know my methods . . ."

"Mac, which . . ."

He heard no more until he was roughly shaken.

"Mac! Wake up!"

Like a fireman reacting to an alarm, he sprang from bed and grabbed his pants. "What?"

"It's Karen! On the phone! Someone's in the house."

"For Chris' sake, tell her to get off the phone and out of the house!" Already on the way to the office where his gun cabinet was located, he called out, "I'm on my way!"

Chapter 20

Clouds on the horizon had brought an early end to Sarahville's day and, moving steadily eastward, had formed a heavy overcast. Now, nearing midnight, ground fog had been added. Mac's visual world extended no farther than the flashlight-lit circle in front of him. Raising the heavy machined-aluminum five-battery Smoke Slicer to see ahead merely brought the fog to swirling life. He reached the creek to find the stepping stones completely submerged.

He had misgivings about his decision to approach the farmhouse cross-country rather than by car. His reasoning had seemed sound; the police would arrive before he could get there by road. He splashed through water that reached halfway to his knees.

If the intruder had a car, he was probably long gone. But if he was on foot . . . Mac hit the opposite bank running, risking a fall on the rough ground. The police would block any attempt to cross the road to the south. Escape to the east meant a long run across an open field. The direct route through the barnyard meant crossing the creek where it formed a waist-deep pond—deeper now. That left the path through the graveyard.

Mac switched off his light and slowed as he neared the top of the rise. The first tombstone was a patch of black in the darkness. He paused to listen. Nothing.

Moving cautiously, gun drawn, he strained to see. A momentary breeze thinned the fog on the hilltop, leaving lower levels a milky white. As he reached the second row of stones, a car turned onto the farm's driveway. A second car stopped on the road and began to play a searchlight along the ditch. Another light appeared farther east. The cars had taken up positions without sirens or flashers. It was doubtful that the searchlights could reveal much, but the intruder would probably not risk it, and would be forced back in Mac's direction.

Crouching low, he moved to the third row, stopping at the only tall monument in the graveyard. A marble angel with welcoming arms that marked the grave of Tusnelda Schneider. A slight sound to his left! He switched on his light and took aim at a small form that bounded away.

Mac rose from his crouch, cursing silently. Spooked by a rabbit! Any hope of surprise gone, he swept the light over the graves before him.

The faint sound of a siren grew rapidly louder. Not another police car. Surely all Sarahville owned were already on the scene. He turned to see the road. An ambulance! Karen? Something had happened to Karen while he was up here chasing rabbits! He took one step toward the path.

A blow behind the right ear dropped him to his knees, gun and light falling.

Pain rose from the back of his neck, spread across the top of his skull, and forced his eyes shut. A wave of dizziness caused him to clutch the earth to keep from falling off.

The pain became a dull ache and the sound of running footsteps through the brush told him the attack was over. Mac retrieved his flashlight, rolled to a sitting position, and leaned back against the angel. After a moment he struggled to his feet, clung to an out-

197

stretched marble arm as a second wave of dizziness came over him then passed.

Mac found his gun and holstered it. With police on the scene, coming out of the fog waving a gun could get a man shot. He made his unsteady way down the path, calling out his name in response to a police challenge. He arrived at the farm in time to see Karen Cannelli being helped into the ambulance.

He felt a surge of relief that she was not being carried. The fog began to lift, replaced by a light rain.

Emergency rooms on Friday nights (and into Saturday morning) are busy places. Karen and Mac, among the walking wounded, were relegated to a bench opposite the admitting nurse. Mac insisted that all he needed was an aspirin, but no one paid any attention.

Karen had appeared dazed in the ambulance. She now leaned back, eyes closed, face drawn and white.

"Karen?"

"Yes?" She did not open her eyes.

"Feel up to telling me what happened?"

"It's kind of vague. Can it wait, Mac? I don't feel so good."

"Sure. Just take it easy." He tried to relax, wishing he could get a cup of coffee.

After a silent half hour a doctor approached them. He spoke briefly to the police officer hovering nearby, then came to Karen's side. "I'm sorry we don't have space in the emergency ward right now." He checked her eyes, and the bump at the back of her skull. "I'm going to order an x-ray, and then we're going to admit you for overnight observation."

"Overnight? Is that necessary?"

"Even if the x-ray doesn't show a fracture, and I don't think it will, there's no doubt you have a concussion. We don't want to take a chance with that." He ignored Mac and went to the admitting desk.

Mac was about to ask Karen again what had happened when the automatic doors slid open and Abby appeared.

Face drawn and white, she paused to scan the room, then rushed to Mac. "Are you all right?"

"Fine."

Abby glanced at Karen. "What about Karen? She looks terrible. Why aren't they doing something for her?"

"The doctor just saw her. She'll be okay."

The stiff set of Abby's face relaxed a bit. She touched his face. "They said you were hurt."

"I'm fine. Really."

"Then why didn't you call?" Her voice rose. "You go charging up a hill waving a pistol —"

"I didn't wave —"

"— like the cavalry at the Alamo —"

"There weren't any —"

"— in the dead of night." She glanced along the wall, where other sufferers had put aside their pain to listen with interest. She dropped her voice to a hissing whisper. "The least you could have done is call!"

Mac grinned up at her. "You called the police, jumped in the car, and headed for the farm, right?"

"Of course. You didn't expect —"

"Who would have answered?"

"Don't change the subject. You . . ." Abby laughed. "Well, okay. But why did they tell me you'd been hurt?"

Karen had straightened up a bit during this exchange and opened her eyes. "He was hit on the head, but I guess his head is harder than mine. It doesn't seem to bother him."

"I was lucky," Mac said. "The blow fell as I was moving away. Gave me a headache, that's all."

Abby touched his face again. "Oh, Mac." She sat beside him and took his hand. "Private eyes on TV get hit on the head a lot, but I *can't* believe it's good for you."

Mac was still trying to think of an answer to that when a nurse pushed a wheelchair up to the bench. "Mrs. Cannelli? We're going to Radiology now."

"I'm feeling better." Karen stood up. "I can walk."

"The ride's included in the price, so you might as well take it." She took Karen's arm firmly and guided her into the chair. In a moment they disappeared around a corner in the corridor.

Jack Taylor erupted through the door. He was followed, at a more sedate pace, by Metlaff. Mac rose to intercept them.

"Take it easy, Jack. Karen's okay."

"Where is she?"

Mac explained Karen's status, which did nothing to calm Taylor. "I knew I shouldn't have let her go home alone."

"Where were you?" Mac asked. He glanced at Metlaff, who had drawn a cigar from his pocket, thought better of lighting it, and stood rolling it between his fingers. "And why bring a lawyer?"

"What? Oh. Metlaff caught up with us at the Tavern tonight and insisted I come to his office. He drove me home. There were cops all over the place."

"I suggest," Metlaff said to Mac, "you hold the questions I see forming in your mind. When the opportunity presents itself, I will brief you on what you need to know. In the meantime you are not to question Mr. Taylor." He turned to Jack. "And you are not to answer any questions."

Taylor nodded. "When can I see Karen?"

Mac shrugged, and they waited as patiently as they could, until the doctor emerged to check up on Mac. He said Karen had been moved to a room for what was left of the night. No visitors.

After listening to Mac minimize the extent of his injury, the doctor agreed that he could leave. "Just keep an eye on him, Mrs. McKenzie. If he becomes drowsy during the day, has any problem with his vision, dizziness, or anything else out of the ordinary, call your doctor at once."

With Abby's promise of vigilance, they adjourned the meeting to the sidewalk, where they huddled under a marquee out of the pouring rain.

"When do I get that briefing you talked about, counselor?"

"I have to take Mr. Taylor home, get"—he glanced at his watch—"two hours' sleep, and catch a plane. I'll call you on my return Monday."

"That long? What am I supposed to do in the meantime?"

"There isn't a great deal to be done over the weekend in any case. The police have no present basis for moving against our client, and are unlikely to find one in the near future. So the delay shouldn't matter." With that he turned up his coat collar, drew his hat more firmly on his head, and headed for his car at a waddling run. Taylor trotted easily behind him.

The McKenzies, holding hands, followed suit.

Mac was never at his best in the morning, but today was worse than usual. He had slept till ten and felt vaguely guilty about it. Sitting on the edge of the bed, he cataloged a series of aches and pains. At least the lump at the back of his head was not throbbing. Unless he touched it. The rain had ended, but a tree outside his window still dripped, and the sky was gray. He dragged himself into the shower and managed to wash away some of his troubles in a torrent of hot water.

He arrived in the kitchen as Abby was sliding two eggs onto a plate that already contained bacon and potatoes. "How did you manage to get the timing just right?" he asked.

"When you turn on the shower, every pipe in the house protests."

Mac sighed. "Did you have to mention that? Do you

201

know what it'll cost when we have to replace those old pipes?"

"Shut up and eat."

"Aren't you having any?"

"I've been up for hours. Had breakfast long ago. I couldn't eat a thing now." She took a slice of bacon from his plate. "I called Jack. He's going to pick up Karen at eleven."

"Then she's all right?" Mac peppered his eggs liberally. "When can I get her story?"

"We're going over at one. Will you feel human by then?"

"Did Jack say whether anything was missing?"

"Not that he can tell. The dining room window was broken. The police didn't find anything inside, and the rain washed away any trace outside." She poured a cup of coffee for herself and took a piece of Mac's toast. "Was it just a burglary, do you think?"

"Could be, but then again—"

"Okay, we both think it's connected. But what was he after?"

"Only one thing I can think of. That box we brought home."

"For what? The birth certificate?"

"Any way you look at it," Mac said, beating Abby to the last slice of bacon, "it's not likely. If our villain knows we've seen the thing, nothing is gained by stealing it. If he doesn't, then why not let us find it? He must know we'd come up with the Albrecht name. All the certificate does is confirm that." He finished his bacon. "Maybe he's after the envelope."

Abby poured Mac a second cup of coffee. "Who would know about that? Or putting it another way, if the killer knew about the envelope and didn't want it found, why wait till now to go after it? It's been there for years."

Mac nodded and pushed his plate aside. "I guess I'm ready to face life again. Too bad Metlaff's not in town.

I'd like to hear what Taylor told him."

"Doesn't seem right just to let things slide. Isn't there anything we can do before he gets back?"

"Stan's working on the birth certificate and the envelope, but he's not going to get anywhere on the weekend," Mac said.

Abby started to clear the table. "I thought we might talk to everybody again. So I phoned them all while you slept the morning away. Everybody is gone or busy."

"At this point," Mac said, "I don't know what we'd ask them. I'm sure Stan will check alibis for the burglary."

Abby went to the window and looked out at the gray and dripping day. "If you're right about the killer being a World War II German agent, that eliminates the women, doesn't it? I mean, you're not thinking there was a Mata Hari involved, are you?"

"No. But wives have been known to aid and abet."

"What do you suppose I'd do? I mean, if it was you . . ."

Mac came up behind her and put his arms around her waist. "Probably seduce Bedford into silence."

Abby laughed. "Now there's an unlikely story." Leaning back, she said, "Alice Hillman is pure steel under that giggly exterior. She might do it, but she's too young."

"How old is her husband? Do you know?"

"Young." Abby took Mac's hand and led him back to a kitchen chair. "That leaves the Rhines and the Arlys."

Mac said, "While you're at it, don't forget Rudy."

"I did forget."

"And Josie," Mac said, sitting down.

"You mean because of Rudy? Yes, I'm sure she'd do quite a lot for him. I bet Elmer can tell you all about her." Abby sat on Mac's lap. "Why don't you give him a call?"

"Now?"

"In a little while."

Whatever Abby had in mind for the interim was not to be. The screendoor to the porch sounded its usual protest on being opened, and then slammed shut. "You have to do something about that spring," Abby said as she rose. "It rattles dishes." Footsteps crossed the porch as she opened the kitchen door. "Good morning, Stan."

"How's old hardhead?" Stan removed his yellow rain gear. "Can his eyes focus yet?"

"They managed to focus on breakfast, so I guess he's all right."

"Just remember, you only get so many hits on the head before you start to lose it." He pulled off his boots and stepped into the kitchen. "Of course, in his case, I'm not sure you could tell the difference."

"Good thing you stayed in bed last night," Mac said. "For a change the Sarahville police performed efficiently."

"Sergeant Tompkins is a good cop. Or at least he was before Almeir got to be his boss. Now he has a little trouble remembering what's his job, and what's mine."

"A little bureaucratic infighting?"

Stan helped himself to coffee and a chair at the table. "He knew damn well my investigation involved Taylor and the Schneider farm. He should have notified me. Instead he got Almeir out of bed. Almeir told him to treat it as a simple burglary—which it might be, I'm not saying that—but he said don't bother Pawlowski until morning."

"Don't you have a detective there at night? Didn't he know about it?" Abby asked.

"Yeah. But you call in, an intruder in the house, the blue suits respond and deal with the situation, whatever it turns out to be. Then they should preserve the scene and report to my guys. This time they waited till the day shift came on."

Mac briefly touched the back of his head and suppressed a wince of pain. "Well, you couldn't have done anything in the dark and the rain anyway."

"I could have checked the inside of the house before everybody tramped through it. I could have checked the graveyard before it turned to soup. I could have checked the whereabouts of some people."

"Does that mean Taylor's off your list?"

"Hell no. If this is a straight burglary and assault, it don't affect things one way or the other." Stan got up and found an ashtray in the cupboard next to the sink. "But that was for me to decide, not John Almeir."

"Anyway, I see by your boots on the porch you've been enjoying the great outdoors," Mac said. "What did you find?"

"What you'd expect. Mud." He sat down and lit a cigarette. "So I came to get your story."

Mac related the events of the previous night, leaving out the attack of the killer rabbit. Stan had enough on him as it was.

"I'll say one thing," Stan said. "Tompkins was on the ball. As soon as you stumbled into the farmyard, he sent a man up the hill. The rain had just started. He could still see by the trampled weeds your sparring partner headed toward Main. One of Tompkins' cars made a sweep down Main just before that, and the only candidates for getaway car were in the Running Fox parking lot." He put out his cigarette and finished his coffee. "So he checked the people inside and accounted for all the cars. And none of the customers looked like they'd been wading in the creek."

"What does all that tell you?" Abby asked.

Stan shrugged. "Maybe the guy lives around here and got to his house without being seen. Or he slipped past us and got to a car parked farther out of the area. But Tompkins don't buy that last one."

"You have a list of people in the Tavern? Anybody we know?"

"The Rhines. The bartender says Al Rhine was gone for a while. He noticed because Helen struck up a conversation with a guy at the bar. Her and Al had a few words about it when he got back."

"Where did Al go?"

"Claims to the washroom and then to look for Rudy Wilking. Wanted to talk price on renting the upstairs for a company party. Never found Wilking, so no confirmation. But the Rhines were both warm and dry, so it don't mean much."

"Anybody look for wet boots in the washroom? Or the car?"

"No. They missed that."

"So what's your next move?"

Stan got up and shoved his chair under the table. "Julie tells me I'm fixing the tile in the bathroom. So I better get at it."

Mac walked to the door with him. "This isn't just a straight burglary."

"I don't think so either. Could have been after that box you left with me."

"How're you coming on the envelope?"

"The FBI put me on hold. And Michigan's closed for the weekend, so there's nothing on the birth certificate either. I'm gonna forget the whole case until Monday."

The McKenzies arrived at the Schneider farmhouse promptly at one. Jack Taylor led them into the parlor, where he had installed Karen on the sofa with a pillow behind her head. There was a pot of tea on the end table.

"The doctor said to keep an eye on her and call him if she gets drowsy or throws up."

Karen looked much better than the last time Mac had seen her. "I wish you'd stop fussing, Jack. I feel fine."

"Jack's right to fuss," Abby said, sitting down opposite Karen. "A concussion is nothing to fool with."

"Up to telling your story again?" Mac asked. "I'm sure you've told the police, but I'd like to hear."

"There's not that much to tell." She waited for Jack to join her on the sofa and took his hand. "Metlaff wanted to see Jack in his office. I dropped him there and went to Lou's for gas. He was closed and I had to go all the way to Streamwood. The attendant noticed the left rear tire was low. He found a nail, and I had it fixed. So it was late when I got back here."

Mac leaned against the mantlepiece. "I take it there wasn't anything outside to warn you? We know there was no car."

"Not a thing. We'd left the hall light on, and it was still on. The police found a broken window, but you can't see that from where I—"

"Did you come in the front or the back?" Abby asked.

"Back. It's the dining room window that's broken, and you can't see it from the drive or the back of the house. I decided to make coffee in case Jack wanted some when he got home. I'd just filled the pot when I heard a floorboard squeak. It sounded like it was in the front bedroom, upstairs. That's when I called."

"The smart thing at that point," Mac said, "would have been to get out of the house and drive to the nearest phone."

"That's what I say." Jack put a protective arm around her. "To hell with the burglar, just get out."

"I can see why, at the time, you might not think of that." Mac left the mantlepiece and sat on a chair separated from Abby by a round table. The table held a terra cotta woman in flowing robes with a lamp growing from her head. He leaned forward. "But why call us? Why not call the police directly?"

"Just panicked I guess. Maybe I thought you'd get here quicker, living so close. Anyway, Abby told me to get out of the house. I almost did." Karen frowned. "Then I did something really stupid."

Jack's short laugh held no humor. "Stupid is the word all right."

"There hadn't been a sound since the first squeak, and I began to think I'd made a fool of myself, calling for help. It could have been the sound of a very old house settling, or maybe the wind. So I tiptoed over to the swinging door between the kitchen and the dining room and opened it to listen."

Mac sighed. "You didn't."

Karen hunched her shoulders and stared at her slippers. "I know. But the house was perfectly quiet. The dining room was pitch dark. I opened the door a little farther and felt for the light switch. In doing that I stuck my head partway into the room, and I guess somebody tried to knock it off. That part's kind of hazy."

"You could have been killed," Jack said.

"The next thing I remember is a terrible headache and somebody pounding on the door and light flashing through the window. I managed to get up and stagger down the hall to the front door. According to the policeman, I opened the door and fell on him."

"So you didn't see or hear anything useful," Mac said. "I suppose the intruder heard you come in, and as soon as you went to the kitchen, he tried to slip out through the dining room window. He may have heard you telephone and went to the door to eavesdrop. He was caught by surprise and struck you so that you wouldn't turn on the light and see him."

"Are you sure nothing's missing, Jack?" Abby asked.

Taylor shook his head. "There's not much to steal anyway, except a couple of antiques Karen says are okay. But you'd need a truck, and this guy was on foot. Probably looking for cash. There isn't any."

"Forget about cash," Mac said. "How about something that might relate to the graveyard, or the murders?"

Taylor and Karen turned to each other, obviously startled. Taylor put his arm around her. "You think it was the killer?"

"It's a possibility."

"But—how—I mean what could he be after here?"

"The box!" Karen exclaimed. "It must be the birth certificate!"

"That settles it," Taylor said. "You're not staying here. We're going to your apartment until this is over."

Abby said, "Why not stay with us? There's plenty of room. And we can make sure Karen is never alone." Karen and Abby argued the point briefly, but Karen's objections were merely polite. It was decided Karen and Taylor would come for supper, prepared to stay.

"Metlaff ordered Jack not to tell me anything about this case," Mac said, "but—"

"I don't understand," Karen said. "Why would he do that?"

Mac looked at Taylor, but could read nothing in his expression. "I assume Jack told him something that he doesn't want reported to the police. If I hear it from Jack and fail to pass it on, I could have license problems." He turned back to Karen. "But I can ask you a question. Right after you and Abby got back from Mrs. Linsdale's, you went to Jack. I assume you told him the story as you had heard it from her. Right?"

"Yes."

"Bits and pieces," Taylor said. "I never got the whole story."

"I guess that's right," Karen said.

Mac looked from one to the other. He made no attempt to hide his disbelief. "Why not? It would be the natural thing to do. Just start at the beginning. She said and we said and she scratched her head. Why not?"

Karen got up and walked to the window. "I think I'm feeling better." She stood with her back to the room. "I came here. Jack was working on his car out back. I said, 'You'll never guess what we found out.' I pointed toward the graveyard. 'The man up there isn't Goldfarb,' I said. 'His name's Albrecht.' Jack wasn't surprised. He took me inside and told me—things. I never finished my story."

Taylor joined Karen at the window and put his arm around her.

"This is absolutely maddening," Abby said. "We're trying to solve a mystery, our client knows all the answers, and his lawyer won't let him speak. It's insane. Well, *I* don't have to worry about a license. Mac, leave the room!"

Mac laughed. "Settle down. We've guessed most of it anyway." He spoke to Taylor. "Somehow, a German soldier, a noncom, arrived in Sarahville during the war. He worked here under the name *Albrecht*. You probably know his real name. We don't. One way or another, he died and was buried as Goldfarb. That was your Uncle Henry's attempt to conceal the fact that he had harbored an enemy in time of war."

Taylor turned from the window. "How did you know?"

"If he says 'elementary,' " Abby said, "hit him."

"Assuming that we're right," Mac continued, "what's missing is the man's real name, how he got here, and the identity of the other German."

"Other German?" Taylor advanced on Mac. "What other German?"

Karen came to Taylor's side. "The police just drove up."

"I'll let them in," Abby said. "Don't say anything important while I'm gone."

"You don't know about the other man?" Mac asked. "That's disappointing. Because he's our killer."

Stan walked in carrying a walkie-talkie. "Mr. Taylor, I'm afraid I'll have to disturb you again. I have another search warrant."

Anger flared in Taylor's eyes. "You tore the damn place apart last time. What the hell do you expect to find?"

"This warrant is for the barn," Stan said. He handed

the writ to Taylor. "Sergeant Henderson is out there now."

The radio in Stan's left hand came to life. "Cap'n? Got it."

"Got what?" Taylor asked.

"One Luger. Nine millimeter," Stan said. "Not seven six five. You have the right to remain . . ."

Chapter 21

The rain on Saturday—a downpour in the predawn hours, intermittent showers late afternoon and evening—measured over three inches, more in southern Wisconsin and Lake County. Rain returned on Sunday morning with moderate intensity, but its steadiness indicated it was settling in for the long haul.

Karen roamed through the house, ashtray in hand, staring out of each window, sitting briefly, then resuming her obsessive circuit. Abby tried to divert her with small talk, but eventually trailed off into helpless silence. By noon Abby felt Sunday had already exceeded its allotted twenty-four hours. No one clamored for lunch, but she put a tray of cheese and cold cuts on the table and invited anyone interested to pick at it. She ate an apple and watched Mac manufacture a sandwich. He took it with him back to his office, where he had spent the morning.

By one o'clock Karen was well into her second pack of cigarettes, but at one point, with an expression of disgust, she threw it in the trash. Ten minutes passed before she fished it out and lit another.

That was the last straw for Abby. She grabbed Karen's arm and pulled her toward the stairs. "Come on, let's get the Master Detective to tell us what he's up to."

They found Mac in his chair, facing the window, with his feet on the sill. His eyes were closed, and his breathing was slow and regular. Abby's eyes narrowed and her lips tightened. "If he's sleeping, I'll kill him."

Mac removed his feet from the sill slowly. He turned his chair and leaned on the desk. "I was in deep thought."

"Do you always snore when you're thinking? Just what have you been doing while"—she glanced toward Karen—"while we've been worrying ourselves sick?"

"Well, for one thing, I've been trying to run down this guy who knows about POWs. If you think that's easy on a Sunday, wait till you see the phone bill."

"Is that important?" Abby asked. "Jack must know who the mysterious Albrecht really is. He must have told Metlaff and Metlaff will tell you."

"Probably. But in the meantime I'd like to clean up some loose ends."

Karen slumped in a chair. "Did you find him?" Her tone was listless, the question a mere attempt at conversation.

"Yes, as a matter of fact. I did."

Abby leaned on the desk. "Mac, don't be infuriating. What did he say?"

"The POWs who escaped were recaptured within hours, or at most, days. Except one. He's still out there somewhere."

"After all these years?" Abby glanced at Karen to see if this news had penetrated her gloom, but could detect no flicker of interest. "So it's possible Albrecht was—"

Mac stopped her with a shake of his head. "The missing man is fluent in English."

Abby shoved the telephone aside and perched on the corner of the desk. "That's all you've got to show for your time?"

"I've also been talking to Mrs. Dancer, trying to run down Metlaff."

"And what does Laverne have to say?"

213

"He's somewhere in Baltimore."

"Surely she has a number where he can be reached."

Mac chuckled. "That's just what I said. It seems he goes to Baltimore about three times a year, and he never leaves a number. When I asked why, she said that was none of her business, and certainly none of mine."

Abby's surprise was evident. "Oh." Her left foot kicked gently at the desk. "Do you suppose . . . ? No. Not Metlaff. When is he due back?"

"Noon tomorrow."

That brought the first sign of genuine interest from Karen; she put out a half-smoked cigarette and laid her ashtray on the desk. "Will he get Jack out? What do you think?"

Mac smiled reassuringly. "No problem. I've asked Stan to hold off transferring him until Metlaff gets here."

"Transfer?"

"They usually transfer prisoners to Cook County Jail."

Abby saw that this last remark had plunged Karen back into gloom. "Don't worry. Mac knows who did it. It's just —"

"You know?" Karen stood up abruptly. "Then why is Jack still in jail? Why haven't you told the police?"

Abby made an apologetic face at Mac. "I wasn't supposed to say that, Karen. I'm not sure why, but no doubt the Great One will explain."

Mac sighed deeply. "The idea was to *avoid* explaining. Look. I don't know who killed Bedford. Or Ketchall, and probably Albrecht. I have a strong suspicion. That's all. The trick is to find a way to check my hunch. So far I haven't figured out how to do that."

"That's the part I don't understand," Abby said. "If we're right, the killer is living under a false identity. What's so hard about proving it? Any number of things won't check out. Where he went to school, relatives, fingerprints maybe."

214

"All that takes time. If I do it myself, it could take a year, unless I get lucky. Remember, this guy has had decades to smooth the rough edges of his story. He's probably got good documentation by now."

"Jerome Bedford did it. It didn't take *him* a year."

Mac stood up. Leaning against the window frame, he looked out on Twilly Place. "I know. That's what's driving me quietly nuts. How did he do it? All I can think of is that something was taken from his apartment besides the grave marker. Something we'll never find."

"I suppose that must be it," Abby said.

Karen's breathing had quickened during this exchange. "The FBI! You said it was another German, maybe a spy. Couldn't they do it faster?"

"Karen, first I'd have to convince them my suspicion was worth their effort. Even then, he'd clam up and they'd have to dig it all out the hard way. And in the end all they'd have is a case for deportation. Proving he's not who he says he is doesn't prove murder."

Karen picked up the ashtray, but not having brought cigarettes with her, she put it down again. "But if this man is being investigated, wouldn't that mean—"

"That Jack would be off the hook? I wish it were that easy. Once Jack was arrested, Stan lost control of the case. Only the State's Attorney can drop the charge. And with a positive firearms identification, it'll take more than a theory by McKenzie to convince him."

"Who is it, Mac?" Karen slumped back into her chair. "Who did this to us?"

Mac shook his head. "No, Karen. If I tell you, you're liable to act on it. The first time you pass him on the street—"

"He's right, Karen. Best leave it to Mac. He'll find a way out." Having dutifully promoted the party line, Abby's own resentment welled up. "Of course, that doesn't explain why he won't tell his wife and associate."

"You don't know either?" Karen asked.

"All he'll say to me is, 'You know my methods, Watson.'" Abby was pleased to see a faint smile from Karen. "But I'll tell you one thing. We're not going to just sit around waiting for Metlaff. Mac, there must be something we can do before Karen and I go stir-crazy."

"Right. We're all going out to dinner. And we'll talk about everything except this case."

Karen looked doubtful, but prompted by Abby she nodded. "Well, all right. But not around here, please. I don't want to see anyone. They'll ask about Jack and—" She fished a tissue out of her sleeve and wiped at a tear.

"Sure, wherever you say," Mac said hastily. "We'll go to the Milk Pail. Or Pheasant Run."

Karen began to cry in earnest.

"Well, okay. Then how about Arnie's," Mac said.

Monday morning was crisp and clear; Karen's mood could perhaps be described as limp and muddy. Thankful for that much improvement, Abby rolled down the car window. "Now that we know the way, the trip doesn't take that long," she said. "We're almost there."

"I don't understand why we're going back to Mrs. Linsdale, but anything is better than sitting around waiting," Karen said.

"We detectives like to clear up all the loose ends."

Karen's laugh was brief, but genuine. "Abigail McKenzie, girl detective."

"Now you sound like my husband. But there *is* a loose end. The connection Jerome found. That's the person he had an appointment with the night he was killed."

"How can Mrs. Linsdale help?"

"Maybe the connecting link was in that box she kept for Henry Schneider."

They drove in silence for a mile, then Karen said, "Jerome looked through the box a long time ago.

That's when he got the picture, remember?"

"At that time he hadn't found the grave. Maybe didn't realize the significance of what he saw. Now, if he had another look when he came to see Mrs. Linsdale—"

"She might know what he found!"

"And whether he took it away with him."

Mrs. Muntner was waiting at the door when they arrived. She ushered them through the house.

Noting that Mrs. Muntner's hair was in disarray and there was a smear of mud on the blue workshirt she wore, Abby asked, "Have we come at a bad time?"

"No, it's all right. All that rain over the weekend gave us a foot of water in the basement, but I've got things under control."

"Oh, I'm sorry. I noticed this morning the creek behind my house was out of its banks."

"The radio says this is a temporary break. The rain'll be back later."

"Maybe we should come back another day," Abby offered.

"No, really. Mother was pleased to hear you were coming back." She opened the door to the sun porch. "She gets very little company these days."

Abby smiled and took Alma Linsdale's frail hand. "I hope we're not a bother, Mrs. Linsdale. There's just one little point we want to clear up."

Alma Linsdale smiled. "Sit down. Sit down. Lovely day, isn't it? Would you like some tea?"

"No, thank you." With Mrs. Muntner's problem in mind, Abby said, "We can't stay long. We were just wondering, Mrs. Linsdale. When Jerome Bedford came to see you, did he look through Henry Schneider's things?"

Mrs. Linsdale frowned. "Jerome . . . ?"

"Bedford."

"Oh, that peculiar young man. I believe he did. Bea, do you remember?"

217

"Yes, Mother. You made me watch while he spread everything out on the dining room table. To make sure he didn't take anything."

"Did he seem to find anything of special interest?" Abby asked.

"Yes, he got quite excited about somebody's birth certificate. Wanted to take it with him, but Mother wouldn't hear of it."

Mrs. Linsdale's eyes had followed the flow of question and answer with no more than polite interest. "Bea, do you suppose we could have that tea now?"

Mrs. Muntner smiled, patted her mother's hand, and left.

Abby sighed. "Well, I don't know where that gets us."

"Maybe while we're here we should ask about the picture," Karen said.

"Might as well." Turning to Mrs. Linsdale she said, "There should have been a picture of Henry and Camilla. Did you—" Abby stopped abruptly. Alma Linsdale's color had deepened and she placed her hands on her breast. "Oh, dear," Abby said, glancing toward the door in hope that Mrs. Muntner was returning. "It's all right if you kept it, really."

"I didn't think anyone would miss it. And it reminded me . . ." Mrs. Linsdale started to rise. "I'll get it for you."

Abby reached out and touched her arm. "No, keep it. Please. We just wanted to know where it was, that's all."

"You're sure? Mr. Schneider won't mind?"

"Schneider? Oh, you mean John Taylor. No, he won't mind. There's another copy anyway."

Abby was relieved to see Mrs. Linsdale's color return to normal. Just one more question, and then they'd chat for a while so the old woman wouldn't feel cheated by the briefness of their visit. "Just so we know where everything is, was there anything else in the box

218

that you—any other keepsake?"

Mrs. Linsdale sighed. "I suppose you guessed the reason. They look so much alike."

Abby noticed Karen squirm in her chair, and shared her uneasiness. "It's not necessary to—we don't want to pry."

"I thought, you know, after Max died, Henry would . . . But then Joseph came along."

Startled, Abby and Karen looked at each other. "Albrecht?" they both said.

Alma Linsdale turned toward the window. She arched her back and smiled, her voice almost inaudible. "He loved me, you know." She looked at them over her shoulder, pursed her lips, and lowered her eyes modestly. "They both did."

Abby held her breath, afraid to snap the spell that had enveloped the old woman, but Karen shook her head and said, "You mean Henry and Albrecht?"

"Oh, yes. Of course, there wasn't anything between Joseph and me. But Henry thought there was. He was quite angry. Said he knew a few things he could tell if Joseph didn't stay away." She stroked her cheek and settled back in her chair.

"What things, Mrs. Linsdale?" Abby asked.

"What?"

"What did Henry know about Alb—about Joseph?"

"Oh. I don't know. He only said it the one time. Just before . . ." Mrs. Linsdale massaged her stiff fingers and turned back to the window. A cloud passed over the sun and she drew her sweater around her. "It was an accident. I'm sure." She nodded her head. "I'm sure."

The silence lasted for a long minute. "Henry got so moody after that. We hardly ever talked anymore. And the farm got rundown. Most times he wouldn't answer when a body rang the bell." A tear escaped her eye. "I thought, maybe, after Max was gone . . ."

Abby got up and touched Mrs. Linsdale's shoulder.

"I'm sorry. We didn't mean to upset you." There was no response.

Mrs. Muntner entered with a pot of tea and two cups on a tray. "I've brought us a nice cup of tea, Mother."

"We're sorry," Karen said. "We didn't mean to—"

"It's all right." Beatrice Muntner put down the tray. "You didn't know. Would you mind seeing yourselves out?"

Abby and Karen escaped quickly.

The all-volunteer Sarahville Police Department took over the old bank building in 1947. When progress required a salaried force and enlarged quarters, the mayor and the other village departments climbed on the bandwagon and proposed a modern Municipal Center. Debate over the bond issue was lengthy and spirited, construction delays were many, and the new facility was not ready until the spring of 1957.

By then the center was too small for all who wanted to move in. Turf battles over the limited air-conditioned space approached the level of civil war. A newcomer, and politically unconnected, Stan was the first casualty; he was required to detect crime from the second floor of the old bank.

His revenge came with the record-setting rain of July 1957, when the mayor's desk floated into the hallway of the new building. Water damage brought to light latent defects, shoddy construction, and the participation of the mayor's lumberyard as sole supplier of materials to the contractor.

Stan met Mac at the side entrance of the no longer new center, and passed him through to the basement interrogation room. Mac sat at one end of the linoleum-topped table. Stan leaned against the wall.

"Why didn't you search the barn with the first warrant?" Mac asked.

"The warrant should have included outbuildings and

grounds, but it didn't. Typical screwup."

"But you didn't take a second crack at it just to cover a mistake."

"True. We had an anonymous tip. Told us right where to look. The caller said her kid was playing in the barn and found it. She didn't want the kid involved. Wouldn't leave a name."

"You believe that?"

"Taylor elects to stand mute on advice of counsel. Counsel is out of town. I'm hoping you'll get him to open up."

"Metlaff will be back this afternoon," Mac said. "Why push it?"

"State's Attorney wants him transferred to Cook County. Right now. By the time he gets processed and bail can be arranged, which the State's Attorney will jack up as high as he can, it'll be another twenty-four hours."

Mac studied Stan. "So why does that bother you?"

Stan shifted his weight from his left leg to his right, scratched his chin, folded his arms. "I don't like the way this is shaping up. But it's too late to let go."

"I don't like it either, but what's your objection?"

"That grave business. Anonymous tip that ties Taylor to Bedford. Another one that turns up the gun—"

"Cops live off anonymous tips."

"Yeah. Okay. Look—find out what you can. If word gets out, I can't guarantee the State's Attorney won't ask you what he said. But I won't ask. You decide what to tell me."

"Won't they expect *you* to ask me?"

"If the mayor hears I left you alone with the prisoner, his buddy Almeir will do the asking from now on, and I'll be checking parking meters."

Stan left. Mac leaned back in his chair. If he persuaded Taylor to talk, what were the odds it would damage his defense? The fluorescent light buzzed and flickered. Mac looked up and saw the dark silhouettes of dead flies through the plastic diffuser. He sighed. With the murder weapon found on Taylor's property, the case against him could hardly be worse. Mac stared at the wall, where periodic dampness had raised bubbles in the green paint. One of the bubbles was starting to peel. Would a jury believe it had been planted? Not without an alternative suspect. Could he give them one?

Stan returned and led Jack Taylor into the room. "Twenty minutes," he said. "No more."

Taylor needed a shave and, judging by the bags under his eyes, a night's sleep as well. He slumped into the chair opposite Mac. "Metlaff coming?"

Mac shook his head. "We don't have much time, so let's get down to it. If Metlaff were here, he'd tell you to tell me the whole story. As things stand, it's the only way you can help yourself."

Taylor looked around the room, uncertainty etched into the furrows on his brow. "I don't know. I don't see how anything I tell you can help. And Metlaff—"

"The hell with Metlaff. Whatever you tell me stays with me, unless I can see a way to use it to get you out of here. And don't forget, whoever killed Bedford and Ketchall also attacked Karen. She could be in danger." Mac knew that was highly unlikely at this stage, particularly since she was staying with him. But if Taylor believed it . . .

"Okay." Taylor stood up. "I've been worried about that too." He started to pace the small room. "I'll tell you what I know." He frowned. "Let's see. I guess it starts when I got the box from Mrs. Linsdale. There was a ledger book in with the other stuff. It had dates in one column, German writing next to each date. Looked like a journal of some kind."

"Where is it now?"

"I'm coming to that. I had a shipmate, German immigrant, just got his papers. I sent it to him. Asked if it was worth translating. Just curiosity, you know?"

"Couldn't you have found someone local?"

"At the time I still thought my being a Schneider was a secret. Anyway, my friend skimmed through it, and when he got to the burial, he translated that part and sent it to me. That's when I tried to drop the whole damn project."

"Because Henry Schneider harbored an enemy soldier?"

Taylor stopped his nervous pacing and sat down. He rubbed his forehead. "Actually, he didn't know about Dietricht until after the war. Maybe he suspected earlier. I don't know."

"Dietricht? That's the man's name?"

"Feldwebel Herman Dietricht. Feldwebel means—"

"Sergeant. I know." Mac nodded encouragingly. "Go on. We don't have much time."

"Dietricht started working on the farm in '44. Claimed to be a Jewish refugee. Hard to find farmhands then, so Henry didn't ask too many questions. It was a chance for Hans, his father, to speak German, and they got to be good friends. Otherwise Dietricht kept pretty much to himself. The three of them would drink a few beers up at the tavern on Saturday night, but that was about it."

"When did Henry tumble?"

"Like I said, he must have suspected something was phony. But what brought it to a head was Alma Linsdale."

"Linsdale! What does she—"

"I'm coming to that. Henry and her must have had something going. He doesn't say so in so many words, but it must have been that way. He said Dietricht started 'bothering' her, whatever that means. So he went through Dietricht's stuff. Found a letter he wrote to his sister."

"The envelope?"

"I guess so. Her name wasn't mentioned, so I didn't make the connection. Seems he entered the country in some roundabout way from Argentina. If he said why,

223

or mentioned the other German you were talking about, Henry didn't put that down."

"Okay. Dietricht would be cagey in his letter. In case it was intercepted at the other end."

"Yeah. Henry said it all became clear when he found a military patch and put two and two together. So Dietricht was being real cagey, or it would have been clear without that."

"Speed it up. What did Henry do once he knew?"

"Confronted Dietricht. Demanded to know who and what he was. Dietricht gave him name, rank, and serial number, I guess. Said he was a deserter, wanted to stay in the U.S. Henry said, 'Turn yourself in, or get turned in.' "

"If Henry didn't know until after the war was over, and then told him to turn himself in or else, why worry?"

Taylor sighed. "You haven't heard the punch line. Dietricht agreed, but said he owed it to Hans, who was dead by then, to finish the harvest first."

"And that's when he had the accident?"

Taylor leaned back, legs outstretched, hands in pockets. "Henry went out to the field where Dietricht was working. Dietricht tried to brain him with a rock." He shook his head, as if in disbelief. "Henry didn't make a long story out of it. He knocked Dietricht down and ran over him."

Chapter 22

Stan held his watch to the small window in the interrogation room door and drew a finger across his throat. Mac stood up. "Where's the journal?"

"Karen has it," Taylor said. "The translation too."

Mac paused at the door. "Not that it matters, but why so hot to protect the family name? You once said the Schneiders were strangers to you."

"My grandfather died in the First World War. My father in the Second. I was a career Navy man—Korea, Nam." He shrugged. "And Karen—she got me hooked on all this family history business . . ." His voice trailed off.

The door opened and Stan said, "Time."

Mac nodded to Stan and left the building. He glanced at the sky and noted the clear sunshine of the morning was gone. He sat on the concrete steps at the front of the Municipal Center. Good news, bad news. The bad news was that Henry Schneider killed Albrecht. He had suspected Albrecht was the victim of his comrade in arms—a much stronger motive for a cover-up than merely wanting to stay in the U.S. But that was offset by the identification of Dietrich; the theory of the second German now had enough weight to bring in the Justice Department. And there was always the possibility that war crimes were involved, an even better motive.

A line of dark clouds, the leading edge boiling, moved rapidly out of the southwest. Would the Feds move quickly enough to save Taylor from trial? Would they find a connection to the Bedford and Ketchall killings? If not, Taylor could still be convicted.

Mac got up as the first drops fell. More than the Feds, he needed the State's Attorney's attention. Some way to get the charge dropped until the smoke cleared. Some overt act that . . .

He ran for the side entrance, arriving just as the squadrol left with Taylor. A uniformed officer, about to enter the building, turned to block Mac's way.

"Is Captain Pawlowski still here?" Mac asked.

The officer pointed in the direction of the departing wagon. "He just left."

Damn! The trip to the lockup at Twenty-sixth and California would take an hour each way. Allow an hour for paperwork. Three hours. Stan should be back in time, but meanwhile he had to meet Metlaff.

"Can you get a message to him?" Mac asked. "It's urgent."

"What message?"

Mac hurriedly scribbled in his pocket notebook and tore off the page. "See that he gets this as soon as you can. Please. Can do?"

The officer glanced at the note. "Doesn't make a lot of sense."

"He'll know what it means."

The Running Fox Tavern tour was a sellout. The entire Sarahville Historical Society, less Karen, attended. Rudy, counting the house, noted Mac's absence.

"He had to see Jack Taylor," Abby said. "And from there he went to meet Metlaff's plane so he can brief him. Karen is going with him. He'll be here as soon as he can."

Lunch in the upstairs dining room was served buffet-style, leaving both Rudy Wilking and Josie Horvath free to join the group. "We are normally quite busy at this time of day," Rudy said, "so this is for us a pleasant break in the routine."

"I expected to see that backhoe making the mud fly," Al Rhine said. "What's the holdup?"

"They did begin on schedule — but the rain, you know. Seepage from the rising creek has made them fear the activity of their equipment could collapse the subcellar roof and cause the sides to fall in."

"What difference does it make?" Jean Arly asked. "I mean, the whole idea is to fill it in anyway, isn't it?"

Al chuckled. "I think the plan is to fill it with dirt, not excavating machines."

Abby studied the group as they passed down the line, filling their plates. What should have been a festive occasion seemed permeated by a general unease. The reason became apparent once they were seated at the long table.

Helen Rhine gave it voice. "I feel just terrible about Karen. Jack Taylor seemed so right for her."

Alice Hillman's voice, normally capable of scratching glass, dropped to a lower register. "Just terrible. They were such a romantic couple."

"He's not dead, you know," Abby said.

"But she wouldn't —" Alice's voice moved back up scale. "Now that she knows he's a cold-blooded killer —"

"You're moving a bit fast there." James Farrell impaled a morsel of smoked fish. "Can't hang the boy till we get the trial out of the way."

"Jim is quite right," Rudy said. "We mustn't jump to conclusions. After all, we have not heard the evidence."

"H.A. can tell you all about the evidence," Jean Arly said, picking at her potato salad.

His wife's words halted H.A. in the act of piling corned beef on rye bread. "Now Jean!"

Al Rhine laughed. "Ever think of getting yourself a

syndicated column? Call it 'From the Horace's Mouth.'"

H.A.'s smile looked as though it had been strained through his teeth. "They found the murder weapon in Taylor's barn."

"I didn't know the police had released that news," Abby said.

"Connections," he said, and turned his full attention to his plate.

"Old Horse always has a connection," Al Rhine said. "Come on, reveal your source for once."

H.A. shrugged. "You know how it is with the Fire Department. Twenty-four on, forty-eight off. Lots of them moonlight, or have a little business on the side. I do the books for one."

"So that's Fire," Al said. "What does he know about Police?"

"He does arson, when there is any. Knows most of the police, some real well."

"Do they have any other evidence?" Rudy asked.

"Motive." H.A. bit into his sandwich and they waited while he chewed. "Something to do with the parking lot plan." Turning to Abby he asked, "Is your husband going to drop this business now?"

"Oh, no. Jack had nothing to do with the murders. Mac knows who did. It's just a question of time now."

Questions came from every direction. She was tempted to utter a politicianlike "no comment," but said, "You'll have to ask Mac."

"He *is* coming, isn't he?" Josie asked.

Abby checked her watch. "I hope so. Maybe he'll catch up with us on the tour."

Reminded of his role as host, Rudy turned the conversation to the purpose for the gathering. He talked at length, beginning with the English settlers who built the tavern, adding anecdotes of the deeds and misdeeds of subsequent owners. He concluded with the apocryphal story of Al Capone's final illness.

The group then clustered around him while he explained that the upper floor had once provided lodging for travelers, the conversion to private dining areas taking place around 1910. The tour skipped only Rudy's living quarters, which Abby judged must be rather small. As they finished up in the kitchen, she noticed Mac slip in at the back of the group.

"I see we have been joined at last by our local Sherlock Holmes," Rudy announced. Heads swiveled and mouths opened, but Rudy said, "No, no. Hold your questions, please. Our next, and last, stop will provide a proper ambience for a tale of mystery and murder."

He opened the cellar door. "The stairs are narrow and rather steep, so please use the handrail."

The party descended, led by Rudy. Mac and Abby brought up the rear. "What's happening?" Abby whispered.

Mac shook his head. "Tell you later."

A single bulb hanging from the ceiling gave dim light and created deep shadows among the rows of shelving and stacks of beer cartons. Rudy walked confidently to the center of the stone-walled cellar, his head clearing the beams by two inches. Al and H.A. were slightly shorter than Rudy, but they ducked involuntarily nevertheless.

"As you can see," Rudy said, "this is where we store our provisions. The walls are of the type of stone deposited in this area by the last glacier. They were constantly turned up by the plow, and provided early settlers a ready supply of building material."

"Where does that door go?" Alice asked, pointing to the east wall.

Rudy grasped the wrought-iron handle and pulled. The four-foot-high door opened with some effort, revealing steep stairs that disappeared into darkness. A dank odor seeped from the opening. They could hear the sound of trickling water and the hum of a sump pump.

"This leads to the other cellar, which is at a lower level and extends beyond the surface building. The shrubs at the back of the tavern are directly above it and prevent parking over the rather ancient roof. As we discussed earlier, it is the reason for the excavating equipment."

Jean Arly, moving closer, smiled up at Rudy. "Surely you don't expect us to go down there."

Josie said, "Excuse me," and passed between them.

"No, no. It has become dangerous."

"If I'd known, I'd have taken pictures before it's all gone," Helen said.

"I have already done so," Rudy said. "For the Society's files."

"Very thoughtful," Helen said.

"What's it good for?" Farrell asked. "I mean, originally?"

"There are several theories. The most likely, it seems to me, is that it was an entrance to the brewery, which we know had a very deep cellar. You all know—well, perhaps the McKenzies do not—the brewery was built by the family which also owned the tavern. It was quite small, but could supply local needs at lower cost than bringing beer from Chicago by horse-drawn cart. Closed by Prohibition, it eventually burned and was razed."

"And now it's a parking lot," Al said. "Damn shame."

Rudy pointed down the stairs. "Perhaps this was an entry tunnel and was preserved as a storm cellar." Rudy chuckled. "One aged romantic, a regular patron when I first purchased the tavern, insisted it was a vault used by Capone. He claimed the owner was merely a front. Well, perhaps. The only thing certain is, it has become a nuisance."

"The way the creek's rising, it may be more than a nuisance pretty soon," Mac said. "You have six inches of water in the parking lot." His words were punctuated by a muffled roll of thunder.

"No doubt there is even more water down there in the subcellar." Rudy shrugged, dismissing the problem. "This method of concluding the tour was not planned, but clearly the fate of Jack Taylor and the future of Karen Cannelli is weighing on us all." He nodded to Josie, who wheeled a cart, containing glasses and several bottles of wine, to his side. "Mac, Abby tells us you believe Taylor to be innocent."

Mac looked at Abby and raised an eyebrow.

"Okay, Poirot," Abby said, "explain." A sharp crack, signaling a nearby lightning strike, startled the group. "But not in endless detail. I'd like to get home before the house floats away."

Mac held up a glass to be filled. "This case seemed to begin with the death of Jerome Bedford. The physical evidence didn't lead anywhere, so the police searched in Bedford's past, among his acquaintances, for a motive. Nothing suggestive turned up." He passed the glass to Abby and took another. "It began to look like there was nothing to do but wait around for a break."

"Did I hear you right?" Farrell asked. "Did you say, 'seemed to begin'?"

"Right. It really began over thirty years ago. But I'll come to that."

Mac paused to sip his wine. "Jack Taylor came along, enthusiastic about a scheme to move the Schneider graveyard. Shortly after that Abby found an unexplained grave. As you all knew, or suspected, Bedford had found the same grave. Next, we discover Taylor is about to lose a potentially profitable inheritance if he can't assure the bank, by May first, that he can move the graves. So Stan—Captain Pawlowski—now had a motive, and his only suspect."

Al Rhine had already finished his wine and was looking for a refill. "So why didn't they arrest him?"

"They needed some connecting link between Bedford

and Taylor. Of course Taylor was near the scene that night, as were several others, including me. So Taylor *may* have had opportunity."

"But that wouldn't be enough for the police," Farrell said.

"There was more. An anonymous caller, a woman, reported seeing Bedford enter Taylor's motel room two days before the murder. If true, that would supply the missing link. Valueless as evidence without confirmation, the tip did increase police suspicion.

"The question of means next arose; the long arm of Pawlowski reached all the way to San Diego and found a witness to Taylor's possession of a Luger pistol. Taylor claims the caliber of his gun was different from that of the murder weapon, and that it was stolen from him two years ago. He failed to report the theft, suspicious in itself, and his story is unsubstantiated."

"If this was a jury, I think we'd have a verdict by now," H.A. said.

"Worse to come," Mac said. "The murder weapon has now been found on Taylor's property. That also came about because of an anonymous tip—also by a woman."

"The same woman?" Helen asked. "Oh, how silly! They were both anonymous."

"Regardless of that, the murder weapon clinched it, and Jack Taylor's been arrested."

Abby scanned Mac's audience. There was no doubt he had their full attention, except for Al Rhine, who by gesture was telling Rudy it was time to open another bottle.

"But apparently you do not agree with the police," Rudy said.

Mac outlined his objections to the police theory much as Abby had heard earlier. "Actually, the police aren't entirely happy either, but they can't ignore the evidence. However, acting for the defense, and prodded by Abby's conviction that Taylor's innocent, I tried to look at the case from a different angle."

"There isn't any other angle," H.A. said.

"No? Let's see. If we assume Taylor's innocence, what can we say?"

Jean Arly, nervously twirling her glass by the stem, said, "There really isn't *anything* to say, is there? I mean, no one else had a *reason,* did they?"

"We'll come to motive," Mac said. "Start with Agnes Ketchall. Agnes spoke up at the SHS lunch, and promptly died. Her death occurred so quickly after she spoke that the killer must be someone who was there, or who heard about it within the hour."

Alice Hillman's eyes narrowed and she spoke softly. "That's what I figured."

"That's a bit of a jump, isn't it?" Farrell objected. "Are you sure the murderer didn't know, before the lunch, that Agnes was dangerous to him?"

"Possible. But the killer had to know she was going directly to the graveyard in order to intercept her there."

"Logical," Rudy said. "Unpleasant, but logical."

"With that to narrow the field," Mac said, "let's look at Bedford's death. Assume, as the police do, that he had an appointment with his killer. His demeanor and remarks make it highly unlikely that the person he was to meet was at the same SHS meeting that he attended that night. You all see that, don't you?"

Grinning, Al said, "At least I see you just dropped me and Helen from your list."

"I'm sure we were never on his list," Helen said.

"Don't kid yourself." Raising his glass, Al said, "Well, here's to us, Babe."

"If that line of logic was right, it left a short list of five," Mac said. "As I, or Abby, talked to each one on the list, it became clear that two told deliberate and unnecessary lies. At that point my problem was how to choose between them."

H.A., at the wine cart for a refill, asked, "What lies?"

"I don't think I should say. Not at this stage. Let's turn to the peculiar circumstances of the extra grave." He summarized the successive discovery of the names *Goldfarb* and *Albrecht*. He reviewed the evidence that Jerome Bedford had followed the same path of discovery, and had done so with the foreknowledge of still a third name, learned from a grave marker that had since disappeared. Then he explained the paradox of a man knowing only basic English having a U.S. birth certificate. "Of course you could invent theories to account for that, but not convincing ones."

Mac paused as Rudy abandoned his wine cart to draw closer. "At that point, I put together a theory, built mostly of straw, that had the identity of the man in the grave as central to the mystery. What did we know about him?"

Josie, who had stayed in the background until now, moved forward. "Not a hell of a lot, the way you tell it."

Helen Rhine took the empty glass from Al's hand and set it on the cart. "That's right. It doesn't seem as though you know anything at all about him."

"I know his native language was German," Mac said. "And thanks to Jim Farrell, I suspected he had been in the German Army."

Attention now focused on Farrell. "Right," he said. "Henry Schneider sold me some stuff. There was a German sleeve patch included."

"Remember," Mac said, "the man arrived in Sarahville during World War Two. His story, that he was a Jew, didn't hold up. His whole background was apparently fabricated."

"War criminal!" Alice exclaimed. "Like that movie with what's-his-name. You know. And the dentist—"

"Or an escaped POW," Farrell said.

"Probably a spy," Helen Rhine said.

Al Rhine snorted "Spying on the Schneider farm? For what?" He retrieved his glass and sidled toward the wine.

"Those were all possibilities," Mac said. "Some more likely than others. We've since ruled out the POW theory. The patch tells us he was a noncom, not a high-ranking Nazi. And spoke poor English at best, so not a trained agent." Mac paused and surveyed his audience. The ham's enjoying this, Abby thought. She smiled. He does do it well.

"So I added more straw to my theory," Mac continued, "and came up with a second German. One who could arrange for the Albrecht birth certificate, who could fit into an American community. And perhaps someone who could arrange for anonymous tips to the police—by a woman."

"Lets me out." H.A. tried to smile, managing a brief twitch of the lips. "Not old enough for a decrepit Nazi."

Abby noticed that Josie had disappeared again.

"Don't be ridiculous," Helen said. "He can't mean—" Turning on Mac, she said, "You can't, can you?"

Mac ignored the question. "The second German must have arrived about the same time as Albrecht. He must be of an appropriate age."

At first the group stared at Mac. Then they glanced quickly at their neighbors. Their thoughts were obvious, and voiced by the obvious Alice. "You mean this Nazi is—one of us?"

"There are several candidates. And weeding them out could take a long time. But we got a lucky break."

Startled, Abby's eyebrows rose. What break?

Jean Arly echoed her thought. "Lucky break?"

"Henry Schneider kept a journal. It was found some time ago by Jack Taylor. Unfortunately it's written in German and Jack was unable to read it. Out of curiosity he photocopied two pages and sent them to a friend for translation."

Abby observed Mac carefully. His face was calm, almost impassive, and his eyelids drooped a bit, as though he were sleepy or bored. A sure sign he was up to something snaky. There was a con on.

"Jack's thought was that if the journal was family history, he'd get the whole thing translated. If it was just farm business, it wouldn't be worth it. Well, the results are in, and to our surprise the pages he chose explain who this Albrecht really is."

The group maintained a tense silence. Except for Alice. "Who? Who?"

"He was a sergeant in the German Army. His name was Herman Dietricht."

"How the hell did a Kraut sergeant wind up in Sarahville?" Farrell asked.

Mac shrugged. "Maybe we'll find out when the rest of the journal is translated. But the most interesting part is the last sentence on the photocopy, as translated. Let's see if I can quote it exactly." Mac closed his eyes, as if concentrating.

Abby felt like applauding.

He opened his eyes, slowly scanned the audience, left to right, and said, "I have read the letter which Dietricht last wrote to his sister. There he mentions his superior officer. Imagine my surprise to find it is . . ."

"Is who?" Alice asked. "Is who?"

"That's where it ends. The journal's sitting on my desk and just as soon as I've discussed it with Metlaff we'll get it translated."

"Have you told the police?" H.A. asked.

"No. I work for the defense. Metlaff first."

"I understood that's where you were this afternoon. With the lawyer."

"Metlaff didn't show. He's expected on a later flight."

Helen Rhine, eyes narrowed in concentration, said, "But you don't have to understand the language to read a name."

Mac sighed. "You're right, of course. Unfortunately there is no name. I guess Henry described him some other way. Maybe by his trade, like 'the village shoe-

236

maker' or"—he smiled—"his property, as in 'the tavern owner.' Just kidding, Rudy."

Mac sipped the last of his wine and placed the glass on the cart. "In any case, we'll know by tomorrow." He glanced at his watch. "I had no idea it was so late. Sorry to break away, but Abby and I have to hurry if we're to meet Metlaff's plane."

Beginning to get a glimmer of what was going on, Abby said, "With the rain, we better leave for O'Hare right from here."

Rudy sighed. "If that is all we are to hear, then perhaps this is a good time to close this most fascinating meeting."

The group, silent, reluctant to leave, began moving up the steep, narrow stairway. Rudy busied himself at the wine cart. Abby stopped to thank him for his hospitality.

As H.A., the last of the group, disappeared through the door, Mac said, "We have to go, Abby."

They were halfway up the stairs when Josie suddenly reappeared, blocking the door. She carried an object wrapped in a towel. The outline looked a great deal like a gun.

"Mac! Abby!" Rudy called. "Will you join me for a last drink? The learned attorney can always take a cab. And I feel we have more to discuss."

Abby looked at Mac apprehensively. "Honey, you haven't done something stupid, have you?"

Chapter 23

"So," Rudy said. "All is discovered, as they say."

The rumble of thunder seemed to originate in the thick stone walls, surrounding them with muffled sound. "Not all," Mac said.

"Come, come. It is clear you know a great deal more than you have told us." Rudy moved under the light, his face passing into shadow. "I have felt your hot breath on my neck more than once."

"I don't know who you are—yet."

Rudy handed a glass to Abby. She accepted it with her right hand, the fingers of her left digging into Mac's arm. He kept his eyes on Josie. She stood on the lowest step, and there was no longer any doubt what she had carried wrapped in a towel; the gun was fully visible. "And I'm not sure why you feared discovery so desperately," Mac continued. "Nazi war crimes?"

"Certainly not. Quite the contrary." Rudy handed him a glass and returned to the cart.

"What then?" A Luger's shape is distinctive, not to be mistaken for anything else. Josie held it in the flat of her hand, as though she were offering a tray of pastry. Either she was afraid of guns or she was supremely confident.

"Where's *your* gun?" Abby whispered.

"Home." He patted her hand.

"I was—I *am* Leutnant Hans Earhart." Rudy shook his head and smiled briefly. "After all these years the

238

name sounds strange to me. Even then, the title of rank made me feel like an actor on the stage. I fear I was not cut out to be a warrior."

Mac was having trouble giving Rudy his full attention. Why had he exposed Abby to this risk? He should have known things wouldn't go as planned. They never did.

"I was assigned to the Abwehr," Rudy continued. "You know—military intelligence. On the staff of Admiral Canaris. And thankful, I might add, to be where shots were never fired in anger."

"And Dietricht?"

"Feldwebel Dietricht was a driver assigned to the Abwehr."

"Go on."

"You know, of course, that the admiral was not a great admirer of der Führer. As a matter of fact, it sometimes seemed the Abwehr spent as much time giving intelligence support to the anti-Hitler plotters as it did gathering information about the Allies." He turned toward the stairs. "Josie, dear, come have a glass of wine."

As she approached, Mac carefully measured the closing distance and gently removed Abby's hand from his arm. Rudy held out a glass to Josie with his left hand and extended his right to take the gun. Josie's eyes were fixed on Rudy and her chin trembled slightly.

Rudy, on the other hand, seemed entirely at ease. "Did you know the Abwehr supplied the bombs used in several attempts to assassinate Hitler? Quite true." He took the gun from her, grasping it by the barrel, and pointed it toward a startled Mac, butt first.

As Mac gingerly accepted the weapon, Rudy continued. "I fully agreed with the idea of blowing him up, but I will not deny working in that hotbed of intrigue where nothing was quite what it seemed filled me with apprehension. Hitler seemed to lead a charmed life, and the plots failed one after another. If Canaris fell,

Hitler's net would be cast wide."

Mac looked at Abby. She seemed a bit more relaxed now that the weapon had changed hands. He withdrew the Luger's clip and checked the chamber. It was empty. "How many Lugers do you have?" he asked.

"Just the one." Rudy lifted his own glass, bowed to them, and drank. "I do not pretend to the heroism of those who carried explosives on suicide missions to rid us of the madman. So you can imagine my delight when the old man assigned me to carry funds to Argentina. They were, he said, to meet the payroll of his agents in the Americas and to finance certain secret operations."

"Was that the usual way?"

"No, this sort of thing was normally done through the diplomatic pouch. I suspect Canaris was preparing a safe harbor against need. If so, as you know, he failed to act quickly enough. Or perhaps he changed his mind and elected to go down with the ship.

"Why choose a junior officer for such an important mission? You may wonder, as I did. But consider. If the next plot succeeded, senior staff would be needed in the Fatherland, would they not? At least, that is my guess.

"On my arrival in Argentina—did I say Dietricht was assigned as my aide and bodyguard? Well, that's obvious, isn't it? Before depositing the funds in the accounts Canaris had designated, word came from a friend in the embassy that Colonel Oster had been placed under house arrest and Himmler was moving to take over the functions of the Abwehr."

"Colonel Oster?" Abby asked.

"Colonels implement what generals and admirals conceive. Admiral Canaris was an enigma, always in the background, constantly touching and testing the strands of his web. Oster was a driving force, one around whom others rallied. It was clear to me that, by daring to arrest the admiral's closest aide, Himmler was closing in; the conspiracy could not remain a secret, and executions must soon follow. At that moment I decided not to return."

"What about Dietricht? I don't suppose he was as well informed as you."

Rudy frowned. "Quite true. And I did not expect he would be in any danger. If I disappeared, he would present himself at the embassy and be sent home. So I thought. But the Gestapo, in their heavy-handed way, took him off the street. I witnessed this and followed. They were determined to extract information from him that he did not possess. The poor fellow was—" He turned away abruptly. "I won't bore you with the details of our escape from the Gestapo. We eventually arrived here."

There was silence for a moment, then Rudy turned back, smiling. "So you see, I am not such a bad fellow after all."

Mac put his glass on a case of beer. Abby took his hand. "Did you think of going to the authorities?" she asked.

"Briefly. But we were free, which is to be preferred to the life of a prisoner of war. And there was the money. Some in U.S. dollars, the rest in easily converted currencies. No Reichsmarks. I suppose greed played its part."

"How about when the war ended, and POWs were being repatriated?"

"Well, by then that would not have suited me at all. Here I was, an American saloon keeper, my business bought with tax-free money. Back in Germany, I'd be reduced to scrabbling in the rubble with the rest of them. Besides, I had lived here briefly in my youth and always wanted to return. It seemed fated. More wine?"

Abby and Mac both declined and Mac put the pistol and its clip next to his glass. "Why Sarahville? Weren't you afraid of standing out in a small community?"

"I had some acquaintance with Chicago and thought

I could easily merge into its German-American population. Also, it seemed safer away from the Atlantic seaboard. The problem was Feldwebel Dietricht. He had no facility for language. He could keep his mouth shut, but lacked the agility to improvise when questioned.

"I worked as chef and sometime bartender. My employer preferred his produce from the farm, rather than the Water Street market, and frequently sent me to Sarahville. It seemed an ideal spot for Dietricht, himself a farmer before he was conscripted. He was to say, if it were ever neccessary, that he was part Jew, escaped from Germany before the war. I also became aware that this tavern was for sale, and quickly took advantage of that."

Mac removed one beer case from a stack of three, the remaining two making a convenient height for Abby to sit. "How was that refugee story supposed to square with the Albrecht birth certificate?"

"Forgive me—would you like to go up to the barroom? It would be more comfortable." Mac looked to Abby. She shook her head, and Rudy continued. "The certificate was merely a starting point for obtaining other documents. If it ever came to the point where Dietricht faced any serious inquiry, the game was up anyway. Eventually he would learn, we hoped, to blend into the background. At that time he could use his share of the money to purchase a small farm.

"Albrecht and old man Schneider, Hans Schneider that is, became good friends. They spoke German; Dietricht should have spoken English only, to improve himself. All that *Kaffee Klatsch*. Sooner or later he was bound to give himself away."

"Is that what happened?" Abby asked. "He gave himself away?"

Rudy shrugged. "Perhaps. The trouble began when he met the widow, Alma Linsdale. Henry Schneider resented Dietricht's attentions to her." Thunder rumbled again and Rudy turned toward the low door to the subcellar, head tilted, listening. "At first Hans Schneider managed to keep the peace. Hans died in the winter of '46." Rudy turned back, eyes fixed on Mac. "That's it, isn't it? That was my first mistake."

Abby looked to Mac. "Mistake?"

"Right," Mac said. "You told me you knew Hans. In fact, he was a regular customer. Then, when I asked about Goldfarb, you said you had just bought the tavern about the time he died. An unnecessary lie. I guess you were intent on putting as much distance as possible between you and Dietricht's grave."

"You know my methods . . . !" Abby exclaimed. "How was I supposed to know that? I wasn't there!"

"I beg your pardon?" Rudy said, clearly puzzled.

Mac grinned at Abby. "You weren't there, but I told you about it."

"You did not!"

"Pay no attention to her," Mac said. "Go on, Rudy."

Looking from Mac to Abby, as if expecting another shot in the skirmish, he pressed on. "It occurs to me I compounded my error when you asked about Albrecht."

Mac, to urge Rudy on, said, "So Hans Schneider no longer stood between Henry and Dietricht. What happened then?"

"The trouble between them smoldered through the summer. And then somehow Henry learned Dietricht's true identity. He issued an ultimatum. Dietricht rushed to me with the news. He said Schneider knew nothing of me, and whatever happened, he would keep my secret." Rudy frowned and passed his hand across his brow as if to smooth the furrows. "But the government would want to know all the details of how he got here. Eventually he'd mention the money, and they'd want to know what became of it. Sooner or later they would give him a choice—cooperate fully and go home, or keep his secrets and be jailed."

Rudy clasped his hands behind his back and began to pace, his shadow shifting rapidly as he passed to and fro beneath the light. "I tell you, I came very close to murder then. I said as much, and Dietricht himself was in a rage. He vowed to shoot Henry and bury him in his own graveyard!" Rudy stopped pacing and turned to face them. "Well, that brought me to my senses, and I demanded his weapon. When he left me, I believed I had convinced him to forswear the Linsdale woman, agree to leave the area if necessary. Perhaps even offer a bribe."

Josie came to Rudy's side and took his hand. He regained his former calm. "But as you know, that was not the outcome. A tragic accident intervened."

Mac said, "I have reason to believe you weren't as convincing as you thought. Dietricht did try to kill Henry."

Rudy nodded. "Perhaps—yes, I am not entirely surprised. There was an altercation then? And Henry—?"

"That's what Mrs. Linsdale has suspected all these years," Abby said.

"Henry's journal confirms it," Mac said.

"You mean there really *is* a journal?" Abby asked. "I thought that was just one of your scams."

Mac raised an eyebrow. "How could you suspect me of such a thing? Of course there's a journal."

"What—"

"Let the man talk," Mac said. "Go ahead, Rudy."

"When Henry passed Dietricht off as a relative, that gave me pause to wonder, but my doubts were submerged in relief. Now no one would look too closely into the Albrecht identity and find it to be false. As for the absence of Albrecht, Henry let it be known that he had moved on, as itinerant farmhands so often do."

"So you were safe," Mac said. "And the years passed. But by now, assuming you've been as respectable as you seem to be, you could probably get a sympathetic hearing from Immigration."

Abby looked at Josie, standing silently at Rudy's side. "Particularly if you were married to an American

244

citizen."

Rudy squeezed Josie's hand and smiled at her. "In recent years I occasionally thought of that. Thirty years of blameless, law-abiding life *should* count for something. The result could well be resident status and a chance to apply for citizenship."

He frowned, disengaged his hand from Josie's, and refilled his own glass. "Then I would think of the uncertainties. The money. Who had rightful claim? Could I lose everything? Had I violated the tax code or currency regulations? And most worrisome—would I be believed?

"I entered the country in wartime, on my own two feet, bearing a large sum of money. Would they assume I came as spy or saboteur? Would they be vindictive enough to prosecute so long after the war?" He stared into the bottom of his glass, as if it held the answers. "Perhaps not. Probably not. But why take a chance?"

He looked up and smiled briefly. "So I continued as I was. And took care, until now, not to entangle Josie in my affairs."

"Until Bedford unearthed you."

"No, not Bedford. Taylor and his parking scheme. It seemed certain that the Goldfarb grave, which had been forgotten, would play a major role. Taylor would have to look for relatives and would discover it was not Goldfarb. Well, you can see the consequences as they have, in fact, unfolded. Not that I foresaw it all clearly—but the potential for a problem was certainly there.

"So I floated my own parking scheme. The idea was that as soon as Taylor hit a snag with his, mine would be accepted. That would end Taylor's interest and the Goldfarb grave would be again forgotten." He picked up an unopened bottle of wine. "I'm sorry. I forget my duties as host."

Both Mac and Abby shook their heads. "No thank you," Abby said.

Rudy put the bottle back on the cart. "Unfortunately, events moved too fast," he said. "Your charming wife discovered the grave and the investigation was launched before Taylor's proposal ever reached the village board. To make matters worse, it seemed in some way to be tied to Jerome Bedford's murder.

"I still had hope. Perhaps the investigation would end with the Albrecht identity, and Bedford's death would remain an unsolved crime. Then matters were further complicated by poor Agnes Ketchall's tragic end."

He spread his hands, shrugged his shoulders. "What to do? My options were limited. I could give myself up and hope for the best, but where that option had presented some uncertainty before, you can imagine the difficulty now. I would instantly be the chief suspect in two murders.

"The other option was to pray. And as it became clear that the police were focusing all their attention on Taylor, the wisdom of that course seemed demonstrated. But I continued to worry about your championing of Taylor's interests. And tonight it was obvious you had focused on me. Your story of the journal was intended to spur me to a revealing action."

"You're losing your touch," Abby said to Mac. "The mark saw right through you."

Mac thrust his hands in his pockets and walked to the stairs, his mind in confusion. "I hate to say it, but I believe your story. And that means I'm still short one killer."

Rudy gave a short laugh. "You can hardly expect me to be sorry about that."

"I counted heavily on motive and did what Stan always warns me against." Mac sat on a step. "I got ahead of the evidence. There were two candidates, but I can't think of any conceivable motive for the other one. It just seemed so obvious that the second German must be Bedford's killer."

Abby sniffed. "And you accused Stan of clutching at

246

straws!"

"Well, you have to admit I found my man, even if he isn't a murderer."

"What will happen to us?" Josie asked. "They won't . . ." She put her arms around Rudy and laid her head against his chest.

"Now, now," Rudy said. "I'm sure it will be all right." His face, turned to Mac, said he was not as confident as his words indicated. "I understand why you came to suspect me, but surely that wasn't fully convincing."

"It was a question of fitting you to the pattern," Mac said. "You matched perfectly. Arrival at nearly the same time as Dietricht. The right age. Present at the SHS lunch, but not at the SHS meeting. And then there was the burglary."

"Burglary! How did that point to me?"

"Metlaff met Karen and Jack here, in the tavern. He asked Jack to meet with him in his office. You were in a position to overhear that, and would assume Karen was going along. A tip-off that the farmhouse would be empty. Then, when the police were searching for the intruder, they had reason to believe he came here and they looked over the crowd for signs of someone having fled through wet underbrush. But they didn't see you, and Al Rhine claims he looked for you and you weren't around."

"I see. As a matter of fact, I was down here wrestling a case of scotch into the dumbwaiter. They never opened the cellar door."

"Sloppy," Mac said.

"Anything else?"

"A minor matter. Your speech pattern."

Rudy chuckled. "Josie has tried in vain to make me more 'hip.' Is that correct? But I am an old dog, I fear."

"All right, Great One," Abby said. "Explain why you got us into what could have been a real mess. I mean, suppose Rudy *had* done it?" Realizing she had just ad-

247

mitted buying the whole story, she said, "He didn't, did he?"

Mac shook his head. "It seemed safe enough with the whole group here. As Rudy guessed, the idea was to spook him into another break-in. The journal is on my desk and Stan and his minions are guarding it. If he'd gone for it, we'd have a felony arrest and a basis for getting the State's Attorney to suspend action against Jack. In the meantime the FBI would get into the case, and who knows what they might turn up? At least Metlaff would have plenty of dust at hand to throw in the eyes of a jury."

"What do you suppose Stan will say when you tell him he's been hiding in the bushes for nothing?"

Mac shuddered. "The other thing I was hoping for was a long shot. Maybe we could trace the gun back to Rudy through German records, if they still exist."

Rudy nodded. "That was my thought also. That's why I surrendered my weapon to you. Unlike many officers who bought the newer Mauser, I had only the original-issue Luger. Obviously it is not the murder weapon."

"Right. Just a coincidence, I guess. Wait! You said Dietricht gave you his sidearm. Was that a Luger too?"

Rudy placed his hand on his forehead. "I had forgotten. Even though I mentioned it this very evening—of course I have not seen it for many years. Perhaps this would be a good time to go upstairs, and I will get it."

They started to act on Rudy's suggestion. Josie asked, "Where is it?"

"In the office safe, well to the back and behind some ledgers that go back to when I first bought this place."

"No, it isn't."

"But I am sure—"

"I moved the ledgers looking for your gun. It's usually in the safe, unless we have money on hand. But I found the gun in the desk drawer."

Rudy had stopped halfway up the stairs, and in the

silence that fell, the sound of running water could be heard coming from the subcellar. "I hope the sump pump can keep up," Rudy said. "The leakage gets worse each year when the creek overflows to the parking lot."

"Could the gun be anywhere else?" Mac asked.

"We must search—but no, I think not."

"I'll look again." Josie ran up the stairs while Rudy turned back to where Mac and Abby had stopped.

"Three Lugers in one case. That's stretching things," Mac said.

Abby held up four fingers. "Don't forget the one Jack used to have."

"But surely, the murder weapon cannot be Dietricht's. It has always been locked in my safe."

"If I'm right about the other candidate for the honor you just missed, access to the weapon is no problem. But motive—why would he care if—" Mac stopped suddenly and grasped Rudy's arm. "Rudy! What happened to Dietricht's money?"

"The money? The State of Illinois has it. After seven years, inactive accounts are turned over—"

"How much?"

"Let me see. There was originally about one hundred and ninety thousand, so with accumulated interest—"

"My God! It must be nearly a quarter of a million!" Abby exclaimed.

Josie reappeared at the cellar door. She stumbled on the top step and caught at the handrail.

A dark figure loomed behind her. "Two hundred and thirty-two thousand, seven hundred and thirty seven dollars, and sixty one cents, to be exact," Horace Arly said. "Stand clear of that gun, McKenzie. All of you, move over there." He gestured toward the east wall with his pistol. "You're going wading."

Chapter 24

Mac took a deep breath and exhaled slowly, forcing discipline on nerves that had curled his hands into fists and knotted his stomach. "Well, H.A.!" He reached for Abby's arm and guided her backward, away from the stairs. "You're just in time to finish out the story for us." He managed a calm, conversational tone. "Tell me, how did you get your hands on the money?" He angled toward a row of shelving where a quick shove might give Abby shelter, if Horace Arly fired.

"Quit stalling, and move that way!" Arly jerked his head in the direction of the low door, revolver aimed at a point between Mac and Abby. They moved as he directed. Rudy waited until Josie joined him before obeying.

Arly descended far enough to keep them covered. "Open the door."

"Now, just a minute, H.A.," Mac said. He turned, at the same time giving Abby a small shove backward. He stepped to one side, placing himself between her and the gun. "Whatever you have in mind, it won't work. I wasn't fool enough to come in here without backup, you know."

To Mac's dismay, Abby reappeared at his side. "That's right," she said. "My husband is *not* a fool. The police are outside now."

The gun wavered, swinging from Mac to Abby, then settled again on Mac. Arly's laugh sounded more nervous than amused. "That's not what you said a few minutes ago. I heard the whole thing from up there." He gestured toward the top of the stairs with the gun. Mac took one step and H.A. jerked it back to center on his chest.

"I guess you outsmarted me, all right, H.A.," Mac said, hoping to delay Arly as long as possible. Once inside the subcellar door, their chances diminished. "I knew it had to be you or Rudy, because—"

"Because I was at the lunch and not at the meeting," Arly said. "I can add it up for myself."

"Right. That's what I told Stan Pawlowski. So you see, he'll know who to look for."

Arly's lips curled in contempt. "Yeah? All that fancy theorizing and you forgot Alice Hillman. She fits too."

"Helen Rhine played chauffeur for Alice after the lunch." Mac noticed beads of sweat on Arly's brow. "By the time she was dropped at home, it was too late to kill Agnes. Besides, she doesn't have a car."

Rudy stepped forward and placed himself in front of Josie. "You also mentioned a lie, I believe."

"That's right," Mac said. "The flu was going around and H.A. used that as an excuse for missing the meeting. Of course, he was actually busy setting up Bedford's killing. Probably came here and, with easy access to your safe, took Dietricht's gun, then broke into the schoolhouse."

"How do you know that was a lie?" Rudy asked.

Arly took a step toward them. "Shut up and move!"

They both edged backward. "Everybody else was laid up for a week. H.A. was back here, working on your books, he claimed, the next day. Probably wanted to get the gun back in your safe as soon as possible. So it would point to you."

Visibly agitated, Arly's voice boomed and echoed in the stone-walled cellar. "Get in there! Or should I throw your dead body down the stairs?"

Afraid Arly was about to panic and lose control, Mac said, "Easy, H.A. We're going." He turned to Rudy and said, "Better do it." As Rudy began shepherding Josie toward the door, Mac turned again. "How did you find out about the money in the first place?"

"No more talk."

Mac took Abby's hand and they moved slowly toward the low door. "Just tell me one thing, H.A. How did you find out Albrecht was dead? Or did you know the whole story?"

Arly's chuckle sounded more at ease, now that the situation seemed back in his control. "You mean all that German crap? Didn't have a clue. Didn't know where Albrecht was buried either, till Bedford turned it up."

"I have to hand it to you, H.A." Mac crammed as much admiration in his voice as he could muster. "I wouldn't have the nerve to clean out those accounts. If you didn't know Albrecht was dead, he could have showed up anytime."

"Not a chance. Where would a farmhand get that kind of money? Then he takes off, leaves it all behind, and his birth certificate to boot? Doesn't take a genius to figure out we're talking hot money."

"You did the Schneider taxes," Mac said. "Is that where you ran across the certificate?"

Arly descended another step. "Schneider had a fit when I asked about it."

"And I suppose you ran across the Albrecht accounts in Rudy's safe?"

"A bundle of passbooks. Then I check up on our Heinie friend here. He came out of nowhere with a fistful of money to buy this place. So I figured he put Albrecht at the bottom of a gravel pit, took the cash, but didn't have the nerve to go after the accounts."

They all clustered at the subcellar door. Abby said, "But Jerome kept what he found a secret."

"The fool. Hints here. Hints there. Had to make himself the center of attention. Then Karen said he looked through her junk pile for the name *Albrecht*. I had to find out what he knew." Arly's smug expression hardened, his voice turned harsh. "Enough talk. Open the door."

Rudy complied. The hum of the sump pump was barely audible over the sound of trickling water.

"Inside. Be quick about it. I've got a lot of ground to cover."

Rudy hesitated in the doorway. "We are going to be quite damp, I fear."

"Just one more thing, H.A.," Mac said. "Why did you break into the farmhouse? You didn't care what was in Henry's box, did you?"

"Hell no. I went to plant the gun."

"Bad mistake, H.A. The police had already searched."

"I know that. Think I'm stupid? Henry sometimes kept cash under a floorboard in his bedroom. If the cops had missed that, I could put the gun there. But the board was pulled up, so they must have found it. I had to stash the gun in the barn later." He came closer. "Into the pool, kiddies."

Rudy bent almost double to clear the doorway. "Be very careful. The stairway is steep; almost a ladder. And in bad repair. Stay near the wall."

"Isn't there a light?" Josie asked. She followed, keeping one hand on Rudy's back.

"No." His voice reverberated, as in a cavern.

Mac took Abby's arm and urged her through the low door. Arly pushed his gun in Mac's direction. "Now you."

Mac ducked his head and took a step inside. He turned and peered out. Was there a slight tremor in Arly's hand? Panic in a man holding a gun could be deadly. "How did you get Bedford to meet you in the schoolhouse?"

"Told him I had inside info on the grave, from a client. Had to meet in secret, so nobody would know I violated a confidence. He lapped it up."

"From what I've heard, I guess he would," Mac said. "But why care what he found? You already had the money, didn't you?"

"The damned publicity hound was going to the newspapers with his story. A grave with three names. If somebody picked up on it, they'd trace the bank accounts in no time. Then they'd look for the guy who claimed the money after Albrecht was dead."

"That was a tight spot, all right. So then—"

"Shut up and move!"

Abby touched Mac's arm. She whispered, "He's on the edge. You better come."

Mac moved cautiously sideways, feeling for the step with his foot, eyes fixed on Arly. His muscles tensed. This was the moment. If they were to be shot like fish in a barrel, it would be now, before they disappeared into the sheltering darkness. Sweat broke out on his forehead. Could he guess Arly's next move? Throw himself down the stairs, carrying them all into the watery pit, in time? Broken bones were better than a bullet in the back.

The stairway swayed under him and Josie screamed.

"Stop!" Rudy shouted. "Too much weight! Let us get to the bottom first!"

Mac jumped back into the upper cellar and reached back to grab Abby's hand. He hardly recognized Arly's voice, thick with fury.

"Get back in there!"

"Now hold on, H.A.! Give them a chance to get down first."

Arly, holding the pistol with arm fully extended, swung to the left and fired. The bullet threw splinters from the door jamb. "Move, or I shoot you where you stand!"

Mac hurriedly shoved Abby through the door, hoping

the others had moved off the stairs. As his weight joined Abby's, he heard the shriek of nails pulling free of rotting wood. He grabbed her arm. There was a momentary sense of floating, then they jumped into darkness as the structure gave way.

Chapter 25

Mac struck the water with Abby's scream and Rudy's curses ringing in his ears. He scrambled to his feet, coughed up a mouthful of the muddy brew, and pulled Abby up with him. The door above slammed shut. The dim light disappeared. He encircled Abby in his arms.

"Are you all right?"

"I think so." She clung to him.

"Everybody all right?" he called, his voice echoing in the narrow chamber.

"We seem to have survived," Rudy said.

Josie's voice quavered. "It's like a grave down here."

Rudy, whatever he felt, sounded calm and reassuring. "Don't let imagination take over, *Leibchen*. This is merely an inconvenience. The only danger is pneumonia from standing knee-deep in cold water."

"Rudy's right," Mac said. "If we can't figure a way out, all we have to do is wait for somebody to come get us."

"How long will that be?" Abby asked.

"Quite a while," Josie said. She seemed a bit calmer. "We're closed tomorrow, because of the excavating."

"Won't the workmen come? Won't they get suspicious and call the police?" Abby asked.

"No, they won't come," Rudy said.

"If they stopped because of seepage before," Mac

said, "they won't work under these conditions. How bad does it get, Rudy?"

"If there are six inches of water in the parking lot, then the stream is out of its banks and has overflowed the wetlands to the north. When that happens, the intersection of Main and Harper also floods."

Abby said, "Good Heavens! We could be here for the next forty-eight hours. This is going to ruin my shoes!" Her tone was light, but her grip on Mac tightened.

Mac laughed. "That's my girl. First things first."

"First thing is, get us out of here before Josie and I get pruney."

A glimmer of light showed along the bottom of the door, and as his eyes adapted to the dark, Mac began to make out some features of their prison. Rudy and Josie clung together near the north wall, just past where the stairs had ended. Mac and Abby had their backs to the south wall. The chamber was no more than five feet wide, and the far end was invisible in the dim glow.

"I could tolerate this a lot better if it weren't for the smell," Abby said.

"God, yes," Josie said. "I think I'm going to be sick."

"You'll get used to it," Mac said. "Remember Ed Norton? He got to like it." He looked to the ceiling. It was perhaps six feet from the floor, causing Rudy to stoop. But it rose sharply at the tavern end to accommodate the doorway to the upper cellar. He reached behind him and felt the same dressed stone construction as the tavern foundation. Stepping past Abby, to where the down slope allowed him to touch the top, he said, "What's the ceiling made of, Rudy? It feels smooth."

"Reinforced concrete."

"Not part of the original, then."

"No, no. Much later."

"How far underground are we?"

"Five feet below the parking lot, rising to within two feet of the surface at the top of the door."

Mac waded to a spot directly below the door, carefully pushing floating wood aside as he went. He explored the threshold with his fingers. It was merely an extension of the cellar floor that projected several inches into the space where the stairs had once been. Rising on his toes brought his eyes above the sill. All he could see was the cellar floor. When he turned away, it took a moment to readapt his eyes to the dark. "Does the door lock?"

"No," Rudy said. "It has a latch, however. Wrought iron."

"We should be able to do some damage to wrought iron. Give me a hand." His answer was the sound of Rudy's splashing approaching.

"Don't leave me!" There was an edge of panic in Josie's voice.

"Come along, then. Join Abby." Rudy's progress was slow, and Mac assumed he was being careful to avoid the flotsam. "It's less claustrophobic at this end."

They waited for Josie, and Mac said, "If you give me a boost, I can grab the doorknob and pull myself up onto the sill."

"Sorry to disappoint you," Rudy said, "but there is no doorknob."

"What the hell kind of a door doesn't have a doorknob?"

"The outside, as I said, has a simple lift latch. There is a wrought-iron handle to draw the door open. The latch cannot close itself accidentally, so the door can be opened from this side by merely pushing. No need for a knob."

Mac sighed. "Well, hanging my toes on a two- or three-inch sill wouldn't give me much leverage anyway. Any ideas?"

"None. An efficient prison, I fear."

"This is better," Josie said. "Standing under that low roof gave me the creeps."

"I am also grateful for the headroom," Rudy said. "I

258

was getting a stiff neck."

They might all be grateful for headroom if the water continued to rise. Mac kept the thought to himself, but felt sure it had not escaped Rudy.

"A man that keeps lockpicks in his attaché case isn't going to let a simple latch keep him in," Abby said. "Is he?"

"Sometimes the simplest locks are the most effective. But . . . fish around and try to find a thin piece of wood." Mac began feeling through the floating debris.

"What for?" Josie asked.

"We can boost someone up to the door. Maybe there's a gap at the edge. To get something through and lift the latch."

The sound of something heavy being pushed or pulled across the floor above them interrupted his search. A sound of breaking glass and a heavy thud reverberated through their cell. Then silence.

Rudy spoke first. "He has apparently moved the wine rack and tipped it against the door." His voice seemed to fade a bit. "I would say our chances of getting out that way are now nil."

"Rudy," Josie whimpered.

"Well, now what?" Abby asked. "Should we all gather around and sing 'Ninety-nine Bottles of Beer on the Wall'?"

"Are you sure there aren't rats?" Josie asked. "I thought I felt—"

"No rats," Rudy said.

Barely able to see his surroundings, Mac could not read expressions. But he could see Rudy reach out to the wall for support, his head drooping. Mac drew close and whispered, "Problem?"

"Yes. Falling debris struck my leg. Felt faint for a moment."

"Bleeding?"

"How can I tell? We are all soaking wet."

At Mac's insistence, Rudy took his hand and guided

it to the spot on his left leg, halfway up his thigh. The pant leg was torn. "Can't tell much, but we'll assume it's bleeding. Give me your tie."

Josie spoke sharply. "What's going on?" She splashed across the room and gripped Rudy's arm.

"It is nothing. Scratched my leg, that's all."

"Oh, God. In this sewer?"

"Let Rudy lean on you," Mac said, "while I tie this around. It'll protect it. He'll be fine."

Abby joined them and touched Josie's shoulder. "I know it's not the most pleasant odor, Josie, but it's just rain water percolating through the ground. I don't think he'll get infected. It's just muddy, that's all."

Mac finished his makeshift bandaging and Abby drew him aside. "How is he, really?" she whispered.

"Don't know. But he felt faint, which may mean bleeding. If so, I'm hoping the tie will stop it."

"I suppose, when we get out of here, we'll all find cuts and bruises we're not aware of." She pressed close to him and in normal tones said, "Have either of you had an idea yet?"

Mac felt Abby shiver. He became aware of the cold biting into his own legs. No one answered her.

"Listen! Josie said.

Silence, except for the trickle of water.

"I hear nothing, *Leibchen.*"

"The sump pump. It's stopped."

"Perhaps the power has failed. The storm."

"No," Mac said. "The cellar light's still on."

Rudy drew Josie closer. "Calm yourself. The pump is of little use anyway. It merely pours water back into the parking lot, where it promptly leaks back in here."

Mac raised himself to look under the door in time to see Arly's shoes disappear in the direction of the stairs. "I take it the sump pump switch is in the cellar?"

"Yes."

"It seems our friend is trying to fill the pool." Abby clutched his arm and he heard a gasp from Josie. "Not to worry. Even if the chamber did fill, we're safe at this end. The water, if it ever gets that far, which I doubt, will run under the door, and that's a big cellar out there."

"Sure, Josie," Abby said, her breathing a bit uneven. "The ceiling right here is at least ten feet high. The water can't rise that far."

"But it's a foot higher than when we came down here," Josie said. "The radio said the creek wouldn't peak until noon tomorrow."

"Did they say how much above flood stage?"

"Three feet. If the rain stopped."

"Nothing to worry about," Rudy said. "The parking lot has never had more than eight inches of water, and that was in the flood of '57. On that occasion this subcellar came within a foot of the door. And I'm sure conditions are not nearly that severe this time."

But the subcellar walls were now many years older, Mac thought. Unless the leakage slowed, the lower chamber would fill within the next few hours, leaving them just the space nearest the door.

"I was here in '57. We had three inches in the upper cellar," Josie said. "Don't you remember?"

"Even so—"

Josie's voice rose. "Down here, that's over my head, Rudy!"

"We'd still be okay," Mac said. "Plenty of lumber from the staircase. Enough to keep everybody afloat."

"Sure, Josie," Abby said. "Our biggest worry is a bad cold." She punctuated the sentence with a sneeze. "Let's change the subject. Somebody explain about the money."

"Money?" Josie asked. "What money?"

"The money Arly stole."

"A large sum of money presents its own problems," Rudy said. "Once Dietrich and I had established identities as Albrecht and Wilking, we split the money and set up a number of bank accounts, none so large as to draw attention." His voice faded gradually. He paused and took a deep breath. "I withdrew my share to buy this tavern. Dietricht's remained scattered over six states."

"Why did you keep the passbooks?"

"I would have liked Dietricht's share to go to his heirs. But how? I hoped some means would occur to me. Eventually I forgot them. They remained at the back of my safe."

"Where Horace found them." Abby sneezed again.

"Rudy!" Josie called. "The wall's vibrating!"

"That was quite a sneeze," Mac said.

Rudy place his head against the wall. "There *is* a slight vibration."

The quaver of fear returned to Josie's voice. "What if the water's weakened them? What if the whole place collapses?"

"Perhaps it is a pump operating somewhere. Perhaps in the basement of Farrell's store across the street."

"That must be it," Mac said, although he was sure a small pump could not make itself felt at that distance. But no other explanation suggested itself.

Abby left Mac's side and went to Josie, her hand outstretched. "Whatever it is, I'm sure the place isn't collapsing." She gripped Josie's hand. "Don't let—"

A dull thumping sound from overhead interrupted her. There was a low moan from Josie, hushed by Abby. Silence. Then a scraping noise.

"Sounds like somebody shoveling snow," Abby whispered.

"Snow?" Josie whispered. "What—"

"That kind of sound. When the shovel scrapes on the sidewalk."

"The backhoe!" Mac exclaimed. "Rudy, how far did they dig before—"

"They exposed the roof above the stairs out to four feet from the tavern wall. Tomorrow the engineer will inspect, to be sure no damage is done to the foundation. Of course! I had forgotten. He will be out even if no work is to be done."

Mac craned his neck back to look at the ceiling, but could see nothing in the gloom. "I don't think we have that much time. Everybody! Back away. All the way back!" He grabbed Abby's arm and pulled her with him, ignoring the floating lumber with its projecting nails.

"What is it, Mac?"

"Horace is getting impatient. He's figured out how to start the hoe and he's trying to speed up the flooding."

Mac was dimly aware of Rudy and Josie approaching, but they faded from sight in the deeper darkness at the end of the low chamber.

"That makes no sense," Abby said. "He should be on his way to Canada. He can't expect the water to rise to the top of the door—can he?"

"No, he can't—unless the flood is a lot worse than we think. We'll move forward as the water rises and—" Mac stopped abruptly. "If we *can* move forward."

Rudy gasped. "He may bring down the roof and trap us back here!"

"Or bury us!" Josie shrieked.

"The bastard!" The thought of Abby buried in this stinking crypt drove Mac into a rage. "I'll kill him!"

"But why?" Josie wailed. "Why didn't he shoot us? Why make us die like this?"

Mac held Abby's head against his chest, as if merely human strength could hold off tons of concrete and earth. "He wants it to look like an accident. We came down, the stairs collapsed, the roof gave way."

"What can we do?" Rudy's voice sounded as if speaking were an effort. "There must be some way to stop him."

"If he makes a hole big enough to get through before the whole roof goes, I'll get to him. So help me God, I'll get him!" Mac, conscious that he was losing control, not thinking clearly, loosened his grip on Abby. He tried to visualize the dark space they were in, the slab that served as a roof. The first break would come at the high end, where the hoe was operating. "Rudy, you'll lift me on your shoulders. After I'm out, try to shove the ladies through. Until I nail Horace, I can't help, and you can't afford to wait. Win, lose, or draw. This end of the pit'll fill in minutes."

"Sorry to let you down." Rudy's voice was barely audible. "I don't think I can do that."

The scraping stopped and they heard the sound of a laboring engine. There was a loud cracking noise followed by a cataract that poured through a corner of the roof. Mac started forward, running with difficulty in the waist-deep water. He could hear the others splashing in his wake.

He reached the corner that had been breached and looked up. Too high. No way to reach it without help. He felt a tug at his arm.

"Lift me!" Abby said. "I'll stop him somehow!"

The opening was no more than four inches wide. Steel clanged on concrete and another crack appeared. He turned and pushed her back. Another crack, then a low creaking, like a ship's hull stressed by waves. The sound grew louder, became a crashing roar mixed with splashing water. A giant claw reach through the hole where the roof had been.

Mac grabbed Abby, rushed forward, and lifted her to his shoulder. She clutched at the wall and struggled up, a knee on each side of his head. He felt the pressure ease and knew she had grasped the edge of the hole and was pulling herself upward.

"Get out and run for it," he shouted.

After near total darkness, the roof opening to the night sky seemed to flood the hole with light. He saw Abby disappear over the edge and turned away. "Josie!" he called. "You're next."

"Mac!" she screamed. "Help me! It's Rudy!"

264

Rudy lay facedown in the water. Mac grabbed him under the arms and lifted, all the while praying Abby had gotten clear. "Hold him!" He shoved Rudy against the wall, where Josie could support his weight, and ran, laboring against the water's density, to the opening. As the backhoe shovel began to withdraw, he leaped forward and grasped the boom, rising out of the hole with it.

Horace Arly was a silhouette at the controls. Another figure appeared at the side of the hoe, climbing to the cab. Abby! The boom drew the blade back, digging into the side of the pit, bringing Mac close to solid ground. He jumped.

Sliding in the water and mud, Mac twisted around to face Arly. The backhoe lurched forward, drawn by the blade biting into the stone wall. Arly rose from his seat to fend off Abby's clawing fingers.

Knowing what was about to happen, Mac shouted, "Jump, Abby!" She fell more than jumped. He saw her scramble away on hands and knees.

The backhoe tilted forward then plunged ten feet to the bottom of the pit. Only the loader bucket protruded aboveground.

Sound was still echoing off the stone walls when the broken concrete slab above the pit tilted downward and the water-saturated clay began slowly sliding off its edge like a curtain of molasses.

Mac ran to the loader bucket and climbed back into the pit, wondering what Horace Arly was doing. "Move, Josie!" he shouted. "Drag Rudy this way!"

He reached the cab. It was empty. He slid off, dropping into chin-high water. Rudy had roused himself to hold Josie's head above water. Mac grasped her, boosted her up, and placed her hand on the hoe's boom. "Climb!" She pulled herself upward and Mac pushed Rudy onto the boom, where he clung, not moving. "Hurry!" Josie caught Rudy's hand and urged him to climb.

Mac caught a movement from the corner of his eye and turned as Horace Arly, muddy water dripping from his face, lunged at him. Mac braced himself against the machine at his back and raised his foot, planting it squarely in his assailant's chest. Arly stumbled backward, falling.

A rumble vibrated through the water as the stone wall on the right began to give way. Ignoring Arly, Mac leaped for the boom and scrambled upward, thankful to find Rudy had managed to crawl free.

There was a sickening, sucking sound as the overburden accelerated its slide.

Horace Arly splashed erect and reached out as the concrete slab tilted farther, hesitated, then fell. The jagged end of a reinforcing bar rammed into his back, forcing a scream from his open mouth. Eyes wide, he disappeared under a thousand cubic yards of water-saturated clay and gravel.

Mac wearily dragged himself from the wreckage. The rain had stopped and the clouds were thinning. He saw Abby kneeling at the pit's edge, hands clasped as if in prayer.

Chapter 26

Several days of baking sun had turned the top few inches of soil to a friable consistency and the grass to a brilliant springtime green. The odors of cooking greeted Mac and Abby at the farmhouse door.

"Come on in," Jack Taylor said. "Karen's gone crazy. She's baking a ham, roasting a turkey, and she's made four pies. We should have invited all Sarahville."

"Ice cream!" Jason said.

"Later, Jason. After dinner," Jack said.

"Good heavens, Karen," Abby said. "Who's going to eat all that?"

"Well, maybe I got a little carried away. But I just love this huge old kitchen." She left the kitchen range and put her arms around Jack. "And I feel like a bride doing her first big dinner."

Abby sat at the table and drew Jason up on her lap. "Who else is coming?"

"Rudy and Josie. I'm a little nervous about cooking for a couple of pros." Turning to the window, she said, "I think they're here. No, it's Captain Pawlowski."

Jason jumped down and ran to the door. "Can I see your gun?" he asked as Stan entered.

"Sorry, Jason. It's against police rules. I can only show it to the bad guys."

"What's up, Stan? Mac asked.

"Couple of loose ends." He took a book from under

267

his arm and handed it to Jack. "Here's your family journal. The Feds have the birth certificate. I don't think you'll get that back."

"Thanks, Captain. I'm going to have the rest of this translated when I get a chance."

"And one question for Sherlock, here. You got anything on Jean Arly you haven't told me about? State's Attorney says it's put up or shut up time."

"No. One small thing, but it won't help."

"So spill it."

"Jean Arly told Abby she had never heard of Goldfarb. Yet by then everybody, including her husband, knew Bedford had been asking about Goldfarb. Just trying to put distance between herself and the murder, I guess."

Stan shook his head. "Half the people I talk to lie on general principle."

"Then she won't be prosecuted?" Abby asked.

"With Horace Arly dead? It's too hard to make the case."

Jason stood on tiptoe and tried to peek under Stan's jacket. Karen picked the boy up and placed him on Jack's lap. "Tie an anchor on this, sailor." Turning to Stan, she said, "Jean must have known what Horace was up to, don't you think?"

"You *know* she made the anonymous calls that got me into the slammer," Jack said.

"Can't prove it. But the IRS wants to know what happened to the stolen money—so her troubles aren't over. And this Dietricht business isn't the only scam Arly pulled. Going through his files has been a real education."

"Speaking of the IRS, what about Rudy?"

"Ask him. He just drove up."

Rudy Wilking, sporting an ebony cane and a slight limp, entered with Josie Horvath on his arm. They greeted everyone, commented on the delicious odors drifting up from the oven, and assured Karen they were delighted to have someone else do the cooking for a change. Mac repeated his question about the IRS.

"Since I brought the money with me when I entered the country, they have ruled there is no tax due. There will be an audit of my affairs, but all should be well. Whatever else Horace was, he was a good accountant."

"And Immigration?"

"That proceeds slowly, but there is reason to hope."

"Time for me to get back to work and let you folks put on the feedbag," Stan said.

"Remind Julie," Abby said. "Dinner next Sunday."

"And if I didn't mention it before," Mac said, "I'm glad it wasn't you standing out in the rain waiting for somebody to break in." He grinned. "Glad for my own safety, mainly."

Stan chuckled. "That really made the week for me."

"This is something I missed," Rudy said. "I understood Mac had arranged with you to trap me. You were to have surrounded his house."

"Yeah. He left me a note, but it was intercepted. John Almeir figured if there was going to be an arrest that'd break the case, he was going to be the one to get credit." Stan's laugh was infectious. "He hid in the bushes while Mama Nature poured cold water down his neck for five hours. Didn't even give up when he heard the commotion at the tavern. Figured it was a traffic accident."

"I remember it was you who took charge," Josie said. "Shipped us all off to the emergency room."

"I hate tetanus shots," Mac said. "My arm aches for two days."

"Serves you right for playing Lone Ranger. Next time call a cop."

"No next time," Mac said. "After damn near getting everybody buried alive, that was definitely my last case." He put his arm around Abby's shoulders. "I'm going to retire and let my wife support me."

Karen looked surprised and turned to Abby, who

merely smiled at Mac and said, "We'll talk about it later."

Mac's sigh was heartfelt. "You mean talk again—and again—don't you?"

On his way out, Stan grinned. "See you later, gum-shoe."

Karen opened the oven door and peered in. Closing it, she said, "It'll be at least another half hour. Why don't we go in the parlor and have a comfortable seat?"

"If you wish, although I am quite comfortable here," Rudy said.

"Me too," Josie agreed. "Reminds me of when I was a kid. We always sat around the kitchen and talked."

"Suits me too," Mac said. With Karen overruled, he continued. "Rudy, you mentioned being familiar with the Chicago area. How did that come about?"

"I was conceived in Chicago, if you can believe that, but my father returned with my mother to Germany. I missed being a native-born American by a matter of two weeks."

"Talk about bad luck," Josie said.

"For some reason my father insisted I learn English. Then, he returned us here to busy himself with the German-American Bund. I spent several formative years in New York and Chicago. The only cloud in my sky in those days was the Bund. I was required to attend youth camps and engage in all that goose-stepping nonsense."

Josie laughed "Can you imagine Rudy goose-stepping?"

"You are too young to remember, Mac, but Spankno-bel, at that time head of the Bund, fled to Germany to escape a warrant for his arrest. We escaped with him on the ship *Europa*. What my father had to fear I never learned."

"And you were drafted?"

"No. My father tried to get me to join him in the party. I had no taste for politics, and less for the Nazis. So he used his influence to obtain a commission for me in the Army. Familiarity with America and facility with the language led to my assignment to the Abwehr. All in all, I have been a very lucky man."

Josie reached over and patted Rudy's hand. "Lucky? Doesn't sound like luck to me."

"When I think of what happened to others . . . But enough of me. What occasion are we celebrating today?"

"It's kind of a bittersweet occasion. We're celebrating the release of my jailbird," Karen said, squeezing Jack's hand. "And we're saying good-bye to this old house."

"No chance the bank will give you an extension?" Mac asked.

"Why would they? With Dietricht buried up there, it would take months to clear the legal hurdles, maybe years."

"You left this at our place," Abby said, handing Jack his rolled-up map of Olde Sarahville. "I've been doodling on it. Hope you don't mind."

Jack tossed it aside, shrugging. "I'll use it to start a fire in the fireplace tonight."

Abby retrieved the map and unrolled it on the table. "Before you do that, take a look."

Karen bent over the table and studied Abby's doodles. "Jack, look at this!"

Jack joined her. After a moment he straightened up laughing. "By God, I think it'll work!"

"Would someone enlighten me?" Rudy asked.

"Take a look," Jack said. "Abby's put a fence around the graveyard and surrounded it with a park. Here, along the creek, she's put a line of shops and a footbridge."

"But the parking," Josie objected. "Where's that?"

"The old barn out back is about to collapse," Abby said. "Jack planned on stores there. But by building along the creek across from our place, there's plenty of room to park right here behind the house, all the way

271

down to the creek. And everybody parking here will have to walk past the new stores on the way to the bridge."

Jack nodded, then looked at Mac. "What do you think?"

"Beats me," Mac shrugged. "That's Abby's department. I'm just a part-time ribbon clerk."

"Oh, Jack! It's perfect," Karen said. "And with the publicity about Sergeant Dietricht's grave, I bet business will be fantastic!"

"An excellent plan," Rudy agreed. "And although I deplore notoriety, recent events will not hurt business at the tavern, either."

Mac laughed. "That's even better than Capone's fatal illness."